All
Eyes
on
Her

Also by Red Dress Ink
and

Poonam Sharma

GIRL MOST LIKELY TO
(where *Bend It Like Beckham* meets *Sex and the City!*)

All Eyes on Her

Poonam Sharma

RED
DRESS
INK
TM

ALL EYES ON HER

A Red Dress Ink novel

ISBN-13: 978-0-373-89551-9
ISBN-10:   0-373-89551-8

© 2008 by Poonam Sharma.

www.RedDressInk.com

Printed in U.S.A.

ACKNOWLEDGMENTS

My thanks...

To the females who have made my life difficult, because you taught me how to protect myself and, incidentally, gave me another idea for a book.

To my editor Kathryn Lye, whose enthusiasm over the *evil eye* concept convinced me that I was onto something.

And, of course, to my agent Lorin Rees, who although he is male, always seems to appreciate what I am trying to say.

For envy, which separates the girls from the women. And for the animal inside all of us, who merely demands respect and a little fresh meat before she will allow us to rise above.

one

IT IS BETTER TO BE ENVIED THAN IT IS TO GO UNNOTICED, MY mother's voice echoed in the back of my mind. And I would have agreed with her on principle; however, if I leaned any farther to the left to avoid being seared by Stefanie's jealous gaze in that Friday morning meeting, I'm sure I would've toppled right off of my chair. For the record, there were eight other junior associates at our Beverly Hills law firm hoping for the same two promotion slots. I was handling a key client, and I did take my career very seriously. But even I wasn't cocky enough to believe that Stefanie's ill will had anything to do with my superior job performance. Rather, I knew that my being the only other female candidate was the reason why she made a habit of watching me as if there were a bull's-eye centered on my forehead.

"Interesting choice of footwear for a firm-wide meeting," she had sneered in the elevator an hour before. As if my open-toed pumps were too much for the office. Luckily, I knew better. These emerald green Diors were as suitable as they were scrumptious.

Maybe she just didn't like me. And if so, then I really didn't have the time to wonder why. Being the only Indian girl in my Hermosa Beach high school taught me to let the curious stares of others roll right off my back. It was just one of the many side effects of never quite fitting in.

Although I'd never actually done anything to Stefanie the office tension was becoming a problem. How obvious could she be? And why would anyone choose to wear their emotions on their sleeve for everyone to see? To me, that would've been like wearing my naughty-nurse costume to a law school reunion. Or my bra as a hat. Completely illogical. It's not that I was dead inside. It was just that I'd learned to not let my feelings run amok. The casual observer might've assumed that since I didn't react, I didn't care, but I consoled myself with the knowledge that at least my fiancé, Raj, knew better.

Or…well…he used to.

Judging by his recent silent treatment, maybe Raj needed a reminder? I glanced down at my BlackBerry for the eighth time that morning. No new messages.

Two weeks, I thought. *And still not a word from him. Men are such women sometimes.*

Really though, he'd completely overreacted. I had every

intention of helping him understand why…just as soon as he got around to returning my call. Or calls. All right, fine. *Two calls, two e-mails and one text message* in the fourteen days since he took that consulting assignment in London. The thought of him cutting me out of his life so easily made me want to hurl my BlackBerry at the wall. Of course, that kind of outburst at the conference table wasn't an option. Unless you were a client, in which case even trying to smoke the conference table itself would have been forgiven. Not to mention that nobody would ever find out about it—we at Steel Associates would make sure of that. Appearances are everything in Los Angeles, and so much more at our firm, which catered to the stars. Steel was the most sought-after marital mediation and divorce boutique in the city. Composure was our corporate culture as much as discretion was our hallmark.

"It's true that our clients rely on us for our legal expertise. But they also expect us to help them steer clear of the headlines," Niles, a senior partner, began. "I understand there have been some…complications with your case. Monica, would you care to elaborate?"

All eyes were on me. Silently, I berated myself for using Raj's going AWOL as an excuse not to bother with my eyebrows. To begin with, I was a noticeably tiny brunette scurrying around in The Land Of The Seven-foot Model. Beyond that, I chose a professional career in a part of the country where "trophy wife" was considered a legitimate aspiration. I was used to the women in tight-fitting tracksuits and spray-tans who clogged the checkout lines at every Whole Foods on the west side, waiting to buy a single avocado. I was not used to being the center of this much attention. I stifled the urge to check my face in the confer-ence-room window.

"Gladly, Niles." I cleared my throat. "And I want to assure you all that despite recent news, this case of Camydia hasn't been nearly as difficult to handle as some of the others I've had."

Trust me, it's not what you think.

Dubbed "Camydia" by the popular press, Cameron and Lydia Johnson had started their relationship as Hollywood's "it" couple. They had been a publicist's dream-come-true, since they appealed to every imaginable demographic. Lydia was a feisty, buxom and ivory-skinned brunette from a South Philadelphia ghetto. She began singing in a racially diverse inner-city gospel choir and soon topped the Bill-board charts. Cameron, on the other hand, was the son of a mildly successful African-American stockbroker from Harlem, and the product of a top-notch private-school edu-cation. His rebellion against his overbearing single father was to reach for a basketball in lieu of an SAT review book. The pair met at an A-list party mixing celebrities and professional athletes when each was at the height of their career. And the kind of fireworks that ensued could be seen from here to Las Vegas.

But in the two years since they'd shacked up together in a twenty-million-dollar Malibu mansion, things had taken a turn for the worse. On the release date of her latest album, Lydia's former agent wrote a book claiming that she lip-synced on tour. And the rumor around the area locker rooms was that Cameron's hard partying habits had landed him in danger of losing his NBA contract. Put more succinctly: few things will kill a celebrity marriage quicker than the hint that someone's public stock is about to decline. The couple's newly conjoined name, which did indeed rhyme with the venereal disease, was the media's way of underscoring the fiery state of their current affairs. In particular, there were rumors that Cameron had been seen about town with an unidentified blonde.

"With that said," I continued, "we suspect a leak from someone on Cameron and Lydia's household staff. Paparazzi swarmed the Malibu mansion just as they were leaving in separate cars on Saturday night. Although Lydia assures me it meant nothing, since she was headed out for dinner with a girlfriend and he was meeting some buddies at the gym. The rumor in the celebrity rags this morning is that they have each been spotted with other people. So this week we'll be focused on damage control."

Steel Associates was the Navy SEALs of celebrity divorce law. We handled everything from counseling to mediation to divorce, depending on the case. To be sure, we earned a premium for our public-relations-minded strategies in a city where gossip was worth its weight in gold and divorce wasn't just the topic of tragic statistics. To our clients, divorce suggested far more than a broken heart or a depleted bank account. In this city, it might spark a public-opinion shockwave. Who would get the house in Napa? Who was responsible for the ongoing psychiatric treatment of their Pomeranians? What about the care and feeding of the entourage? Just how much of a popularity drop would the divorce cost them among the 18-34-year-old female demographic, and how would it affect record sales? Would it make a difference if they waited to announce until after the Emmys?

These were serious questions, all, and that's why the celebs came to us first. Short of an actual computer spreadsheet into which we could pump all the variables and estimate the costs to both sides, Steel gave the best advice money could buy. Because either alone or in pairs, these folks typically wanted to consider their options, estimate their settlements and minimize the potential damage to their careers.

Loosely, my job was one-part mediator, one-part lawyer and one-part marriage therapist or celebrity spin doctor. Although with Cameron and Lydia lately, that title seemed to be all celebrity babysitter all the time. Given the current state of my own engagement, the marriage therapist part was a laugh. One nice side effect of my career choice, however, was that I instinctively minimized the collateral damage in my own life, as well. I had been wearing my ring on a chain around my neck ever since my engagement three months before. As long as people still noticed the chain peeking out from my collar, I was fine. Other than my cousin

Sheila, nobody knew that Raj and I were, in his words, *taking some time.*

"Since when do we believe everything our clients tell us?" Stefanie interrupted me, smiling widely and refusing to blink. "Have celebrities suddenly become reliable?"

Everyone laughed on cue, and so did I.

"Certainly not," I answered graciously, as if we were all just the best of friends. "I'm simply trying to make sure everyone is up to speed on the new developments in the case. That is what we're here for, right, gentlemen?"

Stefanie was as cool as a cucumber under pressure, and she despised me for at least visibly seeming the same. Had I not known better, I would've sworn that one of the thick and serpentine waves of her long, brown hair actually lifted itself up off her shoulder to hiss at me. Indeed, had my superstitious Indian grandmother been in the room, she wouldn't have hesitated to lick her finger and slide it right across my cheek, as a makeshift shield for the dreaded evil eye. Had I been anything short of convinced that it would fuel every popular corporate stereotype about a woman's inability to play well with another, I might have chosen to react to Stefanie. But I drew a deep breath, threw my fellow female colleague a wide, bright smile, then paused and turned my attention toward Niles.

"After all, Cameron and Lydia are very important clients for our firm."

By the time Cameron and Lydia had first contacted us, they were only in what we referred to as *Phase 1.* In private, they were fighting like cats and dogs and contemplating a trial separation, but were still too emotionally attached to each other to commit to it.

"I agree…" Jonathan, my fellow junior associate and co-counsel, chimed in. "As such, we've prepared a preliminary asset-split recommendation to present to Cameron and Lydia."

I began passing copies of our internal brief around the table. Asking for input from everyone always reflected favorably on a Junior Associate, and Jonathan and I were working together to make a good impression. Not that he needed any of my help. Jonathan had that rare but potent blend of stalwart optimism and moral relativism that meant he was born to practice law in Los Angeles.

"But I thought this was a mediation case." Niles feigned surprise. "When did they move into 'division of assets' territory?"

Snickers around the room.

"Yes, well," I explained. "Our strategy is to show them a version of an asset split and hope they'll take it as a wake-up call. Seeing their life divided up like this might actually force them to reconsider."

Silent stares from every direction. Do-gooders didn't last very long at our firm.

"Naturally, we'll get our billable hours either way."

The tension in the air noticeably dissipated. Niles looked up from his copy of the brief, and added, "All right, all right. I can appreciate the creativity as much as anyone else. But if that is the strategy, you should suggest they each take one of the twin pomeranians. Our clients may be too narcissistic to risk their bodies and their lifestyles by having children, but I'll bet that the idea of splitting up the 'mock children' will get them divorcing in no time."

He was right to be sarcastic. About 75% of our cases skidded right past mediation and landed in divorce. And Steel made a bigger profit in a shorter period of time when the husband and wife divorced immediately than when they opted to "reconsider." Niles made it clear that he wanted this case closed soon, and normally I would have agreed. In fact, I probably would have nudged them not-so-gently in the direction of the courthouse because the more cases I completed in a year, the higher my bonus. But with Camydia, I wasn't convinced. Unlike most of my uber-famous clients, these two didn't fight like they wanted to hurt each other…they fought like they *needed* to hurt each other. A perfect example was the first time they had sat down at Steel Associates with Jonathan and myself.

"I told her it wasn't me in that goddamn hot tub." Cameron buried his face in his massive hands before running them over his bald head. "She could believe that stupid tabloid, but she can't believe me. What the hell?"

Hunched over in a chair before us, he seemed about as helpless as any client I had ever seen. Jonathan and I simply listened, sympathetically, trying not to be blinded by the twinkling of the canary diamond solitaire on his pinky finger, or the studs the size of testicles protruding from his earlobes.

"It'd be one thing if I did it." He licked his upper lip and wrung his hands. "But I didn't do what they said I did. And she doesn't even talk to me about it! She just swallows whatever her goddamn publicist feeds her! And then I have to hear it from my agent that my own *wife* is taking off with her girl-friends to Cabo San Lucas for a week. I got home from practice one day and she was out! How you gonna leave town without even telling your man first? Without even calling him?"

I resisted the urge to hug him, knowing as I did what it felt like to be left without a forwarding address. Instead I fingered the chain around my neck. But before I could run the risk of looking as if I was taking sides by trying to console this head-shaking, hand-wringing tree of a man, Lydia whooshed back in from the ladies' room.

"Oh, so now I gotta tell you where I'm *goin'* every minute of the day?" she spat at him, taking a seat and ripping off her white-rimmed sunglasses to reveal striking and furious blue eyes. "Do I always know where you are, Cameron? *Huh? Do I?* Oh, or maybe you just own me?"

After crossing her legs she brought her puffy, defiant eyes to rest on mine.

"What the hell is she talking about?" Cameron looked from me to Jonathan. "How am I supposed to deal with a woman like this?"

"What I am talk-ing about, Cam-ron," she overenunciated, "is reality. Somethin' you lost touch with."

"Pshhhhhh…whatever," Cameron protested to no one in particular, leaning back in his chair with a neck and eye roll in her direction.

"Lydia," I jumped in. "I hear you. You want equality. And Cameron, you want communication. These are good goals. Although the first step is empathy. Lydia, Cameron was just telling us how your reaction to the tabloid article made him feel. The key in reconciliation is to separate emotions from actions, and then try to improve communication. Once you understand each other's motivations, you can decide if and how you can function better as a couple. Now, are you willing to give this a try, Lydia?"

She sighed, fished a cigarette out of her purse and then signaled with her eyebrows for me to continue. Quoting the building's *No Smoking* policy would've gone over as well as pointing out that her roots were emerging under that chestnut dye-job. I decided to let that battle go and picked another.

"Baby," Cameron murmured, "what the hell? What are you doin'?"

"Nothing," she hissed, blowing smoke in his face. "That's what I'm doin'."

"Do you believe this?" Cameron looked to Jonathan for some male bonding over female irrationality.

"Oh, so my smoking bothers you?" She sat upright, mocking him. "Tell ya what. Maybe you'll get lucky and your new hot-tub girlfriend won't feel the need to smoke after sex. Oh, wait a minute, what am I talkin' about maybe?

You already know whether or not she smokes after sex because you already had sex with her!"

"I didn't sleep with her!" He slammed a fist down on the table beside his chair, causing me to glare a little.

"And I'm not *smoking!*" she fired back, breathing more smoke in his face.

"Hey, guys, clearly there's a lot of hurt and confusion in this room. But let's remember why we're here. We want to be productive and try to make sense of the situation together. You've taken the first step by coming to us, so now let us try to help you, okay?" I asked.

Cameron nodded like a schoolboy who'd just admitted to putting glue in another child's hair during nap time. Lydia didn't acknowledge me.

"Cameron," I tried, "why don't you tell Lydia how you felt about her reaction to the story. Remember—don't place blame, and don't attack her actions. How did her leaving suddenly make you *feel?*"

Lydia rose to look out the floor-to-ceiling windows of our skyscraper. The city lay prostrate before her, and the mountains waited patiently in the distance as her husband beseeched her.

"Lydia, when you took that trash rag's word for it, without even talkin' to your man first, without even hearin' his side of the story, I felt like you weren't on my side anymore. We used to be on each other's side. Always. I always knew you had my back."

"And?" I led him along.

"And, I felt…abandoned." He blinked his eyes hard and sniffed.

"Don't do that, Cam," she warned him, twisting around to reveal the dragon tattoo climbing up her right shoulder. "Don't even think about it. I am not your mother. You can't blame me for her splittin' on you and your pops."

"It's not about that," he told his hands.

She straightened before asking, "Why can't you look me in the eye when you say it?"

"Baby, I—"

"No! Don't give me that!" she yelled and gestured with the lit end of the cigarette. "I see the way your dumb teammates look at me. They're laughing at me, and I don't know why! You have the balls to say that I'm not on your side? What about you bein' on my side for once? What about not letting them *laugh at me!* I'm your wife, damn it. Not some stripper you guys called up to the room in Vegas and think the wives won't find out about it!"

"Look, it's like I told you," Cameron attempted to get a word in.

"Like you told me? What did you tell me, Cam? Huh? I can't remember the last time I got a straight answer from you. Are you tellin' me now that you were never in that hot tub with her?"

He hung his head.

"Answer me!"

"Not…" he started, his voice rising about twenty octaves "…not exactly."

Lydia froze, and I saw a vein in her temple go live. She took a step forward, slammed down her palms, leaned forward on the conference table and dared him to finish his thought.

Cameron wouldn't look up, and Lydia's knuckles were turning white as she dug her lengthy, bejeweled fingernails into the taut black leather of the conference table, so I took the next step for them.

"Cameron, could you clarify that for us?"

"Okay, like…here's what it was. I mean, I was with her in that hot tub." He reached out for his wife. "But it was before you and me even got engaged! You were on tour and it was like…two months since I even seen you. But those pictures from that magazine…they weren't me. That party was at the same place, but it was during the playoffs, and that was waaaaaay after we already got married. It was the same girl with a different guy. I didn't break my marriage vows with her, boo, I swear!"

Lydia was stoic, her unflinching glare burning a hole into Cameron.

After what seemed like forever, Cameron turned to me. "Monica, you said to tell her the truth."

two

MOMENTS AFTER OUR MORNING ASSOCIATES' MEETING I COULD feel Cassie, our team's assistant, struggling to catch up to me. She would have been a lot more aerodynamic if she didn't insist on wearing those five-inch heels to work every day. Besides, compared to my shrimpy five feet four inches, she was practically a giraffe in the first place. Leaping up from her desk just outside the conference room, she tailed me right into my office and kicked the door shut behind me.

"Can I help you?" I smiled conspiratorially, rounding my desk.

"God, she is such a witch!" She popped her gum aggressively for affect.

"Who?" I feigned ignorance, slipping my jacket off of my shoulders and over the back of my chair.

"Oh, shut up." She leaned over my desk as I settled into my seat. "By the way, nice suit. Tahari?"

I nodded, logging back on to my computer. The only daughter of a Greek-American missionary and a woman from Northern India (a Peace-Corps baby, as she had originally described herself to me), Cassie had immediately adopted me as the older Indian sister she never had. Her gratefulness for any connection to the subcontinent sparked my maternal instincts toward her, ever since the first time I noticed the pride with which she ordered everything extra spicy (*I'm Indian,* she routinely informed any waiter within earshot.)

"Great cut." She nodded her approval at my ensemble, which was quite the compliment considering that prior to Steel, she had been in the women's apparel department at Nordstrom's. "Anyway, that's not the point. I can see everything that goes on in that meeting through the double glass doors. Stefanie was staring at you so hard that I had one hand on the fire extinguisher the whole time, in case you actually burst into flames."

"Well, *good lookin' out?*" I tried.

"I got your back."

"It's not that bad." I slipped on my glasses and grabbed a stack of snail mail out of my actual in-box.

It wasn't like I was unaware of the situation; it was more that I felt like it was my responsibility, as one of the few professional females at the firm, to maintain a certain level of decorum.

"Yes it is, Monica." She began watering the potted ficus in the corner, and then paused as if she just realized something. "You know what it is? *Baskania!* It's *baskania!* In Greek, you know? Evil eye? I knew I felt something horrible radiating out of her!"

I shook my head, tossed a letter from the *Young Friends of the Getty Museum* into the trash and reached for another envelope.

"Come on," she said. "I know you know what I'm talking about. What do we call it in Hindi?"

Cassie's mother had all but denied her that half of her heritage while she was growing up, as a protest against having been disowned by her family for running off with the American missionary all those years ago. Consequently, Cassie had never visited India, and spoke little if any Hindi at all. What insight Cassie could claim into any part of her family history came almost exclusively from her immigrant Greek grandparents. And it didn't help that, according to her, the Indian girls at UCLA were less than welcoming to anyone who didn't seem *Indian enough* for them. I told her they were too jealous of her beauty to allow her to play in their reindeer games, but I knew that for her it was small consolation. The way she described it Cassie had the subcontinent to thank for nothing more than her outsider mentality and her deep brown eyes. From Greece, however, came her facility with Greek cuisine, her encyclopedic knowledge of Greek mythology and her tendency to suspect everyone of everything.

Sometimes I was just glad I was on her good side.

"Yes, I know what you're talking about, and you're wrong." I exhaled. "We call it *nazar* in Hindi. But in the old wives' tale—and *it is* an old wives' tale—they say that too many compliments to a healthy baby or a beautiful bride pisses off the gods. It makes them jealous because no human should be envied as much as a god. So the gods take revenge on the child or the bride to mitigate the hubris. And we both know that Stefanie isn't exactly in the habit of complimenting me."

"So what? She smiles at you with that hateful hateful look on her face. It's the same thing." She made herself comfortable in the chair across from my desk. "Besides, Medusa never complimented her victims, you know. She didn't have to. She just dried them up by looking at them and that's why they talk about turning people into stone. She sucked all of the moisture right out of them. Seriously. So kids got diarrhea. Big, strong men became impotent. Women couldn't nurse their babies because they couldn't produce milk. Everybody she hated literally dried up."

"How do you know?" I asked without looking away from my e-mail. "Were you there?"

"Seriously, the myth says that young mothers could no longer lactate!"

"Okay, yuck?" I repositioned my bra around my ribcage with my elbows.

"It may be gross, but it's also universal, Monica. In Greece they would make Stefanie spit into holy water and then have you drink it," she pointed out, with all the self-satisfaction of a child who'd just proven in too much detail to a roomful of adults that she knew where babies came from.

Experience had taught me that Cassie wouldn't leave until she was ready, so I decided to humor her to speed the process along. "All right, fine. You win. Why would somebody who hated me enough to curse me be willing to help me out by spitting in holy water?"

"Well, sometimes the evil eye is unintentional. Like what you said about too much praise…too many compliments… making it accidental. Sometimes it's Medusa, and sometimes it's just too many compliments."

"So being admired has roughly the same effect as being hated?" I raised my eyebrows to demonstrate that it added up. "That's comforting."

"In Mexico they would roll a raw egg over your entire body," she continued, ignoring me. "And then crack it open to see if the yolk was shaped like an eye."

"Kinky."

"I'm serious. And drying up isn't a good thing. First you would have dry skin…then you'd start itching, then lose your hair. Think about it, the evil eye could cause premature aging!" She snapped her fingers and pointed at me with too much satisfaction.

"*Malocchio,* huh?" Jonathan added, having opened the door and invited himself into the conversation. "I don't know much about it, but I do know that when I was a kid, my grandmother used to dribble olive oil into water and then study it like tea leaves to see if we were cursed."

We both looked at him.

"Yeah, she did it whenever we visited them in Iran. She said it was because I was such a cute little boy that the people in the village were probably jealous."

"See?" Cassie insisted.

"*Malocchio*... Isn't that an Italian word? Not a Persian one?" I asked.

"Well...you know the, umm, flavor of the month?" He raised half of what would have been a unibrow were it not for the weekly waxing appointment he didn't think I knew about. "Daniela? She's from Milan, or Florence, or Rome or something. I can't remember. But I know it's in Italy. Anyway, she's rubbing off on me because she doesn't speak much English. Pretty soon I'll run out of Italian restaurants to take her to on the West Side. And you know I don't go farther east than West Hollywood. Oh well, I guess every relationship has an expiration date."

Jonathan was the only man I knew who could be smarmy and endearing at the same time. Kind of like your horny kid brother offering to rub sunblock on your girlfriend's back at the beach.

"Oh, right. Back to you, ladies." He stepped away defensively. "I forgot, it's all about you ladies. Jeez, don't you get sick of talking about yourselves all the time?"

It may be useful to point out here that I know for a fact Jonathan actually spends more on skin care than I do. He was the perfect example of that weird hybrid of raging insecurity and blinding self-entitlement unique to a Beverly

Hills upbringing. The only son of a wealthy Persian family who fled Iran in the 1970s, he had earned his bachelor's and JD degrees at UCLA, had never lived more than five miles away from his parents, and categorically refused to date any woman who wasn't blond and at least five inches taller than himself. The latter fact, as he had explained to me over a working lunch shortly after we both joined the firm, was because all the fun was sure to be over once he decided to grow up and settle down with a nice Persian virgin.

Meanwhile, the fact that he weighed roughly 100 pounds with his pockets full of lead, in a town full of men who looked like walking G.I. Joe's, probably had nothing to do with his need to have the latest cell phone, the newest Maybach, and the *pimpin*-est table at any club he ever set foot in. But Jonathan was good at what he did, we looked out for each other when the workload got too steep, and the demonstrated depth of his family values had long since mitigated some of my revulsion at the double standards by which he lived. Also, he was a good ally to have within the firm because something about his playful smarminess seemed to make our two-timing clients feel at home. Jonathan, clearly, would make partner.

"Anyway, that doesn't mean I'm with you on this home-remedy stuff, Cassie," he elaborated. "I could've done without my grandmother spitting into her hand and rubbing it onto my cheek all the time."

"Are you wearing a pink shirt with that suit?" I squinted at him.

"Daniela said it brings out the color of my eyes," he defended himself.

"Since when does pink bring out brown?"

"I know, I know," he admitted, shaking his head. "I have to break up with her."

"Hmm, I'll get some bottled water for your office anyway," Cassie reassured in the most serious of voices. "So you'll have it handy in case you find yourself starting to dry up, that is."

"Oh, gross." Jonathan winced. "Is this a woman thing?"

"No, it's not a woman thing, you troglodyte. It's a super-stition thing." I shook my head, averting my eyes with a grin. "Anyway, Cassie was on her way out, so you and I should get to work."

The problem with acknowledging another woman's envy is that it implies you actually believe you are somehow superior. And I never saw any reason for Stefanie to envy me. She was attractive, intelligent and a formidable future litigator in my opinion. And when we had first arrived at the firm I had imagined we would be friends. Or at least convivial colleagues. Boy, did I have a lot to learn back then.

Cassie noticed my smirk. "What did you do at that meeting?"

"Nothing. I brought everyone up to speed on Cameron and Lydia's case." I saw her perk up like a puppy that had caught a whiff of kibble. "And I don't plan on telling you anything about it, so scoot."

She whimpered, which would have been annoying coming from anyone else. But since she had started working with us a year before, Cassie had become the little sister I never had. The one with the heart of gold. And the poor taste in men. And the sick fixation on every detail of the personal lives of celebrities. Naturally, it made the opportunity to work at Steel both completely irresistible and supremely frustrating for her.

"Need-to-know basis, babe." I continued, "And you don't need to know the specifics of their relationship. We're lucky we can even tell you who the clients are."

"Fine. But sometimes this *attorney-client privilege* stuff goes too far." She air-parenthesied the words in protest. "Besides, I'm practically family."

"Don't let Niles catch you saying that."

"That I'm family?" She looked hurt.

"That we ought to share privileged information with family," I corrected. "Because believe me, Sheila never hears word one."

"Sheila's only your cousin, Monica. I'm the one who knows all your dirty little secrets," she teased on her way out the door, oblivious to Jonathan's eyes sparkling. "And that makes me closer than family."

Once she was gone, Jonathan swiped my marked-up copy of the Camydia division-of-assets proposal off of my desk. He made himself comfortable on my couch, propped his feet up on the coffee table and started scanning through the notes I had made in the margins.

I seized on the chance to check my e-mail once again. Still no messages from Raj.

"Don't worry so much, Monica." Jonathan peered over his memo. "Whatever these dirty little secrets are, I'm sure we can have them taken care of. *I know a guy.*"

"I don't have dirty little secrets, Jonathan," I said, scowling. "I have a…problem. And I don't think it's anything Bruno can help me out with."

Bruno was one of those wannabe Hugh Hefners littered across the California basin who made local news for depressing real estate prices, erecting neon signs and waving freedom of expression banners everywhere he went. His was the first case Jonathan and I worked on together, and when he came to us he was convinced that his eighteen-year-old stripper wife, Claudia's refusal to keep dancing at his club meant that she was cheating on him. Yes, the strip-club owner was worried that the stripper was cheating on him. In much the same way as a dog owner worries that his dog might be licking itself while he's away. I, for one, was shocked.

Before breaking the news of the impending divorce to his wife, Bruno came to us to find out how much it would cost him. Although he could have gotten the same advice for a cheaper price from any of our lesser-profiled competitors who catered to the rich, if not-so-famous, Bruno, like so many others who worshipped at the altar of celebrity, needed desperately to believe that his life mattered to the general public, and was therefore worthy of Steel-strength confidentiality.

At one point, after yet another grueling day of poring

over his convoluted tax returns, Bruno invited us over to the club for some drinks. Rather than offending the client, I went along to The Cinnamon Lizard for just one drink, and then made my escape on the premise of an early appointment with my personal trainer. Honestly, I hadn't seen that much purple neon lighting since the weekend I spent in Atlantic City. The next morning Jonathan informed me that our client's real name was in fact Eugene Bronstein. A good Jewish kid from the tree-lined suburbs of Massachusetts, Eugene had moved to Los Angeles to reinvent himself after the collapse of his career as a stockbroker and the failure of his first marriage to his high-school sweetheart.

Emboldened by all those shots of Jim Beam, Bruno had decided to brag to Jonathan about the sophistication of his entrepreneurial operation. He gave him a personal tour of the two-story building that housed the most popular of his three strip clubs, located just off Sunset Boulevard. Below street level there were two additional floors, containing an X-rated bookstore, private lap-dance suites, bachelor party rooms, six-person showers surrounded by one-way mirrors, peep shows and even a carpentry shop where Bruno's artisans built and repaired the peep show booths on site. None of these ancillary sources of income, it turns out, had been mentioned anywhere on Bruno's tax returns.

According to Jonathan, their conversation had turned (as I'm sure that it so often does amidst flying G-strings, plentiful rhinestones and women whose breasts refused to shake when they did) toward religion. Being Jewish himself, and a devout temple-goer, Jonathan knew what he had to do. Somehow, before he arrived at work wearing the same suit and reeking of smoke and other people's misery the next morning, Jonathan had managed to help a drunken and re-luctant Eugene Bronstein see the ungodliness of trying to bilk Claudia out of her share of his empire.

Over the next few weeks, we worked out a private settle-ment that took good care of Claudia while sparing Bruno the ugliness of having to report anything new to the IRS. Yes, we were in the business of secrets, and the final one that I had to keep in the Bronstein case was the one belonging to Jonathan. It was his opinion that his big-man reputation simply couldn't withstand the hit of his having convinced someone to do the right thing. And in a way I saw his logic. So I had taken the fall for Jonathan's conscience, claiming to be the one who had forced Bruno to make an equitable arrange-ment. And I made a lifelong friend in Claudia Bronstein (the proud new owner of their house in Palm Springs, along with the third largest strip club in Hollywood) in the process.

"I still can't believe that guy calls himself an entrepreneur," Jonathan mused from the couch a half hour later.

"Meaning?" I looked up from my books on case law.

"Meaning—" he lowered his voice and glanced at the door to make sure that his pesky sense of morality would remain between the two of us "—in my opinion, a real en-trepreneur is someone who makes something from nothing. Like my dad, who used all his savings to build an import business from scratch. He's the perfect blend of an inventor and a salesman. But with Bruno, it doesn't apply. He didn't have to invent or sell anything. People are hardwired to want sex with ridiculously beautiful women, and to be fascinated with depravity, especially in this town. How much of an accomplishment is it when all you're doing is essentially turning the lights on at the crack store to make it a little easier for the junkies, who were already looking to find it? Sure, he diversified into related businesses, but he never had to sell anything to anyone that they didn't already want and kind of need."

In order to keep some semblance of idealism alive within herself, a girl in L.A. has to search for signs of integrity in most men with the resolve of a drug-sniffing dog. Jonathan was one of the good ones, I had long since decided. And my resolution made it so much easier both to work with him and to recognize as a fact how influential in the upper echelons of the local legal community I had no doubt he would one day become.

"Okay. But he's pretty damn proud of himself. As proud as I'm sure wife number three will be…just as soon as she turns eighteen and decides to apply for a job at his club, that is."

"That guy doesn't have much to be proud of." He half laughed, turning his attention back to his work. "Take it from a junkie."

three

Okay, so it's not a dirty little secret in the *"No officer, I have no idea how that horse managed to dress itself up in full bondage gear and climb into a vat of Jell-O"* sense of the phrase. But still, my obsession for the horoscope section of the otherwise god-awful celebrity rag, *Pucker,* always made me feel a little dirty.

So in the end it turns out that my father was right. Family is the truest testament to the concept of karma, since they always get so much farther under your skin than anybody else without even trying. And that much irritation can only have been built up over multiple lifetimes. Case in point… Even though I hadn't spoken to her in a week or more, I was thoroughly resenting my mother's potential satisfaction at the mere thought of my resorting to the horoscopes for advice before I had even checked my weekly copy of *Pucker,* which Cassie left for me in a very nondescript-looking envelope on her desk every Friday afternoon. She referred to the magazine as my dirty little secret because she knew that despite my vocally vehement protests to the contrary, no one at the firm would ever believe I wasn't reading it for the celebrity gossip.

But when you live your life surrounded by celebrities, you quickly find that you have about as much interest in their love lives as you do in their opinions on your love life. Which is to say, none. Once you have seen them standing in line behind you at a Starbucks at 11:00 a.m. on a day when their stylists, hair and makeup people have presumably gone simultaneously AWOL, it's hard to muster any real interest in who they might have woken up next to. Unless of course you're the one that woke up next to them. *I'm far more interested in who I'm sleeping with,* I'd often told my cousin Sheila, who never believed me.

Either way, after work I headed for the parking garage, climbed into my car and locked the door behind me. As I flipped to the page containing my horoscope, a small slip of paper floated out onto my lap. Inside the slip of paper was a single peacock feather. *Of all the weird promotions,* I thought…before clicking on the light and noticing the words scribbled on the paper: *It's shaped like an eye, get it? It's like an amulet. Shut up and put it in your wallet! Love ya, Cassie.*

Laughing, I tossed the feather and note onto the passenger seat. Then I got back to scanning *Hayley's Horoscopes,* praying for something that might relate to me and Raj. After weeding through the useless bits about how some planet is rising in some sector of my chart, and how many years it's been since it did that, I finally got to the specifics. But aside from a warning about unintended consequences for any capricious actions I might be considering this month, it offered up little in the way of help. So I switched to Taurus—Raj's sign. It read in part:

Watch out for an upcoming eclipse, dear Taurus, which will occur in the second week of the month, and most likely affect your home and romance sectors. The planets are intent on misbehaving this month, making it difficult for you to be sure of the intentions of those around you. Trust me when I tell you that this disruptive influence is not only positive, but also necessary for many of you. The frenzied social calendar which will preceed the eclipse will set the stage for a much-needed examination of your romantic priorities, and those of your partner. If you're stuck in a romantic rut, cosmic AAA is already on the way! If your partner has been misbehaving, it might be time to trade them in once and for all. Keep reminding yourself that, while things may start out difficult, they will soon begin moving in the right direction, and you will find your love life in far better shape than ever before.

I couldn't believe my eyes. If the universe and Hayley were conspiring to pull Raj and I apart, then they weren't gonna get us without a fight. I dropped the magazine, shifted into Reverse and slammed on the gas…only to have to jam down the brakes a split second later when an angry woman in a fast-moving SUV honked me back into the moment before zooming by in my rearview mirror. Had I hesitated, I would definitely have slammed into her driver's side. I held a hand to my chest and hung my head to try and regain equilibrium. After catching my breath, I opened my eyes to fixate on the peacock feather watching me from the leather seat beside mine. Feeling like a child who'd decided to run away from home to her tree house on the night of the biggest snowstorm of the year, I looked both ways, sighed and reached for the feather. Folding it into three pieces, I tucked the feather inside my wallet, fastened my seat belt, and then ever so timidly backed my car out of the space.

"That torso is not a toy!" someone yelled at me through the phone at roughly 8:00 a.m. the following morning.

Sliding my SleepyTime terry cloth mask away from my eyes to let in his voice along with the ambient light I replied: "Excuse me?"

"Is this Monica from Steel Associates?" a person who sounded a lot like an English butler asked, and then spoke to someone else, *"How did she get a hold of a mannequin inside the dressing room?"*

"Maybe," I replied, fearing the worst.

"My name is Arthur Wood, and I am the Director of

Private Client Services at Barneys New York in Beverly Hills…*Madam, please refrain from abusing my staff!*…and your client, one Mrs. Lydia Johnson, has caused a bit of a situation at our store this morning."

"A situation?" I sat up, picturing her trying to set the place on fire, and wondering what that might have to do with me.

"Yes, let's call it that. And we do not have the means to sedate her without calling the police, which I am sure you understand would alert the media. You are the only person she is willing to speak with. She has barricaded herself inside of a dressing room, and… *Stop that immediately! Mrs. Johnson!*…. She just threw an iced coffee at my sales associate's head, soiling an entire rack of two-thousand-dollar *Badgley Mischka* gowns in the process! Look here, we are accustomed to accommodating the wealthy and…err… particular, but this abuse has simply gone too far. I will have to insist that you or someone from her team come here and collect her *immediately!*"

Less than twenty minutes later I was tossing my keys at the valet and being ushered in via the secret entrance reserved for the uber-important at Barneys off of Rodeo Drive. As a courtesy to the rich and truly bratty, high-end Beverly Hills retailers routinely arranged private shopping hours during which "Special Clients" could browse their stores in peace. It was a perk intended to spare certain clientele from the prying eyes of paparazzi, who could make millions just by reporting their bra sizes or affinities for brand names which they might not officially be endorsing that season. The retailers' return on this effort, of course, was the insane amount of money that celebrities would drop in their stores in a single visit. But Lydia's psychosis was too much to take, even for them, and now it was my problem.

Awesome.

Lydia, it seems, had called Mr. Wood frantically at 7:00 a.m. that morning to demand a visit to the jewelry department in preparation for a public appearance later that evening. When she arrived, she was belligerent. She insisted on donning numerous precious necklaces and rings at the same time, and then she started sobbing uncontrollably, refusing to take them off. Gasping through the tears, Lydia had suddenly become completely paranoid. She darted up the escalators toward the second floor, keeping the salesgirls at bay with creative sword work from the pointy end of a hat rack she had swiped along the way.

"She's run out of things to throw at us," Wood explained, smoothing his hair back as we hustled to the dressing room. "And at least her yelling has finally subsided. Perhaps she lost her voice. Still, we are meant to open to the public in a little over an hour, and we need her out of here before we can begin the damage control. Can you manage that?"

"I'll try, Mr. Wood, but with all due respect, she's not my child." I did my best to stare past his upturned nose and into his eyes. "We all work for them, don't we?"

"I suppose we do." He unclenched and patted my arm.

"Mind yourself in there, Madam. And let me know if there is anything else you'll require. She's already sent one of my salesgirls to hospital for some stitches across the forehead."

I paused to consider whether Lydia's retainer with Steel covered emotionally fueled assault.

"It was the new golden-snakeskin, four-inch Versace stiletto," he said before looking away. "She had about as much chance as any top model's personal assistant during detox."

"I thought she was just having a tantrum," I said. "I didn't realize she hurt anyone. I'm so sorry."

"As am I. Three inches to the left and that heel would have caught me in the eye," he thought aloud. "No matter. There are at least fifty plastic surgeons within ten miles… We won't be pressing charges." He raised an eyebrow at me. "But we will be expecting Mrs. Johnson to take advantage of our personal shoppers in advance of her next album release, so that she may remain off-site."

"That seems reasonable."

"Well, then, I'll leave you to it."

I grabbed a white silk scarf from a nearby Hermès display, walked lightly toward her dressing room, braced myself and put my ear to the floor.

"Don't shoot, Lydia." I waved the scarf under the door in an attempt to make her smile. "It's Monica. If you're willing to let the jewelry go unharmed, I'll promise to talk to the D.A. about sparing you jail time. I've negotiated lots of hostage situations before, and I know that we can work this out."

A sniffle, but no reply.

"Lydia?" I said a little louder. "Lydia, I'm coming in there unless you can give me a good reason why I shouldn't."

These were the more interesting moments of my job, and sometimes I wished I could have shared them with people outside of the firm. Because who would've believed that belly-crawling underneath the door of a changing room in the DKNY section of Barneys Beverly Hills before the rest of L.A. awakened on a Saturday morning had anything whatsoever to do with the practice of law?

I slithered over the plush carpeting (which was far softer than any sweater I owned) and into the cubicle (which was larger than my bedroom). Lydia was sitting on the floor cross-legged opposite the mirror, absentmindedly examining her split ends. Her hair made mine (which had not yet been brushed) look professionally done; however, her teal-green Juicy Couture track-suit had seen better days, and she was in truly desperate need of a facial. Or Proactiv. Or a vat of cover-up.

Imagine how much money I could make right now with just one snap of my camera-phone, I thought, cursing my morals to hell.

Clinging to her wrists, neck and ears were at least three million dollars worth of emeralds, diamonds and pearls in necklace, choker, bracelet, ring and chandelier earring form. There was even a pearl-encrusted tiara threatening to slide off her head. Over years of working with people surrounded by yes-men, I had learned that the best way to get them to do something was to let them talk first. So I sat up, settled in beside her, folded my hands in my lap and waited.

"When I was fifteen, my boyfriend Angelo Damiano gave me a necklace for our one-month anniversary," she began a few seconds later, while fingering the emeralds imbedded in a platinum, chain-link bracelet on her wrist. "It had this one really tiny emerald hanging at the bottom of a *mad-thin* five-carat gold chain. I swear I had to use a magnifying glass to find it. And it was probably just a chip of green glass, anyways. But it was the most beautiful thing in the world to me back then. I never took it off. I even slept with it on."

"Lydia," I pleaded, covering her hand with my own. "Things will get better. You had a fight, right?"

"You don't get it." She shook her head. "I trusted Angelo. I believed in my man back then. No question. It was me and him against the world. Things was simple. I miss that."

"So this is about your high school boyfriend?"

"It's about Cameron. I know he's cheating on me, Monica. I just know it." She stood up and confronted herself in the mirror. "But the messed-up part is that I don't know if I really know it, because everybody has somethin' to say. They all want to put in their two cents. And the media just wants to rip us apart."

"That's terrible, Lydia, but it's also a fact of public life." I borrowed a line from the boilerplate Steel Associates speech. "I'm here to help the two of you make sense of things, privately. But I still don't understand why you've locked yourself in here."

She turned to face me, her chandelier earrings shimmering at me as an echo of the gesture. "You have any idea how humiliated I am?"

"Oh, don't even worry about that. There's no paparazzi within five miles of the store. No one even knows you're here, other than the staff and me."

"It's not that, Monica. I'm not humiliated that people will find out. I'm humiliated because I don't even know if I trust my own instincts anymore, much less my man. There's just too many people in this relationship, and there have been from the beginning. Me, Cam and everyone else in the world. I don't even know who I can trust…they called my agent and my 'best friend' from my phone before they called you, Monica, I heard them. And they both saw my name on caller ID and didn't even answer their phones. My divorce lawyer is the only person who would take my call. So why would I trust my own husband, or anyone else?"

"Lydia, I'm sure it's not that bad—"

"He didn't come home last night," she cut me off, twisting an emerald ring on her trembling finger. "But instead of assuming that he was practicing late or staying at a buddy's, my mind went to the worst place. It's like I got no real feelings about my own life anymore. I'm just watching it all happen on TV and believing what they tell me, just like everyone else."

She stood straighter before her reflection, as if she was only now recognizing the ridiculousness of the situation. Stiffening her upper lip, she yanked the tiara from her hair and handed it to me. I decided I would have to smuggle her home anonymously in my car.

"So then stop listening to your own hype, Lydia." I rose to my feet and put an arm around her shoulder, noticing that I myself was no prize without makeup on a Saturday morning. "Go home and *talk* to your husband."

She turned to face me with an almost apologetic smile.

"But I'm gonna have to insist that you hand over the rest of those jewels first."

An hour and a half later, I was waiting to leave through the electric gates of Camydia's private driveway. Harold, the paunchy former marine, stood guard at the foot of the mile-long driveway leading up to their Malibu mansion.

"What was it this time?" he asked with a bitter smirk and the flash of a gold tooth as I idled beside his white-shuttered guard stand. "She thinks she looks fat on her new album cover?"

"Something like that," I said, rubbing my forehead to signal that I wasn't up for chitchat.

"I wish I had her problems," he whined. "Paparazzi been swarming all over the gates like monkeys this mornin'. I just turn up the juice on the electric fence whenever they get too close. Usually they read the signs or they hear it crackling and they keep their distance, but once in a while they try touchin' it anyway. Then I get to watch 'em sizzle."

"You're living the life."

"I can't complain," he acknowledged, then bowed his head. "You take care of yourself, Miss Gupta."

"You too, Harold."

As I watched her 30,000-square-foot, sea-facing faux-Spanish hacienda shrink in my rearview mirror I felt more than just pity for Lydia. Because at the moment, the people supposedly looking out for her were only doing it because she paid them, and she knew it. Not that we weren't worth the money, that is. For my part, I had delivered her safely into the loving arms of her waitstaff, instructed them to keep her away from the morning's newspapers and gossip shows at all costs, and convinced her to submit to the healing touch of the most-requested masseuse at Le Merigot spa. Normally, Stefan's heavenly hands were booked up many months in advance. But twenty minutes after my call that morning he was making his way over to Lydia's mansion for an emergency hot-stone treatment.

I deserved a facial and a massage of my own, I decided, and fished the cell phone out of my purse to redial the spa. But when I flipped it open the screensaver of Raj and I reminded me of what I really wanted: simpler times. Times like the beginning of my relationship with Raj—when things were new and uncomplicated between us—and he'd booked us a poolside couple's massage as part of an overnight stay at The Mondrian Hotel for our one-month anniversary.

Rather than make the call, I made a right onto Pacific Coast Highway. I opened the sunroof and skipped through my presets on my radio, looking for something that might take me away. Naturally, Stevie Nicks was belting out "Dreams" and I turned it up, although it made me miss Raj even more.

four

"WHAT'S STRANGE IS THAT THIS DOESN'T FEEL ODD," RAJ HAD told me across the twelve inches separating our poolside massage tables that sunny March afternoon a year and a half before. "Wouldn't you have thought that since we practically grew up together, this would seem bizarre?"

"You only moved back from London two months ago," I pointed out.

To be fair, we weren't moving fast at all. It was true that in the first few years since he had left for college in the UK, Raj and I hadn't spoken much. We had no reason to; he was one of a group of about twenty kids whose parents had settled in Orange County around the same time in the 1970s and formed a mini Indian community to keep us in touch with our heritage. Amid the series of dinner parties and weekend picnics and poolside Sunday afternoons our parents took turns organizing at their homes, Raj was only one of the many boys and girls I grew up with but barely knew anymore.

Yet when my father passed away just after my college graduation, the Raj that I had scarcely remembered had burst back on the scene and was determined to be there for me. It began with the obligatory condolence call, and evolved into a sort of transatlantic e-mail penpal-ship with little more than the hazy image of him, aged seventeen, remaining comfortably etched in my mind. Perhaps the lack of romantic expectation was why we became fast friends. We opened up to each other to the point that when his work as a management consultant for McKinsey & Company brought him back to Los Angeles some three years later, he knew I would be there to receive him at the airport.

I was there, but I wasn't prepared for the vision that was waiting for me when I pulled up curbside to LAX. Besides a much-needed growth spurt and a new truly fantastic European sense of style, Raj had become the sort of man whose stance made it clear that he knew where he was headed. And the moment he saw me the smile that spread across his face was at once familiar and full of things I wanted to discover.

"Yes, and you are certainly not the *proper little girl* I remember," he teased and raised a mischievous eyebrow at me from his massage table two months after we sped away from the airport.

Besides his confidence, his clothes, and the encyclopedia of little British sayings he sprinkled casually throughout our conversations, he had even developed something of an aristocratic accent in all his years overseas. It made me think of horseback riding across the countryside and scoundrels whose flirtatiousness almost compensated for their bad teeth. Looking back on it now, I can see that I didn't stand a chance.

"You're not a bit proper either." I bit my lip, savoring a flashback involving room-service bananas flambé all over my breasts the night before. "I don't remember playing any of the games we played *last night* at those family dinner parties."

"If we had been playing any of those games at those parties back then," he stated resolutely, "I never would have left for London in the first place."

So proper yet so naughty. Like I said, I didn't stand a chance.

"If we had known any of those games back then, our parents would have sent us both away to convents in India," I mused.

"Agreed. But I'm being serious. Our families know each other. My God, Monica, our fathers used to play *thaash* together," he said for emphasis, and then reached to connect us. "We have a lot of history behind us, and yet none of this feels even the least bit awkward to me."

And I remember watching his fingers inch toward me. That strong, familiar hand lifting and intertwining with my own. Until then I wasn't sure what I wanted from all of his

attention. A friendship? A relationship? Something in between? It wasn't that I felt nothing, exactly. It wasn't fire but
it wasn't apathy; and more than familiar, it was comfort. At
the very least I could feel how definitely he wanted me to
be ready for everything he was saying.

And why shouldn't I be? I had asked, looking into those
earnest eyes. *After all, I had known him my whole life. And the
last time I had felt so close to anyone had been in college…so why
shouldn't I give in to this?*

I squeezed his hand, but remained silent.

"I think we should tell our parents that we've been seeing
each other," he said hopefully. "I think they'll be absolutely
thrilled."

And the thing was, I knew that he was right.

Pushing up my sunglasses and tilting the sun visor to
better shield my eyes, I switched off the radio, calculated
the time difference to London, grabbed my cell phone and
dialed Raj.

No answer.

"Listen, honey, it's me," I began. "I, umm…I'm sorry.
You have every right to be angry with me. But we need to
talk about it. So call me. Today."

So I'm not the touchy-feely type. I never said I was.
Besides, men are supposed to respond better to facts they
can use, right? And the fact was that I was ready to talk, so
now it was up to him. But he was so thin-skinned sometimes. And the truth was that he was the one who had over-

reacted. Although I wasn't going to hold a grudge over it. Because in comparison to the irrational behavior I witnessed every day from my celebrity clients, Raj and I were doing fine. He was just testing my commitment by making a mountain out of a tiny pile of salt. Dust, even. And being a management consultant to major international corporations, he was paid to identify proverbial landmines and sandtraps, even where there weren't any. So he probably couldn't help himself.

All right, and in some small part, it could also have been about the peanuts.

"Whatever you fancy, darling," he had told me over the phone two weeks ago as we both converged toward my apartment in the evening. "Just remember to make sure there's no peanuts on the pad thai. And I'll get a bottle of that chardonnay you like. I think you're running low."

He was right, I thought, tossing my cell phone aside. *And how very like him it was to notice that sort of detail.* After picking up the takeout from our usual Thai restaurant in Santa Monica, I made my way home. Sipping on my Thai iced tea, I heaved the door open to find that he had beaten me home. The candles were lit and the table was set. The Maxwell CD reminded us of high school as it played in the background. And the Riedel stemware was dripping with condensation from the chilled chardonnay breathing inside. As usual, he had thought of everything.

He hefted the takeout from my arms, planted a kiss on

me and zipped off to the kitchen. I dropped my briefcase, kicked off my shoes and slipped off my suit jacket. I thought about heading into my room to change clothes before we ate, but something about the image of a man in the kitchen never failed to do it for me. So I snuck up behind him, nuzzled into his neck and indulged in the urge to be playful while he was defenseless, since his hands were busy ladling out the food.

"Madam, as difficult as I know it may be in light of my raw animal magnetism, I'll have to ask you to keep your hands to yourself," he said, putting down a dish of chicken with basil in order to pry my fingers from his lower abdomen and pull them instead toward his mouth. "Because as of six weeks ago, I'm permanently off the market."

Since, in his opinion, I had *such elegant fingers,* Raj always kissed them individually. And to keep it interesting—since he knew how much I detested PDA—he would also lick, nibble and occasionally violate my fingers until I squealed or recoiled in disgust and wiped them on my clothes to make a point. Of course, my protests only encouraged his behavior. Normally it was also his way of teasing me because he knew that I was insecure about my hands. As a child, I used to bite my nails. But on that particular evening, amidst all the nibbling and giggling, he stopped when he reached my ring finger.

"Where is it?" he asked abruptly.

"It's right here, baby." I stepped around to face him, motioning at the three-and-a-half carat princess-cut ring dangling from a chain around my neck.

"I thought we talked about this," he murmured, then switched his focus to the business of the basil chicken.

"Umm…we did talk about it," I said haltingly, following him to the table. I took a seat and folded my arms across my chest. "But we did not resolve it."

"So until we resolve it, you're not going to wear the ring," he huffed and sat down. "God, Monica."

"I am wearing it," I protested, "around my neck."

"Like a noose." He folded his arms to mimic mine. "Once again, your commitment to this relationship is astounding."

"Don't be melodramatic." I waved his comment away, knowing before the words were out that I'd made a major mistake.

Because it wasn't the first time that I had accused him of that, and the hurt registered clearly on his face. Raj had proposed to me during a moonlit stroll along the San Diego waterfront during a weekend getaway. We were sharing an ice cream cone, which he was holding, when he almost tripped over a shoelace. He asked me to hold the cone while he knelt down to tie it, and that was how he managed to catch me off guard.

Monica, he began and looked up from bended knee, *I think I have always loved you. And although it took a tragedy to bring you back into my life, I like to believe that maybe this was the good that came out of that sadness. Your father was an honorable man, and he raised an incredible daughter…who will become a phenomenal mother…and who will make her husband a very lucky man. I have never met anyone I would rather share my life with than you. Will you be my wife?*

I knew that I'd said yes because a moment later he was slipping the ring onto my finger and smothering me with kisses. I assumed the dizziness that followed was the result of some engagement-triggered chemical release in my brain. And I decided the best thing to do was to try to stay calm until things came back into focus. Why ruin the moment for Raj? It was fine. I was happy. Everything was fantastic. Really.

Until he said it. Tucking my hand into the bend of his arm, he took a deep breath and exhaled those fateful words: *Monica Shah.* The air was gone. The world stopped spinning. It was as if I had watched while the door to some small, previously unnecessary room was swung tightly shut. It didn't slam, and it didn't squeak. It simply slid closed, bolted itself tight and refused to entertain the idea of being reopened. Perhaps my own last name had crawled inside, and was packed away neatly in a cardboard box marked "Things I'll Never See Again." Maybe it had been greeted by what little connection I had left to my father, since Indians always believed that after marriage, a daughter no longer belongs to her birth family. It was possible that my detachment to being engaged was a defense mechanism against the idea of my former self being jailed away. None of this had anything to do with Raj, I reminded myself, and went about playing the role of the blushing fiancée.

But the next morning I awoke with his arm around my neck in what for the first time felt so much more like a thick rope than a bear hug. I tried to keep it to myself. I slipped out of bed and into the shower. However, in the time it took to shower and get wrapped in towels, I had realized exactly what I had to do. And I probably should have waited until the room service delivery guy had left before blurting it out, but…

I won't give up my last name, I declared, *for myself or my future children.*

To his credit, Raj tipped and dismissed the confused delivery guy before responding to me.

Good morning to you, too, he replied, and collapsed into a seat before the beautiful breakfast spread. *Okay, look, baby. I can understand you wanting to keep your last name, and I'm willing to talk about that. But on the topic of the children I think I am a bit more traditional.*

Being an adult, I narrowed my eyes and dug my heels in further: *Trust me, Raj. If this is going to be about who's more stubborn, you're not going to win. You're not gonna negotiate your way through this one with me. So don't even try it.*

How can you be so unreasonable? He had gotten flustered. *You aren't even prepared to discuss it! Am I going to be a part of this marriage?*

The thing about me is, I don't tolerate weakness well—in men or animals. It's the lawyer in me I'm sure, but basically I think that if you're dragging the pack down, you should probably be shot or left behind. That's why I reacted so…poorly. I knew it was a bad idea even as I did it…called him the adjective to end all adjectives: melodramatic.

That was the day I learned that even though *both* parties

are usually well-aware of who's more emotionally involved, nobody wants it announced out loud. Whereas a woman would have taken it as an observation, a man hears it roughly translated as: *you're the woman.*

I might have tried to smooth things over, but his silence on the drive back to Los Angeles gave me no choice but to twist the knife. If this was how we were going to start our married life, I reasoned, then I had to set a precedent. So I slipped the ring off my finger and onto a chain around my neck, and it had remained there ever since. Later that night we agreed that we didn't want to fight; everything didn't need to be settled in a day.

Mistakenly, I assumed that refilling both of our wine glasses was Raj's way of putting an end to our Mexican standoff over Thai food that night.

Thank God for reliable Raj, who never ever let things spin too far out of control.

"Actually, I have some news." He spoke in between shoveling heaping spoonfuls of chili-doused pad thai into his mouth. "McKinsey has offered me a one-month assignment in London. They requested that I be on the team since I worked with this client on another project a few years back."

"Mmm-hmm…" I played along, tipping back my glass and dropping my shoulders a bit. "And when would it start?"

"I could leave as early as tomorrow or as late as next week."

"Oh." I rubbed my ring between my thumb and forefinger, concentrating hard on the plate before me.

"A client requesting someone specifically is always good news, so it might even lead to a promotion if I can get enough visibility for the project. Could you imagine if it turned into a full-time offer?"

I'll admit it. I actually laughed out loud. Through a mouthful of green coconut curry.

He glanced up without moving his head.

"Oh, *yeah*," I joked, "because this is the 1920s and all women have to quit their jobs and follow their men across the ocean."

"So you wouldn't even consider it?" He spat out the words and his nostrils literally flared. Not sexy. A little scary, actually.

"Well, I mean…come on…" I was quite the articulate litigator. "It's not really an option. They haven't made you an offer, so we're talking hypothetically here."

"And you won't even consider it hypothetically?" he asked, sucking at his teeth.

"Raj," I said.

"Monica, has this whole thing always just been about *you*?"

"No, of course not."

"I knew what I was getting into when we became friends. Partially this is my fault because our friendship was based on me helping you talk about losing your dad. And it was understandable when we started dating that the focus was originally going to be on you. But I always thought that…in time…in time, things might change. They might become more equal. But they haven't, Monica. And I don't know if that's because of how I allowed this relationship to center around you, or if it's because that's *who you are*."

"I resent that," I began, but then stopped when he held up a hand.

"Oh, crikey!" He choked and dropped his fork, pushed his chair back and rose to his feet.

I was actually shaken by the sound of his yell. Never before had I heard him raise his voice.

"There's sodding peanuts in the goddamn pad thai, Monica!" he said laughingly in disgust, while he shook his head. "And I just lost my appetite."

He stomped straight into the bedroom, leaving me alone to think about what I had done. He didn't help me clear the table, and he didn't face me that night as we slept. When I awoke in the morning, he was gone.

His text message from the airport read:

Decided to leave this morning. Will be in London for at least two weeks.
We need a break anyway. This may be good timing.

It was cold, to the point, and exactly what I deserved. Not at all like him. For the first time since we had gotten together, I thought maybe he wasn't the one with more skin in the game.

And I haven't heard another word from him since.

All right, maybe you can never be certain of anything. But I am at least as certain that I am heterosexual as I am that some hot teen-queen celebutante under the age of thirty will one day make use of Steel's promise that *After your first four divorce proceedings, the fifth one's on the house!*

Still, even I couldn't help staring at the buxom Angelina Jolie look-alike wiggling her way across the intersection of San Vicente and Bundy about twenty minutes later. Unlike most men in my position, I wasn't wondering what it might be like to sleep with her. Instead, I was wondering if such a woman had any idea what it felt like to stare at a cell phone all day, willing it to boil.

Ring. Whatever.

Anyway, I was guessing the answer was no.

But mine did ring, a few seconds later. I sucked in my stomach, straightened my back and plastered a beauty-school-dropout smile across my face. It's instinct. Seeing a woman like that reminds me Raj might be aware of her existence. This forces me to admit that no one will ever be anything but repulsed by the vision of my sweaty, spandexed self huffing to cross the street. Which makes me want to eat an entire bundt cake.

In my closet.

With my hands.

Also, I'm sure that being engaged means he can see me through the phone.

As I pulled over, rummaging frantically through my purse to catch the call before it went to voice mail, I realized that this wasn't like me. I didn't watch other women run. I didn't do somersaults at the possibility of a boy calling. I didn't smile without reason any more than I said my name as if it was a question. All of which meant one thing; my period was coming. Because unlike some women I knew, I only ever spent twenty-four hours each month—the day before my period—curled up in my bed licking trans-fats off my own fingers, watching reruns of *The Golden Girls,* and being convinced that I was fat, inarticulate and incapable of sustaining a normal relationship.

I made a mental note to pick up a pizza, a milk shake and a valium on my way home, yanked my cell phone out of my purse and exhaled.

"Hello?"

"Hello, my sweetheart!" she sang through the telephone in the British accent, which was a legacy of her college days in England. "It's your mommy, darling, and I have got some wonderful news for the both of us!"

This was going to require two bundt cakes.

My mother was understated in much the same way that dating show contestants wear makeup. It didn't help when she upstaged me at my Sweet Sixteen party in a dress *cut-down-to-there,* but it didn't hurt when she told me on the day I left for college that *As long as I was living happily and honestly no matter what choices I made, she would always be right behind me.* Between mother and daughter, the good is just the other half of the bad.

Thankfully, my father always managed to cast her behavior in only the most positive light. And, after all, he had explained to me after a particularly embarrassing incident involving an impromptu conga-line to the tune of "The Rhythm Is Gonna Get You" at my fifth-grade dance that my mother had insisted on chaperoning, she had been hard-wired for drama. How else could she have mustered the courage to defy her parents by wearing those tight blue jeans, which were like a bull's-eye in that small Indian village for the motorcycle-riding, chain-smoking, loner Gujurati boy named Deepak who would eventually become my father?

As the story went, he invited her to meet him for a cup of chai in the bazaar one afternoon during her winter break from college, and she (having grown accustomed to the free-thinking of the 1970s London social scene) decided to accept. It wasn't until the following morning, after news of mom's—or rather, the self-important Renu Malhotra's—brazen public liaison had reached every corner of the village, that word reached her of Deepak's parents already having committed his hand in marriage. An incensed and insulted twenty-one-year-old Renu's immediate response was to march over to Deepak's house, bang on the door, stomp into the family's living room and demand that he marry her as a form of reparation for thinking that he could sully her reputation.

Who could resist such a fiery pataka? he would recount to anyone who would listen, while my mother demurred and waved away any comparison of herself to a firecracker.

A bundook *then?* he would chide.

Do I look like I can spit bullets? she would mock warn him.

Only if I step out of line, sergeant. He would salute, with a clip of his heels for effect.

Do you see how your father mocks me, Monica? she would play along, despite the initiation of my gag reflex. *Whatever you do, don't marry a funny man.*

Happy wife, happy life, my father would say, over the rim of his glasses, before returning his attention to his usual Sunday morning copy of *India Abroad.*

Theirs was the kind of love that every little girl imagines for herself—full of grand gestures, stolen kisses, clandestine rendezvous and passionate choices no one ever second-guessed. I held very firmly to that ideal through most of my formative years. I held on to it through the high school football player who brought me wildflowers, but didn't love me enough to dance in public. And through that shy boy in my college freshman literature class who wrote poetry to me describing a sort of hunger that I never could have felt for him. I held on all the way to the film major with the dimples, who nearly dropped all those copies of his screenplay trying to hold the student union door open for me our first day of junior year.

His name was Alex, and that screenplay was the first of many that I would read and critique for him over the next few years. I can only describe it as the most consuming love I've ever had. Which is probably how it is for everyone, when it really happens, but still...

I might have held on to the grand idea of such a big love

for long enough to let Alex become the man of my life, if I hadn't seen what became of my mother once she lost hers.

One summer afternoon, I came home from lunch to find my father slumped over our kitchen table. My mother stood in the hallway just outside the kitchen. The backdoor key was still in her hand, and she was mumbling something repeatedly to herself about dinner. Later, I learned that there was very little my father hadn't done for us. He had done so much, in fact, that my mother hadn't the slightest idea of the terms of his life insurance, the balance of their mortgage, or the location of the key to the bank deposit box. In short, she was the girl in those blue jeans, wondering where the boy named Deepak had gone.

Two months after my father's death, my mother moved to London to be closer to the extended family who we had visited every summer of my childhood en route to Bombay.

I swallowed and buoyed my voice. "Hi, Mom. Err…okay, so what's the news?"

"Darling you'll never believe it!" Her voice almost rose to a shriek. "I'm moving back to Los Angeles!"

five

MAYBE IT WOULD BE EASIER IF I WERE A LESBIAN. AT LEAST IT would preclude my mother pulling any stunts resembling her telling me "the news" as casually as if she were asking me to pass the mango chutney. Turns out she's not only planned to move back to Los Angeles within a month, but that she's already put the down payment on a three-bedroom Spanish-mission style home in Upper Brentwood. This way, there will be room for the beautiful nursery to which every doting grandmother has a legal right. Letting her in on the fact that my fiancé was AWOL at that point would have been a lot like informing a B-list actress making the walk of shame back to her condo at 10:00 a.m. that the "Director" was really just an extra. Why bother? You can't turn back time.

Mom wanted to know what I thought about a lilac-color

palette, you see, and whether I would object to her hiring a portrait artist, who is apparently *All the rage* according to *Pushy Cosmopolitan Grandmother Wannabe Magazine*, to emblazon likenesses of myself and my newborn baby across one of the walls. *Because these people book up months and months in advance, you know....*

Lacking convenient proximity to a cliff I could hurl myself off of, and confident that being alone at my own apartment that night would virtually guarantee a drunken and tear-soaked attempt to chop off all of my own hair, I swung a right onto Doheny and headed in the direction of the only person who might begin to understand.

"It's because I'm too nice, isn't it?" Sheila asked, swinging her front door open and thrusting an especially appalling dress at me.

"Well, if you mean why did you buy this, then it must be because you went temporarily blind?"

It may sound harsh, but honestly, we're talking all black, long sleeved, knee length, shoulder padded and with an actual beaded trim. She might as well have let a twelve-year-old loose on her ski suit with a BeDazzler and then tried strolling down Rodeo Drive with a straight face. Being her cousin, I knew it was better to investigate before jumping to a conclusion.

"Mo-ni-ca!" She literally stomped a foot on the marble, fists clenched at her sides.

God bless her, Sheila failed to grasp the negative correlation between the pitch of her voice and the gravity of her words to anyone who is listening. Still, she was my cousin.

"What are you babbling about?" I asked, shoving my own situation aside and walking past her and into the living room.

"This! This disgusting dress!" She fell into step beside me, shaking her head and gesturing with that fashion hate crime as if it were a weapon. "She is being so...so...so passive aggressive!"

"Is this about your mother-in-law again?" I dropped onto the white suede couch in their sunroom. "Look, I told you, she's going to treat you the way *you allow her* to treat you."

Tone of voice was only one of the many ways in which Sheila and I were different. Take the copy of *Pucker* laid out on their tree-trunk cross-section of a coffee table for everyone to see. And which I made the mistake of glancing toward. Sheila tilted her head, following the direction of my eyes. A shameless celebrity gossip junkie, Sheila was the last person I would ever admit my *Pucker* fixation to...because she would seize any opportunity to interrogate me about my clients, hooking me up to a lie detector machine, trying to get me to break confidentiality by naming names. Mercifully that day, she was more focused on the issue at hand....

"You don't under-*stand!*" She sniffled. "She knows that it's ugly, because...because how could she *not*? And she knows that I have to wear it, because she bought it for me.

We're all going out to dinner tonight, with Josh's entire extended family! So I'll either look like an ungrateful daughter-in-law or someone who accidentally wandered in from a Bon Jovi concert, circa 1982!"

While Sheila was only one year younger than myself, at times the gap seemed closer to twenty. Hissy fits like this one were part of the reason why I still had trouble thinking of her as a married woman. Her husband was the loving but spineless Joshua. And in the most storybook fashion, they had met one night when she came in to the emergency room seeking stitches for a gash across her forehead.

The kind Jewish medical intern not only sewed her up, but managed not to laugh while she described the spill off her five-inch heels that resulted in a nosedive into the pavement outside a West Hollywood nightclub. She walked all over him, and saw nothing wrong with his lack of interest in getting up off the floor, until she realized that she wasn't the only woman making heel marks on his face. He had been in training, in fact, having spent his entire lifetime balancing on eggshells around his mother. About a year into their marriage it was clear that the coach wasn't exactly thrilled about the idea of another voice barking orders at her team.

"Your problem," I began, "is that you're trying to beat her at her own game by figuring out her rules and then playing them against her. The only way you'll win is if you refuse to play her game at all. When she presumes that you'll spend every other weekend at her place, announce how much you would love to but that you already have plans to go to dinner with the chief surgical resident and his wife, which you are sure she will agree is the best thing for Joshua's career. When she tells you that your choice of lipstick is *interesting,* play dumb and ask her, in front of everyone, to explain what she means by that *because you really value her opinion.* When she insults your food by asking if you would like her extra set of measuring spoons so that you won't be so aggressive with the salt next time, don't laugh it off!"

"But I don't want to be a…a *bitch,*" she lowered her voice, as if the lamp might hear us.

"Fine, then act like a wounded bird," I said and rolled my eyes. "But whatever you do, don't act like it's no big deal. Don't make it so easy for her. Maybe if you're visibly hurt in front of your family, then Josh will finally grow a pair and start defending his wife."

Adept already at the wifely art of choosing her battles, Sheila slam-dunked the dress behind the couch and silenced me with a glance the moment she heard Josh's key in the door.

"So anyway…like I was saying." I shifted gears, widening my eyes and acting about as casual as the kid at Fat Camp with the remnants of a Snickerdoodle clinging to his chin. "My mom says she's moving back to L.A. And she's serious, Sheila. She already bought a house."

"Really?" Joshua asked, bounding in from his bike ride, but apparently deeming himself not-quite-sweaty enough to forgo a kiss to the forehead of his giggling bride. "Is this because of Raj and you breaking up?"

"We did not break up," I warned him, with a cautionary glare at Sheila. "It's temporary. Do you tell him *everything?*"

"Of course she does, we're married. So then you didn't tell your mom about Raj?" he yelled from the kitchen, banging the refrigerator door shut. "But she's your mother."

"She didn't, honey, no," Sheila answered for me after wiping her forehead with her sleeve. "I told you that she's afraid of her mother."

"And what's that supposed to mean?" he asked, leaning against the doorway defensively.

"Nobody's afraid of anybody," I interjected, trying to steer the focus back onto myself. "I haven't told my mom about Raj because there is nothing to tell. We have not broken up. We're taking a breather."

Besides, I thought, reaching for the remote control, *my mother always got way too involved with opinions that were completely misinformed when I let her anywhere near my personal life.* And as if God didn't have just the most perfect timing…

"Hollywood studios are abuzz this week with news of one of the biggest screenwriting sweetheart deals to have been signed by Paragon Pictures in years," some Entertainment Tonight reporter wearing no less than eight necklaces and an entire tube of lip gloss prattled on.

And then they cut to the videotape of Alex.

With that same warm smile. That same humble manner. Those same unmistakable dimples sneaking in an appearance as he sat back and watched the filming from his consultant's chair on the set of the movie that launched his career.

"Rumor has it," the talking head continued, "that the movie studio has just inked a landmark seven-figure, two-script deal with the screenwriter whose first movie, *Like You Mean It*, was the sleeper hit of last summer."

"Oh, *honey*." Sheila sat down beside me. "I'm sorry. You know I only watch that for the celebrity stuff. Let's change the channel."

"Come on, Sheila," I insisted, in a voice that wouldn't have even convinced a total stranger, "don't be silly. I can be happy for him, can't I?"

The first time Alex told me that he loved me was when he came home from a morning run to find me awake and curled up in his dorm-room bed, wearing one of his T-shirts and reading the original version of *Like You Mean It*. I could tell by the way he said it that he'd startled himself, as much because he'd blurted it out, as because of realizing that it was true. Although my first instinct was to drop the script, grab him by the neck and yank him down on top of me, he held me back, asked me to finish reading first, and made me promise to tell him what I really thought when I was done. *Total honesty,* he announced with an idealism that only someone under legal drinking age can muster, *was the only way that this relationship would ever work.*

So like most young couples we managed to be completely honest with each other for the next two years, except, of course, for those little things that we held back. Harmless things, at first, like my insisting that his snoring never bothered me in the least, and his swearing up and down that I was cute when I was drunk. We knew what we had and we shared a quiet instinct to protect it, even from ourselves. It worked for me because by definition a girl's first real love is the guy who feels like family. And it worked for him because rather than feeling skewered by my gut reaction to his work, he told me that he finally felt as if he had someone on his team.

Yes, we kept up a relationship of comfortable truth even through the summer when he tattooed his biceps and bartended on Sunset, while I donned my sensible suit and interned at an emerging-markets hedge fund. At the time, Alex forcing me to admit that I had *gone corporate* to appease my father only made me love him more. But when the summer was over…

"What do you mean *What am I gonna do after school?*" he asked, while hefting my bookcase into the corner of my new dorm room that September.

"I mean that people are applying to grad schools or applying for jobs." I flopped onto the bed and watched him work. "So what are we gonna do?"

"I'm not sure what you're gonna do yet, but I'm sure you'll land on your feet, even if you have to move back in with your parents for a few months."

"And what about you?" I rose up on my elbows.

"Whadya mean?" He blew the hair out of his eyes and

looked up at me. "What's wrong with bartending until I sell my script?"

There was nothing and plenty wrong with it, but what was I going to say? That was when I realized just how committed he was to his writing, and it terrified me. Not because I thought he would fail, but because it might take him a very long time to succeed. And I didn't want that kind of disappointment for him. I came back from summer convinced that it was my responsibility to seek out a career that would work for me, rather than waiting for one to fall into my lap. His summer had convinced him that dedication to writing wasn't enough. Surviving without a safety net was some twisted sort of price he concluded he had to pay *if he was ever really gonna make it*. Encouraging him to seek stability at that point would have been like telling him that I had never believed in him at all. I snapped my mouth shut and swallowed, recognizing that my silence had made the space for the first small fissure in our relationship.

He didn't seem to notice that anything had happened as the months took us into the winter and spring of our senior year. To anyone watching us during the Senior Ski Weekend at Bear Mountain or at the beach in Cozumel on spring break, our rhythm must have seemed unbroken. But every now and then I wondered…how much of our connection rested atop my conspiring to allow him to see himself a certain way? Ultimately, it didn't matter. Even then I understood that I was a young woman in the throes of a connection that she knew she would never forget.

So I accepted, rather than decided, that there wasn't anything I wouldn't sweep under the rug just to keep him inhaling me with those eyes. I had to, you understand, because if I didn't I felt sure that a later, older, wiser version of myself would have never forgiven me.

Just after spring break, Alex had sent copies of his manuscript to a handful of agents. A month later he received his first rejection letter.

"Well, I guess that was Round One," I said, dropping my backpack on my dorm room steps to take a seat beside him. I slipped an arm around his shoulder. "So what are we gonna change before you send it out for Round Two?"

In the weeks leading up to graduation, he collected a stack of rejection letters almost two inches thick. There were enough as it turned out to wallpaper his entire bathroom. We discovered this one morning when we woke up—hungover—to find that was exactly what we had done the night before.

But in the light of day Alex didn't think it was funny. In fact, he crawled into bed and refused to go anywhere for a week. Eventually I had enough of his moping and forced him out when we were to be fitted for our caps and gowns. He came along, but he wasn't the same. And I was very close to being seriously concerned when he burst into the dorm, interrupting a margarita-soaked slumber party with my girl-friends a few nights before graduation, to wave a piece of paper in my face.

"It's from ICM!" he shouted, yanking me up into his arms for what became a twirl around an imaginary dance floor.

"Oh my God!" I slapped both hands to my cheeks before remembering the avocado face mask. "They signed you?"

"No." He ignored my wiping the gunk off on my pajamas, while my roommates poured him a drink. "But it wasn't a form letter this time! This guy, this agent, he says my writing's good…like, *good enough to sell*…if I can just tighten up my plot line. He gave me a few suggestions and said I could send him a new version if I wanted!"

After graduation I had decided to move back home and spend a year temping to keep myself in lip gloss and lemon-drop martinis while I decided where I wanted to land. Alex, as planned, was bartending by night and reworking his screenplay by day, sharing an apartment with a couple of guys in Venice near the beach. He was happier than I had seen him in months. As we rolled into midsummer, I told myself that until I decided to get serious, I had no right to tell him to do so.

However, as the saying goes the only things that truly can change a person are death and divorce. And seeing my mother so helpless in the hallway I had to wonder how long she would have stood there mumbling if I hadn't come home. I wondered while I booked the funeral home with the crematorium to suit Hindu ritual and ordered the flowers for the small family ceremony. I wondered while I sat with Sheila's mother, the lawyer, trying to make sense of our family's finances and pay the inheritance taxes without losing our home. I wondered while I made a list of all of the re-latives in Los Angeles, London and Bombay who needed to be notified, and had to decide which of the elder male relatives would take my father's ashes to scatter over the Ganges River as he would have wanted. And I wondered while I forced my mother to eat something each day, and then stood staring out her bedroom window at the moon each night until the pace of her breathing assured me that her sleeping pills had started to kick in.

The harder Alex tried to connect with me, the more vehemently I told him I needed space. The further I tried to push him away, the harder he fought me for myself. The clearer it became that my mother and I would be lucky if we came out of this owning our home, the more Alex's belief that *love could conquer anything* made me stiffen to his touch. I could tell myself that I was being irrational to regard him as naive, but I couldn't explain myself to him. It was a time when being understood felt like being turned inside out. All I knew was that when he was around he made me feel, and feeling anything at that point simply made me want to throw up. One foot in front of the other was the only way I would make it through this, and I needed to be alone. Then there'd be nobody else left to lose.

So I met him at the Venice boardwalk and told him the one thing that would shake him out of this love, and make him want to run as far away from me as possible.

"I already have a job," he answered, tugging at the grass as we sat in the picnic overlook. "I'm a writer."

"Writing is not a job until you sell something, Alex. Your job right now is bartending."

"So what are you saying? Why all of a sudden don't you think I'm gonna sell this?"

My eyes were fixed on the horizon. "I'm just saying that after all these rejections…this is the real world. Thousands of people are running around Los Angeles with a screenplay to sell, and…and you might never sell a script."

I could feel him staring hard at me, willing me to face him. I could hear him breathing heavily, gathering the steam for his words and then deciding against it. Soon enough, it was over. And he stood up and walked away. No matter how hard I tried to search inside myself, at that moment, all I could find was a very deep sense of relief. I knew that I was alone now, and that I could finally grieve. Because if you take away a man's perception that his woman believes in him, then you might as well just take away the woman herself.

six

I GET A DAY OFF ABOUT AS ROUTINELY AS MEN IN BOW TIES GET invited up for a nightcap. And for me, that's fine, because I knew what I was getting into when I chose the life that I did. So I saw no good reason to look a technical glitch in the mouth that Sunday afternoon when I was unable to log on to the computer in my office. After a few unsuccessful attempts, a message popped up telling me that my password was incorrect and I should contact the IT administrator. Had I known his name or had any interest in really working that day, I might have tried. But the skies were blue, the streets were clear, and I was still overdue for that trip to the salon.

I made a quick phone call to the Georgette Klinger spa, known as much for their signature orange salt scrubs as for the imported champagne and fresh chocolate brownies laid out for guests to nibble on in the plush pretreatment waiting room. Four warm brownies, three glasses of Vueve, and two blissful hours of cleansing, scrubbing, rubbing, buffing, paraffining and polishing later, I was reborn.

The cosmetologist did such a fantastic job with my eyebrows that I couldn't help but admire them via the mirrored double doors of Steel's elevators on my ride up that Monday morning. Unfortunately, the doors opened to reveal a far less pleasing image. Stefanie's beaming smile sent my defense mechanisms into overdrive. I furrowed my brow and clutched my shoulder bag a little closer to my heart, as if it were bulletproof. Maybe she was just delighted to detect my period-induced pimple, I told myself. And maybe, one of these days, I would wake up and decide that rather than fighting, I was ready to age gracefully.

Not likely. Stepping off of the elevator, I remembered the problem about logging on to my computer, and headed straight for the IT help desk.

"Hey, Monica," said some twenty-three-year-old in a singsong voice who I was sure I had never seen before in my life. He stood up to greet me. Judging by his arching eyebrow, I assumed he thought he was flirting. I reminded myself that I was just cranky because of my period, and resisted the urge to tell him that he would have to be *at least this old to ride this ride.*

That might sound harsh, but I'm telling you, he probably didn't even shave yet.

"Hey…you." I tried a smile, wondering who he was meant to be conspiring with, and hoping that I hadn't gotten to know him a little too well at that Cinco De Mayo Company Happy Hour during which there was still an hour I couldn't account for.

"We were expecting to see you earlier this morning," he said, seated again, tapping a few strokes onto his computer and then tilting the screen toward me. "We have never seen anyone try so hard to sneak onto the system using an actual login name. The password automatically resets after fifteen failed attempts when you're outside the office."

"But I came in on Sunday to work and couldn't get into my computer," I said. "I didn't log on remotely at all this weekend."

"Well, someone tried to." He laced his fingers together behind his head, as if he were in charge of IT for NASA. "But no worries, we've reset your login to your direct phone number, and your password to Sphinx. We thought *vgupta* was a little too obvious. You can go into the system now and reset both the login and password to whatever you want. But you might want to be careful about who you tell even your login name to in the future."

I shouldn't have been leaning so far back in my chair to begin with, but when the door to my office burst open, the shock of it sent me sailing backward onto the floor. Clamoring to my knees and curling my fingers over the edge of my desk, I raised my head up ever so carefully. The first thing I noticed was that the door had literally been blown off one of its hinges. And the second thing was that Cameron was headed straight for me. In order to make it easier for him, I backed myself into a corner, and soon enough I was sandwiched between his heaving chest and the wall.

And I have to say that despite the physical threat, it was nice to be pinned against something by someone again.

Oh, and the other thing about having my period is that it also makes me frisky. Go figure.

I tilted my skull back to look into his eyes. There was nothing but anger, and a vein on the side of his neck that was threatening to explode.

Despite everything I knew about him as a man and as a client, my defense instincts kicked in. He was a full two feet taller than me, and easily could have squashed me like a fly. I made a mental note to consider talking to a therapist about the line between adrenaline and arousal, swallowed hard and decided to speak first.

"Cameron." My voice quivered. "Umm…is everything all right?" I smoothed my hair back, composed myself and noticed there was far more hurt than hate in his eyes.

"I thought you were supposed to be our lawyer," he told me, stepping back. "Not *her* lawyer. I can't believe I'm paying your bills and you're on *her* side!"

"I'm working for the both of you, Cameron." I held my hands up before me.

"Then how come you're meetin' with her alone? You

plannin' on giving her a better settlement that I'm gonna get? What else could it be? Ain't nobody left I can trust, man." He stepped toward the window. "But at least with a lawyer, as long as I'm payin' you, I'm supposed to be sure I can trust you!"

"Cameron, you *can* trust me." I turned my chair upright and stepped back into the crocodile pumps I hadn't been wearing when he burst in. "Why don't you tell me what's going on?"

"Oh, I can trust you, huh? Then how come you been meeting with Lydia alone? All I can think is that you're trying to convince her to end this marriage."

"Do you want to end the marriage?" I asked.

He shook his head.

"Then why are you having her followed?" I stood beside him, placing my hand on the window.

"I'm not. But my staff understands that a man has a right to know what goes on in his own house." He looked at me disdainfully. "Even if his wife is worth more than he is."

"Look, I swear that we are not taking sides in this thing, Cameron. That's just not the business that Steel is in. Now I know that things are confusing, but you if anyone should know that you can't believe everything you hear. Or even everything you see."

"Don't play dumb, Monica. You're lawyers, not actors. And I don't believe everything I hear, but I can't ignore what people think they see, either, since it almost cost me my marriage the last time. And maybe you should be more careful, because we're paying you a lot of money to make sure this is all kept on the DL. If my people knew you and Lydia were out in Beverly Hills together this weekend, do you really think the paparazzi didn't?"

An hour after he erupted in my office, I had Cameron pacified and packed off to the home office of an acupuncturist and healer, who'd worked wonders with some of my most difficult clients. I didn't need to know the details, but in one weekend "Doctor" Senji had convinced the world cage-boxing champion, who routinely tattooed himself with the names of the men he had out-savaged, that he had to embrace his inner bully before he could begin to negotiate the terms of his divorce. Even if Senji was doping them up on opium and having monkeys beat them with licorice whips in that compound in Ojai, all I knew was that he was delivering my clients back to me with just enough vulnerability to allow me to get my job done.

Besides, we just added his $5,000 per day to the client's expense tab.

Maintenance informed me that it would take at least two hours to rehang my door, so I headed over to Cassie's desk to see if she wanted to join me in a two-martini lunch at Matsuhisa, which I had every intention of charging to the Camydia account. We were three feet from the elevator when the doors slid open to reveal Stefanie, Jonathan and all of the senior partners laughing and returning from what had clearly been a nice long lunch. One, to which, I can assure you, I had not been invited.

"Oh, *Monica*." Stefanie slathered it on thicker than peanut butter. "It's too bad you couldn't join us for lunch today. You did read the e-mail I sent out, didn't you?"

"What e-mail?"

"The one I sent out on Saturday to make sure everyone got it before this morning. You *do* check your e-mail over the weekend, don't you?" She cocked her jaw to one side. "We're all in this together. We're a family. A team. And we've gotta stay connected. For the clients, you know."

Maybe it was time to call in my favor with that cage fighter.

"I'm sure I would've remembered getting an e-mail about lunch, Stefanie. Perhaps you left me out, by accident?"

"No, I'm sure I included you. In fact, I'm certain of it." Stefanie stuck to the part of the innocent gal pal, shaking her head. "It must have been a computer glitch. Really, you should have your computer checked out. You never know who could be hacking into your files when you're not looking."

Moments later, I was yanked into Jonathan's office.

"So you got my SOS message on your BlackBerry. Don't worry about it, Jonathan. Cameron just had a little outburst about Lydia's tantrum over the weekend. Everything's fine. He's on his way to Senji's compound right now."

"Yeah. That's fine, Monica." He closed the door behind me. "But that's not what I want to talk about."

"What, then?" I tugged at the chain around my neck.

"Stefanie, that's what," he replied, and hoisted himself up onto his desk. Lowering his voice, he leaned toward me, and whispered, "You really have to do something about this little interoffice rivalry of yours. The competition between you two is starting to become obvious. Even to the partners."

"Jonathan, I am not competing with anyone."

"Rrrrrraw!" he mimicked a cat, taking a swipe at me.

"Don't make me hit you."

"Come on," he chided me, smiling. "You had to give me at least one. Seriously, though. You know I'm on your side, babe. I like working with you, and I don't want to see this become a problem."

"So?"

"So…what are you gonna do about it?"

"I'll tell you *what I'm gonna do about it.*" I felt indignant, and was almost shouting. "I'm gonna keep coming to the office every day, doing what I'm paid to do, and expecting recognition for it."

He shook his head at the lifeguard who's only just asked why the heiress isn't returning his calls the morning after. After a few minutes of the staring game, I realized how serious he was.

"I expect the partners to see past this!" I dropped onto his couch, sounding childish even to myself.

"Monica, you never struck me as naïve. All I'm saying is that if I were you, I would do something about it."

I actually wanted to stomp my foot.

"*Why?* Why should I have to engage in this? *Why is it my*

responsibility to teach some other woman to grow up? It's so childish!"

"It's not your responsibility, Monica," he said on a sigh, as if explaining to a guest in rehab why the cough syrup had to be confiscated, "but it is *your problem*. And don't you think that acting like the problem doesn't exist…is kind of childish, too?"

The problem with the insane is that they believe the problem is with everyone but them. Still, as a society we are constantly trying to reason with *people* who we know are neither capable nor interested. I had to do something to diffuse the situation, and I had to do it soon. So, I casually invited Stefanie to help me in the conference room. I cannot tell you why I expected her to give me even an inch. The truth is that I didn't even know what I was going to say until I saw her arrive.

"What can I do for you?" she asked brightly, as if the pink elephant in the room weren't actually doing a striptease.

"Sit down, Stefanie." I folded my arms across my chest and planted my feet opposite her side of the conference table.

"Noooo…I think I'm fine right here, Monica." She tilted her head innocently to one side, and asked, "What's up?"

"I was hoping you could tell me." I circled the table to close the door.

"I have no idea what you're talking about," she delivered, eyes and posture unflinching.

"Fine. Let's just look at the situation, then. You have tried to put me on the spot in front of the partners at more than one team meeting. You managed somehow to invite every junior associate other than myself to the lunch today. And then you accused me very publicly of not being a team player or even checking my e-mail on the weekends. With a smile on your face. You tell me, Stefanie, how am I supposed to interpret that?"

"I can't say that I care *how* you interpret it, Monica. I come to the office to do my job. And I came in here because you said you needed my help on something. So either tell me what you want, or get over yourself, because I have a lot of work to do, and I really don't have time for your little temper tantrum."

The loon spoons a helping of mashed potatoes onto her head at the dinner table and nobody says a word. Then she smiles politely, and asks you to pass the gravy. What do you do?

"I don't want any pretense, Stefanie. I want to know if I have done something or said something to offend you, so that we can just get it out in the open and move on."

"You are such a drama queen," she muttered, searching the ceiling. "Just because you missed out on lunch you're calling me in here to pick a fight? Classic."

"All right. First of all, I am not picking a fight. This is not junior high. Actually, I am doing the opposite because I refuse to lose my cool in public. Stefanie, you can interpret it however you want. But the truth is that I am trying to call for a truce. I don't need this stress at work and I can't imagine why you would want to stir it up."

"Is that a threat?" She seemed almost aroused at the idea.

The loon proceeds to smear cranberry sauce across her lap...

"What?"

"I am not stirring anything," she insisted in a monotone, as if *I* was the one that was insane.

"You can deny it as much as you want, but we both know that it's true. You have hated me since the minute I got here. And honestly, if just looking at me makes you that upset, then I don't understand why you spend so much time staring. But you should know that I will not get into a public pissing match with you, no matter how much you poke and prod me in front of the partners. I will not stoop to that level over nothing. You're wasting your time."

"No, Monica," she spat, clearly incensed at that point. "*You're* wasting *my* time."

"Well I do hope that I'm overreacting, Stefanie. I really hope so. Because maybe I'm an idealist, but I do believe that professional women can only lose as a whole if we don't stick together, or at least stop dragging each other down."

"Whatever, Monica. I have to get ready for a conference call, and you, apparently, have to seek some professional help. We're done here." She threw the door open and strode confidently out.

Not by a long shot, I thought.

seven

"SO..." HE BEGAN, A PIMPLY VERSION OF DOOGIE HOWSER M.D. bellied up to the bar beside me the following evening "...can I buy you a drink?"

The lighting was low enough at Drago that night, but even with an eyebrow raised, junior's clearly college-aged skin couldn't even so much as hint at a wrinkle. And after the last few days of working past midnight, the dark circles under my eyes made it clear that my skin had no intention of bouncing back the way that it used to after all that late-night partying in college. Never underestimate the power of boredom though. Since I was twenty minutes early for my dinner reservation with Sheila, and Los Angeles was one of the funnest places on earth to play the age-guessing game, I threw junior a bone.

"I don't know," I said and turned to give him my most disinterested once-over. "*Can* you?"

"I don't get it." He stiffened, likely frightened or confused, because he left his fake ID at home.

"Sorry." I laughed, deciding to see where this could go, "I don't mean to be harsh, but…don't you think I'm a little old for you?"

"Why?" He pulled his chin back. "What are you, like… *twenty-four?* That's no problem, baby. So am I."

"You're twenty-four?" I nearly spit raspberry seeds from my flavored mojito right onto his face.

"Yeah, I know." He waved away what he had clearly self-translated into a compliment. "I look too professional to be just twenty-four. I get that a lot. It must be the tailored suit."

Well, at the very least I had to give him points for fitting ten pounds of swagger into a five-pound bag.

"Yeah, something like that." I waved the bartender over for a refill.

"So, how about it?" he asked with a big smile. "Can I buy you that drink, now that we've established how old we are? Or do you need to know what kind of car I drive, too? Damn, you L.A. women make a man jump through a lot of hoops."

"We didn't establish my age, honey. We just established your age and an affinity for cranky older women and tailored suits."

"Wow…*affinity.* You're a smart one."

God, dating in Los Angeles could be so degrading sometimes. I wondered what Raj was doing at that exact moment….

"So…you're older?"

I nodded.

"Twenty-six?"

I sighed.

"Twenty-seven?"

"Getting warmer."

"Twenty-eight?" His voice climbed to a pitch that was more than a little insulting.

"I'm twenty-nine years old." I scanned over his shoulder for any signs of Sheila.

"No way!" he protested, as if I'd just told him I could fit both legs behind my head at once. "You're *hot* for thirty!"

"He did not seriously say that!" Sheila hiccupped, while our waiter handed over the menus.

"I think the most offensive part wasn't the fact that he qualified my hotness… I think it was the fact that he rounded up!"

"That's just bad manners."

"Who rounds *up?*" I asked my menu.

"Whatever. At least he was hitting on you. I can't remember the last time anyone hit on me." She held out her ring finger. "This might as well be a massive red circle with a line crossing out my face. You're smart not to wear yours."

"Can we not talk about Raj tonight?" I slurped up the remaining bits of raspberry from my second mojito.

"Then tell me about Stefanie. Has anything happened since you tore her a new one yesterday?"

I shook my head, chewing on my straw and perusing the menu.

"You know this is about being promoted to senior associate, right? If she didn't think you were a threat, she wouldn't be so bitchy to you."

"Good point," I said. "I mean, what else could she have to hold against me?"

"See?" She winked, pointing to her temple as the waitress came over to take our orders. "I know stuff sometimes."

"Trouble in paradise?" I asked, after watching the woman who never ate anything full-fat order an appetizer, entrée and dessert.

She shrugged casually. "The usual."

"Sheila, I haven't seen you order tiramisu since the summer before you went to Fat Camp. Whatever's bothering you, it's gotta be more than *the usual.*"

"Camp Makealeap was for gifted kids," she shot back with a horrified whisper. "And you agreed never to bring that up again!"

"Then don't lie to me."

She huffed into her drink. "The family's going to the cabin for another ski weekend."

At their last fun-filled family trip to Vail, Sheila hadn't felt welcome, exactly. Joshua's mother had planned an entire weekend of activities in advance, and then feigned surprise when Hindu, non-red-meat-eating Sheila opted out of the duck-hunting exercise and asked for something other than beef as an entrée at Smith & Wollensky's. Being the dutiful young fiancée at the time, Sheila bit her tongue. She didn't even flinch when they left her behind on the bunny slope to hit the black diamonds *as a family*.

But the final straw, the one that resulted in a whispered 2:00 a.m. phone call to me from inside their hotel bathroom, was the jacket. Emboldened by Sheila's failure to make a peep in her own defense, monster-in-law had actually gone as far as to tell Josh to change out of the ski jacket that Sheila had bought him as a gift, calling it *frivolous and impractical*. Joshua, blissfully ignorant of anything beyond the tip of his own nose while surrounded by family, had obliged in front of everyone without blinking. Sheila, mere months away from her dream wedding at the time, decided not to make unnecessary waves by forcing him to stand up to his mother until after *I do*.

But time had passed, and the situation never improved. Confronted now with Sheila's sad and tired eyes, I decided to give her permission to take the out she so clearly wanted.

"Why don't you make an excuse?"

"I can't do that," she said, to my surprise. "I won't."

As it turns out, I had underestimated my cousin. The stress I thought I was picking up on was actually anticipation. This time, Sheila had plans of her own.

"Ahem." She straightened up and cleared her throat. "On Saturday morning we have a couple's massage at the spa in town. Prepaid. Nonrefundable. On Saturday night we have dinner reservations for a seven-course prix-fixe tasting menu at the best French restaurant in Vail. They only had a table for two. Prepaid. Nonrefundable. On Sunday morning we're going horseback riding in the mountains. I would have booked my darling mother- and father-in-law with us, on the ride, but I think that three hours would be a little much for a couple their age. And of course…"

"It's prepaid. And nonrefundable." I laughed and shook my head.

"What?" She played dumb. "She can have Friday night. We'll eat Challah and drink Maneschevitz. And if Joshua wants to leave me alone after our Saturday morning massage to go hurl himself down a black diamond with his family that's his choice. But I've got a new red silk number from Victoria's Secret and a jar of chocolate body paint that might make him want to pause and reconsider."

"Who knew being married involved so much strategery?"

"Is that a word?" she asked, while our appetizers were laid out before us.

I shrugged, lifting a spoonful of polenta into my mouth.

"Look, it sounds like a fantastic weekend to me. And you would make up for all the time she stole from you on your last ski weekend. But it is a little passive aggressive. I'm not saying you shouldn't do all these fun things. Though you might also consider telling your husband to be a bit more sympathetic."

Her forkful of warm mushroom salad stopped before her mouth.

"Look, Sheila." I tried my best to backpedal and wipe the look of hurt off of her face. "I didn't mean that—"

"Monica," she said pointedly, and with a wisdom far beyond her years, "wait until you're married."

Sheila's predicament got me thinking about Raj again. Maybe merely entertaining his point of view would help me win back some credibility—or at least a return phone call. So after overtipping the valet in an attempt to offset the negative karma I had generated at the dinner table, I swung a left onto Robertson Boulevard and reached for my phone.

I hit Send and prepared my most ingratiating tone of voice.

Naturally, after three rings there was still no answer.

"Raj, it's me." I was too slow to hang up before voice-mail, so instead I left a message completely contrary to what I'd hoped to convey. "Look...I...I've been giving it some thought. And I get it, okay? It's just...we need to talk. You can't treat a person like this. I know I was a little...difficult... before you left for London. But there really is no excuse for not calling me back. It's just...it's just rude. So...so call me, okay? Okay, bye."

This was getting ridiculous. After being with me for so long, Raj should know that ignoring me would be the cruelest thing he could do. It was very, very insensitive. And very unlike him. In fact, none of this was like him. But at least I still had a chance on the dating scene.

I was *hot for thirty,* after all.

"Is there such a thing as early early onset menopause?" a voice asked. The blaring of my cell phone had woken me at 1:00 a.m. Thursday morning.

"Who covered the catwalk with apple butter?" I mumbled. "Don't they know I'm gonna slip off?"

"Have you been drinking?"

"What? Who is this?" I peeked out from under the covers, opening one eye and checking my hand for signs of apple butter.

"Don't be annoying," Sheila insisted. "So, is there such a thing?"

"Such a thing as what?"

"Early early onset *menopause!*"

"I don't know, Sheila." I sniffed. "I went to law school, not med school. Ask your husband. Okay, good night!"

"No, wait! I can't ask him," she whispered. "I think my period is over."

"It'll come back next month, trust me. And leave me alone. I'm going back to sleep."

"You don't even care?"

I stifled the urge to remind her that since she was married, that guy in her bed was now legally required to care, which was technically supposed to let her spinster cousin off the hook.

"My period has always been five days long," she persisted. "Down to the hour. You could have set a clock by me. Always. Since I was thirteen. And this time it was only three days. So that's why I'm asking. Do you think this means that I'm having early *early* onset menopause? Like maybe I'm drying up?"

"Okay, gross."

"Monica!" she yelled through the phone.

"You woke me up to ask me if you're drying up? Do you honestly believe that?"

"Okay, no… I mean I'm not a maniac." She exhaled, and then thought about it. "Actually, I woke you up to tell you to turn on your television."

"I'm hanging up."

"Turn it on *now!*" she scream-whispered. "Or I'll tell your mom that you and Raj broke up and that you miss her and want her to come stay with you for a month to make you feel better."

"You wouldn't dare."

"You're right, I wouldn't. But I will tell everyone at your office that you read *Pucker.* Just trust me. I swear, I have a good reason for this. Flip to PBS."

"Why are you whispering?" I groped around for the remote on my bedside table.

"Because I don't want Josh to know."

"That you watch PBS, or that you're drying up?" I sat up and flicked on the television, flooding the room in blue light. "What the hell am I watching anyway?"

"Oh *crap!*" she said. "I think I hear him coming. I gotta go hide. I'll call you back from the hall closet, if I get reception."

I found PBS just in time to glimpse a montage of scenes involving various types of primates biting, taunting, roaring and occasionally hurling their feces at one another.

"Welcome back to this special presentation of *Women At*

War. This and other important public programming was made possible by your generous donations to the Public Broadcasting System."

"Sugar and spice and everything nice?" An aggressively eyebrowed host in an argyle sweater beseeches the camera. "Not if you consider the behavior of this two-hundred pound orangutan in the Brazilian rainforest. Unnerved by a younger, fertile female's attempts to attach herself to their group, the elder orangutan roars with anger when the intruder moves toward the vicinity of the alpha male. Eventually she's angry enough to climb a tree and hurl her feces at the potential interloper."

I quickly gathered that this was a documentary exploring competition among female apes from an evolutionary perspective as a means of better understanding human social tendencies.

"It is a generally accepted theory among evolutionary biologists that this behavior is not only traditional, but it is rational. The alpha male represents access to those scarce resources that will ensure the survival of the females and their offspring. Namely, food, shelter and physical protection from predators. Any addition of breeding capacity to the group threatens to dilute each female's allotment of these already scarce resources."

Next, they cut to a tape of a group of black lemurs in Madagascar.

"Of course, hurling feces may be a walk in the park compared to the tragic violence we observe among the female black lemurs of a troop in Madagascar. After the death of their alpha female sparks an upheaval and the need to establish a new female hierarchy, a truly brutal grab for dominance ensues."

Amidst the hooting and hollering from the other females as the largest two duke it out for dominance, one of these pretenders-to-the-throne literally snatches up his rival's screaming infant into her mouth, and swings it up a tree. Perched about twenty feet above the onlookers, including her rival, she shakes the child violently until she is satisfied that it is dead, and then smashes open its rib cage and proceeds to eat some of its inner organs. Seeing this, her competitor simply falls silent, with no other remedy than to watch while the victor makes her point.

"By far the most consistently violent of our genetic ancestors ever to be observed in captivity are baboons. Nervous when another female in the group has a child that might be likely to compete with her own, the female baboon has been known to drop another female's infant, step on it or even take a big bite out of its head when the mother was nowhere in sight. But while mothers who lose their children have little recourse within the pack, there are still those baboons who choose a more indirect approach to stifling the competition.

"Indeed, under the guise of sharing childcare, female baboons routinely enact a more subtle sort of rivalry whereby they will 'accidentally' injure another's infant. One mother had her child passed constantly from adult to adult. Not surprisingly, the infant died within months.

"This behavior is nothing short of brutality." The announcer shook his head. "Even if it is indirect. But in animals, we are raised to believe that it is understandable, even expected. You may be wondering how all of this relates to the behavior of the human species. According to professor of primatology Adrienne McNulty, primate behavior with respect to jockeying for social and breeding position within a clan is almost directly mirrored among humans…"

"We are told time and again as children that girls do not act aggressively," professor McNulty explained from behind her desk. "However, if you look more closely, the evidence actually tells us the opposite. And when you accept that emotional aggression is as valid as physical aggression, and analyze it systematically, it begins to make a lot of sense."

The camera pans over to the host, who is chewing on the end of his glasses, pensively, while the professor continues.

"Fact— As animals, it is only natural that all humans feel the instinct for aggression. Biologically, it is the primary tool at our disposal to contend with the chemicals released in our brain when we feel a physical threat. Fact— We are taught as children that while boys will be boys, girls should make nice, or else risk being considered wild. Fact— Studies have shown that girls begin to develop emotional intelligence far earlier than boys, and learn even before they leave grade school how powerful social status can be. Is it any surprise then that the effects of female emotional aggression not only cut deeper but linger longer than male physical aggression which is usually over once the boys have a chance to physically *duke it out?*"

"According to McNulty—" the host's voice-over narrates videotape of schoolgirls laughing together on playgrounds and in lunchrooms "—social and emotional aggression among adolescent girls is on the rise in this country, and its effects are alarming. Increasing pressure to conform to an unattainable physical ideal makes it easier for girls to tease, harass and essentially perpetrate a form of social death upon one another when competing for status in their social hier-archies."

"Emotional pain, or a stab at the reputation, if you will, takes the place of a physical stab at the heart," McNulty explains while walking a tree-lined academic path alongside the host. "Unlike men, women have not historically won social status in their societies by causing physical harm to their enemies. Rather, in order to compete, women have had to devise clever tools of psychological warfare to make the other feel unwanted, out of place or small. Social ostracization quickly took the place of a punch in the face. And this happens as much among women in large extended families as it does in extended social groups."

An hour into the documentary, my phone rang.

"See?" Sheila squealed.

"Interesting." I turned down the volume. "But what does this have to do with your monthly visitor?"

"Don't do that. Don't say monthly visitor. You're too old to say that."

"Okay, now I really am hanging up."

"No, wait. I'm sorry. It's my mother-in-law. Don't you get it?" she yelped. "She's not ovulating anymore so she sees me as a threat to the resources of Joshua's primary loyalty! That's why she always needs to make me feel so left out! She's trying to cut me down. Establish dominance. She's... she's throwing her feces at me!"

"Sheila, breathe," I urged, trying to stifle a grin. "We'll get you a Handi Wipe."

"I won't calm down! Everybody acts like this monster-in-law crap is okay, and so I am expected to accept it. Look at that hideous dress she bought me. Clearly, she wants to diminish my chances of breeding by making me look totally gross, even if it is subconscious. Because she knows that if I get pregnant then all the attention shifts toward me! Am I the only one that sees this?"

"Honey, I'll grant you that she's an evil witch, but I don't really think she wants to prevent you from having children. Wouldn't that be kind of counterintuitive?"

"Well then she's going to have to choose between wanting grandchildren or wanting status in our family. Or ape clan. Or whatever. Because the stress of this passive-aggressive garbage is drying me up. I swear, I think my hair is starting to fall out."

"Sheila, I'm sure that she wants attention, but I don't believe that your mother-in-law wishes you physical harm. You need to take a deep breath."

"I know, I know." She started talking herself down. "I

know she doesn't have, like, some incestuous tendency toward Josh or anything. But I'm the new lactating female. And she's not gonna get off my ass until she makes me look small in front of the entire family."

"You're *lactating?*"

"You know what I mean."

"And I don't know what to tell you." I glanced at the clock. "You married into that tribe of baboons. So make like a monkey and *groom up* for as long as it takes to make her accept you into the group. It's either that or find a way to finally teach your baboon that he belongs to only you now."

"Groom up?"

"Yeah, weren't you watching?"

"I stepped away to make a sandwich. I was craving ham and pickles."

"Basically, they talked about how certain female monkeys allow others into their groups only if there's some benefit for them. So you should do whatever it takes to ingratiate yourself to a higher-ranking female, so that she'll be on your side, since there's no one else who's gonna defend you. Love your enemy and eventually she will have to love you."

"So you want me to come on to my mother-in-law?"

"Yes, Sheila." I got sarcastic. "That's exactly what I am implying."

She giggled while I wished that I could take a squeegee to my brain.

"I'm kidding," she said, regaining her composure. "Anyway, thanks for listening. I gotta run. I saw a pint of rocky road in the freezer that I forgot we had. I'll call you tomorrow."

eight

I HUNG UP THE PHONE AND TURNED UP THE VOLUME ON THE TV. How Sheila could take any of this stuff literally was beyond me.

"Jealousy among schoolgirls, envy between older and younger women, even competition in the workplace." McNulty continued, "As far back as the fairy tales we grew up with, like Cinderella and Sleeping Beauty, females have been trained to be suspicious of one another, and to resent power imbalances between ourselves and other women. Naturally, we cope by either placing other women on pedestals from which they are destined to fall—begrudging them their humanity—or by simmering with quiet aggression beneath a thin veneer of propriety. When aggression goes underground, and when physical attacks are replaced with emotional violence, can psychological terrorism among women be far behind?

"Woe be to the woman who underestimates her adversary on the playground or in the workplace. Because if there is one thing that holds true across females of the different species and socioeconomic classes which I've studied over the last thirty years, it's that the most vicious attacks are those which come as a surprise."

"So what does this mean for our society as a whole?" the host asks the camera. "Maybe Ms. McNulty should have the last word."

"Humanity is at a critical point in the evolution of our social mores. Never before in human history have we been able to openly acknowledge these issues and recognize their universality. As a culture, we only have two options. Either we can acknowledge woman's capacity for aggression and begin to talk about it openly, or we can start telling our girls what we tell our boys, and let them take it out on each other physically. Maybe then, rather than growing up to be socially anxious, deceptively dismissive or sarcastically aggressive, a larger majority of our daughters can grow up to be the type of women who can get it off their chests and get on with their lives. Even if it means that most of us will have a few childhood scars to show for it."

The upside of having taken care of my mother after dad passed away was that ever since then, while most people were trying to convince their parents that they were no longer children, she presumed I could also take care of myself. The downside was that she assumed I still wanted to take care of her.

"Did I wake you?" she asked me through the telephone, in the moment before I would have drifted back to sleep.

"Of course not." I tilted the alarm clock display away from my face, not even wanting to know how few hours were left until I had to get ready for work. "What's going on?"

"I don't want to upset you, but the situation is that…I have decided not to move back to Los Angeles just yet. Darling, I'm sorry. I've been thinking about it and I am not ready for it. I thought I was, but there are still too many memories of my life with your father there. So I need to ask you to please sell the house for me, and try to get a little more than I paid for it, if you can. Can you do that for me, honey?"

"Sure, mom." I rubbed my forehead, wondering how long it would take me to view, list and sell this house for her, with no real estate experience, and for a profit. "Sure I can."

"I feel so much better knowing that you have Raj there with you," she added, imagining that the middle of the night before a workday was as good a time as any for some girl-talk. "How is he doing these days? You haven't mentioned him lately."

"Oh, fine, Mom." My voice almost cracked. "He's fine."

"Yes, well, good. Very good. Tell him I thought of him

a few days ago when I saw a young man who looked like him from afar, walking here in London. The man was crossing the street in front of my taxi. With some pretty young woman with the most beautiful red hair. He looked so much like Raj that I almost called out to him. Of course I didn't because then I would have ruined the poor man's evening, whoever he was. Anyway, you'll tell him to tell his parents that I said *hello,* all right?"

My father's best friend died of cancer the year that I turned twelve. Ashok Uncle had been my parents' first neighbor when they moved to the U.S., and my parents' only connection to their culture for the first five years of their life here. Eventually, he became my father's partner in his hedge fund. His wife of seventeen years remarried less than two years after his death. Despite my father's having taken it so personally, at the time my mother spoke out in defense of Malika Auntie. In her words, no one had the right to judge her for not wanting to be alone.

We were not raised to be comfortable with being alone, she had explained to me while we were folding clothes. *We went from our father's homes to our husband's homes, and we assumed that by the time we were widows, our children would be grown, so we would grow old in their homes in the traditional Indian style. Like our parents did. Old age was full of family and friends and life, so there was no need for a companion. But life in America is different. No matter how much community we have here, it cannot be the kind of community which will compensate for Malika being alone for the last forty years of her life.*

No love or relationship can ever be perfect; if it could then we would have nothing to fight for. Growing up in the state with the highest divorce rate in the nation, and probably the world, that fact could not have been more clear. Although, there's always the exception because somehow the idea that she could not make room in her heart for another man made me love my mother even more. As much as I wanted her to be happy, I was deeply content with the freedom to believe that their love would outlast even his life.

The problem was it also made me shudder at the total vulnerability of marrying for a love like that of my own.

Why anyone presumed my luck would be better than most at talking Lydia down off an emotional ledge was curious. Why Lydia's agent had my cell phone number on speed dial was questionable. Why he summoned Jonathan and myself to a dilapidated boxing ring way out in East Los Angeles in the middle of the following afternoon was anybody's guess.

But then there were the billable hours.

"Someone better get that goddamn preppy outta my face!"

A cup of dark liquid came flying out of Lydia's makeup trailer, milliseconds after I pulled open the door. Following closely behind the mess was a mousey-looking production assistant, who ran smack into Jonathan as if running for his life.

"I don't care if you have to drive *three hours* to find a goddamned Starbucks this time," Lydia yelled after him. "I want it *soy,* and I want it *HOT!*"

"May I?" I asked, before daring to enter.

"Yeah, yeah, whatever," she said, plopping back into her makeup chair and swinging around to console herself with her reflection in the mirror. "F-ing ivy-league interns. That kid's from Yale and he can't even get a goddamn latte right."

"Lydia," I said, and stepped inside, waiting until Jonathan shut the door behind us. "The deficiencies of an ivy-league education notwithstanding…why are we here?"

"Because my client needs to be made to understand the definition of a contract," Lydia's chubby-cheeked, beady-eyed, suit-but-no-tie-wearing manager answered for her. He smoothed back his remaining piece of hair and kicked away a Chinese divider screen where he must have taken cover.

He held out a pair of pink rhinestoned boxing gloves, which Lydia promptly smacked right out of his hands.

"And my *agent* needs to stop talking to me like I'm an idiot," she snarled, "before I *fire* his ass."

"Is there something objectionable in your contract for this photo shoot?" Jonathan asked.

"Not technically," the agent replied, bending down with some difficulty to retrieve the gloves from the floor. "But certain events could not have been foreseen. And we cannot reneg on the contract, no matter how ironic the event may seem at this point. We could be sued."

"It's not the *event, Marvin.* It's the title." Lydia turned to face me.

"You know that my name is Martin," he corrected her, and then advised us, "My name is Martin."

"Well, since my last album put your kids through college, I think I'll call you whatever I want, *Marvin,*" she scoffed. "Now Monica, do you think it's *unreasonable* for me not to wanna do a photo shoot with the title 'She's Willing to Fight For It,' considering the circumstances, as you lawyers like to say?"

"What circumstances?" Jonathan and I echoed.

Martin slammed a copy of *Pucker* into my hands. "Sources Say Camydia Has Less Than A Fighting Chance" the front-page headline screamed. It was emblazoned in bright red letters across a photograph of Cameron taken in the parking lot of a West Hollywood hotspot the previous night. Seated in the passenger side of his trademark blue sapphire Escalade was an "unidentified blonde" who was shielding her face from the paparazzi.

"This is an endorsement deal for Outlast! It's the most popular sports equipment company on the planet!" Martin pointed out the bejeweled logos twinkling across Lydia's sports bra and satin boxing cloak. "You said you wanted an endorsement deal, and I got you the mother of all endorsement deals. Normally they won't even consider giving them to non-athletes! We've got two hundred extras waiting inside that building to cheer you on, we've got three former heavyweight champions sitting in to play fake judges in the background of the shot, and the entire boxing ring has been lined with pink silk to match your tiara! If you pull out now, it's a lawsuit!"

"I. Ain't. Doing it," she told us forcefully, folding her arms in front of her.

"Lydia!" he hollered.

"You work for me, Marvin. And you are getting on my last nerve. Why don't you go find that pink-diamond tooth cap they promised me? I'm probably not gonna do this shoot, but I'm *sure as hell* not doing it without my *cap*."

"Every hour we wait costs the company an extra hundred K," Martin implored, before sulking out of the trailer. "And it hurts her career, too. This is a marital issue. It's not about Outlast. It's about Cameron. Please, try to make her see the bigger picture. I know it's not what you signed on for, but I didn't expect to be a fifty-year-old man scouring a boxing ring looking for a pink jewel-encrusted snap-on tooth cap."

Lydia ran her fingers over the glittery waistband of her boxing shorts. Jonathan picked her boxing gloves up off the counter and stepped between her and the mirror.

"Maybe not as many people read *Pucker* as you think," he tried.

She stared blankly at him for a second before swiveling her attention to me.

"Go ahead," I said, sitting on the love seat across from her so that she knew she had my attention.

"I can't give 'em what they want." She started tearing up.

"Give *who* what they want?" I asked.

"The media. The goddamn f-ing media." She shook her head. "I am so tired of all this."

Jonathan chimed in, "You feel like you'll look like an idiot if people think you're threatening that woman through a magazine ad, right?"

She nodded.

"And you know what really pisses me off?" Lydia dabbed at her leaking eye makeup. "The media wouldn't have anything to torture me with if these women would keep their hands off a married man. It's not like they don't know he's married. I mean he's not some random guy they never heard of. I'm mad at him, too, but...I don't understand why women always have to go out of their way to hurt other women?"

I said it before even realizing where it was coming from, "Because, deep down inside, some of us still believe that we can only get ahead if another woman falls behind."

"If I may," Jonathan interrupted, lifting the custom-made tiara out of its case. "I have a suggestion. I think there's a way to make sure you don't look weak without you violating your contract."

The interior of the boxing gym was dressed as if the *Queer Eye for the Straight Guy* cast had thrown up all over it. The crowd sat ready to wave tiny logoed penants on cue, while bare-chested and well-oiled waiters with rippling physiques traversed the stands with trays of champagne. A silver-plated icebox full of Perrier bottles stood in place of a water bottle in Lydia's corner. And above the ring in massive lettering there was a banner hanging with the phrase: Strong Women Refuse To Take Life Lying Down.

Lydia squared her legs, tilted her tiara, and then faced off against the camera.

And when they rang the bell, Lydia let go a smirk before swinging so hard that the crowd immediately went wild. She almost knocked that cameraman out of the ring.

nine

After a few more hours of watching Lydia box away her aggression, I decided I deserved a Mango-tini or twelve. So instead of returning to the office, I headed over to *The Wilshire* for their Thursday Night Happy Hour. Amid your usual West Los Angeles mix of aspiring agents in Ferragamo blazers with their barely legal girlfriends, struggling screen-writers in T-shirts and a few days' stubble alongside the real estate agent buddies they bummed their drinks from, and roving packs of men in their fifties who were convinced that they fit in, I made my way to the bar.

Predictably, all of the barstools were taken, and typically, none of the men were in any rush to give up their seat for someone showing as precious little skin as myself. So I scanned for any two people with their backs to each other, and settled on a fortysomething bodybuilder who was chatting up a disinterested, blond Asian woman, and an oppressively tall and awkward-looking Nordic type in a three-piece suit. A good four inches separated them, so I twisted my body sideways and led with my arm. I squeezed my way between them and struggled for eye contact with one of the many bartenders who had forgotten to wear a bra.

I would have lent her mine, but trust me, she needed something a lot stronger.

I was reaching for my wallet when Jonathan interrupted from a corner of the bar. "Put that on my tab, beautiful. Monica's earned herself a drink today."

"Well, she decides to grace us with her presence." Stefanie approached and raised a wobbly glass at me, clearly on her second drink already.

Roaring territorial orangutan: 1.

Latecomer on her first Mango-tini: 0.

But that was about to change. After my afternoon at the boxing ring, I was armed and ready to throw some truly poetic comebacks in her drunken direction.

"You know, Stefanie…" I began, before Cassie interrupted.

"Hey, Stefanie," she said, smiling at me while taking my nemesis by the elbow and leading her off, "why don't you join me in the ladies' room?"

Disappointed, I walked over to Jonathan and dropped my purse on the table.

"So this is a coincidence. Where's Niles and the other partners?" I asked, settling in.

"Don't worry so much, slugger." Jonathan wrapped his arm around my neck and mock jabbed at my jaw with his fist. "I always make sure the positive news about my co-counsel gets back to them. I already told Niles all about how you handled Lydia today. Above and beyond as usual, Gupta."

"But I didn't fix it, Jonathan. You came up with the solution."

"Mere details," he cried and waved the credit back to me. "We all know who makes the connection and who handles mere details on this case."

I noticed Stefanie's reflection. She was glaring at me. In the massive mirror over Jonathan's shoulder. And all of a sudden it started making sense.

"So you're pretty popular these days." I licked some sugar off the rim of my glass just to rub it in, in case Stefanie was still watching. "It must feel good."

He raised an eyebrow at me, and signaled the bartender for another beer.

"It looks like someone has a crush on you."

"Really?" He perked up and asked. "You really think Cassie would go out with me?"

"Cassie? No. I was talking about Stefanie. I think she hates me because we're friends and she thinks I'm a threat to her chances of mating with you. You thought I was talking about Cassie?"

"Mating?" He coughed, nearly choking on the beer.

"I've been watching animal sex documentaries."

"Kinky." He looked impressed. "Is this what you do when your fiancé's out of town?"

"Uh, now you're hot for Cassie?" I wasn't gonna let him change the topic that fast.

He shrugged. I knew I was going to have to work a little harder, so I used the only ammunition I had.

"What is it with the secretaries, anyway?"

"Maybe it has something to do with them being a lot less picky than your average female attorney," he thought out loud. "Or maybe it's just because they're hotter."

I nodded, thinking to myself that I, too, would have been a lot *hotter* if I hadn't spent all those late nights studying for the bar exam. What was I thinking?

"Present company excluded, of course."

"Of course."

"Or maybe it's the image of them licking all those envelopes."

"Ape." I shook my head at him, then noticed my grin had been misinterpreted by one of the earlier fortysome-things—he was raising an eyebrow at me over blondie's shoulder. I quickly tilted behind Jonathan to get out of his line of sight.

"News flash, Monica. We're all apes. Every last one of us. Even your precious fiancé. Deep down inside he's just as disgusting as I am." Jonathan licked his finger clean of the beer foaming over the side of his glass before wiping it on his pants.

"That's comforting. Anyway, I'm not so sure that I even have a fiancé anymore." I twirled the stem of my glass.

"You might want to figure that out before the company party next week." He winked, quickly diverting his gaze toward the glossy waitress gliding by. "It's a great place to pick up pity sex. If you're looking."

"I think I'll pass." I noticed that Cassie was making her way over to us.

"So what are you gonna do with your life if you're too good to sleep with any of us apes?" he asked. "Sit around and stare at the walls all day? Spend your weekends going to the movies alone?"

"Maybe," I replied, watching the Norwegian slip Blondie's coat over her shoulders and lead her out of the bar. "Why not?"

"Oh, speaking of which," he remembered. "Have you seen the commercials for that new movie? The one that's supposed to be a remake of that 1970s movie *Love Story?*"

I scanned the room for signs of more intelligent life.

"It's supposed to be fantastic. I can't ask any guys I know to go see it with me, obviously. And if I go to see it with an actual woman then I won't really see it because, well, I like to take advantage of the dark. But I've heard good things. And it was cowritten by the guy who wrote *Like You Mean It*. So do you want to go see it this weekend? Come on, it's not like you have anything better to do."

I was a ball of nerves when *Like You Mean It* hit the theaters, even though it had been years since I broke up with Alex. I didn't just want the movie to do well at the box office; I wanted this film to put Alex on the map. Being in a committed relationship with Raj by that time, I was completely ashamed of myself. Watching the movie with him was out of the question, of course. Watching it with anyone who didn't know Alex would have cheapened the experience. And watching it with Sheila would have given her license to force me to verbalize and then try to make some sense of my unresolved feelings for him. So I did what any well-adjusted woman who felt as if she was committing emotional adultery would do. I bought a ticket online for the Sunday matinee at a small theater in suburban Orange County where I was sure nobody would recognize me. I drove out there alone in a nondescript tracksuit, minimal makeup and a large pair of generic sunglasses.

I settled into my chair in the back of the theater among the empty rows and the occasional teenage couple who had nowhere else to make out. I clutched my jumbo tub of buttered popcorn and sank deeper into my seat as they rolled the opening credits. And I hated myself for beaming with pride when Alex's name burst forth next to the words Screenplay By.

Mouthing the familiar dialogue of the opening scene where Obama—now a Sudanese refugee working as a busboy—and Ling—now an illegal Chinese immigrant working in the garment district—meet at the crowded lunchcounter of a New York diner in the late nineties, I began to recognize how much had changed. In the last version of the screenplay I saw, the refugee was a former white supremacist recently released after three years in prison for a crime he didn't commit, the immigrant was a tolerance activist and granddaughter of holocaust survivors, and the New York diner was a Halloween Party in San Bernardino.

Despite the Hollywood airbrush, buff and polish, the message of his story hadn't changed. It was about the power of love to transform people against all odds. I smiled at the affirmation that even after all these years he still believed that. But it wasn't until halfway through the film that I got the validation I had been seeking in the first place: the confirmation that he still missed me.

Why does she keep pushing me away? Obama tearfully asks his boss, the kind Italian restaurant owner, on the evening after Ling asks him to forget that he ever met her.

I ever tell you about the Indian chick I used to go with when I was your age? his boss answers, hacking into some veal medallions.

Obama shakes his head.

Yeah, she was somethin', he continues, adding tenderizer. *Real fiery, but a good girl at the same time, ya know? Of course, she left me in the end. She was the only girl I never cheated on, too, 'til I got married. But she was too smart to stick around with me. It turns out she was smart enough for the both of us.*

I do not understand, Obama replies, searching the man's eyes.

The owner pauses, thinks, and then looks directly at Obama. *I always thought I was Italian, ya know? Not white.*

Because where I grown up, there was always a lot of fighting between the Irish, the Polish, the Italians. I thought that my whole life. White people were British or somethin', but they weren't from my neighborhood. Then one day, me and Seema, we're walking down the street, and someone yells out at her something I won't repeat, just because she's walkin' wit' me. And she looks up at me with those big brown eyes, biggest roundest eyes you ever seen…and it's like she's all alone in the world and there's no way I can get to where she is, even if she stood right next to me for the rest of our lives. Take it from me, Obama. You can eat all the lo mein in the world, and you can want to be everything she needs so bad it tears ya up inside. But you ain't never gonna be Chinese, man. And she ain't never not gonna be.

Even though we never had that conversation, the scene stabbed as much as it substantiated something in my memories of him. Did he believe I had broken up with him over race? Of course not. Had he felt there was a part of me he could never reach? I hoped not. Had he taken the screenplay as an opportunity to rewrite our history by implying that he was the one who had decided I was too much to handle? Maybe. More importantly, could I have been so far off target to believe that he had known me better than that?

When I walked into my apartment that night the first thing I heard was Raj, singing along with my Norah Jones CD. Whatever he was making for dinner smelled heavenly. When he heard me in the kitchen, he spun around with an apron across his waist and a ladleful of something for me to try.

I broke into tears. I felt so guilty for having gone to see the movie that I couldn't hold them back. On the one hand I had a cinematic kiss-off from a man who had concluded that we'd never really known each other, and on the other hand I had a real chance of a simple life with a man to whom I would probably never have to explain myself. Effortlessly, he would understand, instinctively, he would empathize, and often, he would make me dinner. I was sure of it.

Raj took one look at my face, set down the ladle, and came over to wrap me in his arms. And then he said those five little words that did as much to make me love him as they did to make me feel more alone than ever:

"I thought it would help."

That was when I recognized the scent wafting through the apartment. My boyfriend was cooking my father's signature dish, Rajma stew, from scratch, to comfort me. Since it would have been my parents' thirtieth wedding anniversary that night.

I buried my face in his neck and considered whether anyone could ever really know me at all. Or maybe, just maybe, I had never given anyone the chance. Either way, I looked into Raj's eyes. Was it presumption on my part? Maybe Raj had been associating the expressions on my face with some catalogue of emotions he'd compiled in his mind because he'd never lost anyone of true importance to him, to death or to anything else. Still, I had the sense even then that he would happily stand beside me, without a hint of resentment and try to make sense of me for the rest of our lives.

★ ★ ★

Why do they even call it Happy Hour? I wondered this Friday morning while ripping off the top of my venti vanilla latte, and tipping it down my throat with both hands. *There were the following facts to consider. That Stefanie wasn't happy when she saw Jonathan buying me a drink. That Cassie wasn't happy when she bumped into an ex she had gotten rid of by claiming she was joining the Peace Corps. That the bodybuilder wasn't happy when, after no less than three failed attempts at getting a coed's number, the only proposal that made its way over to him came from another bodybuilder who was nearly twice his size. The owners of The Wilshire couldn't have been happy with the razor-thin margins they made on the discounted drinks they served just to keep the crowd thick and the impression of their popularity alive. And I certainly wasn't happy when I woke up the next morning with the sense that tiny angry rabbits had entered my apartment through the vents and decided to use my head as a Capoeira drum while I slept.*

Little did I know that at the office the pounding was about to get a lot worse. I logged on to my computer to find that I had only one e-mail waiting for me.

My trip was extended. The client has requested that I stay on.
We'll talk when I get back.
Take care,
Raj

ten

Take care?

Take care?

It was just plain insulting, was what it was.

As if I were someone on a subway with whom he had been making small talk while trying to ignore the homeless guy touching himself five feet away? What kind of a person treats someone like a colleague after having sampled no less than three different Cabernets out of said person's belly button by candlelight at a bed and breakfast in the Napa Valley?

He might as well have asked *if he knew me from somewhere.* Had we not spent the better part of the last few years being one another's best friends? Had I not nursed him back to health after the bad tequila he drank on a dare from that pushy waiter in Puerto Vallarta? Had he not gotten down on one knee and invited me to help him build a Happily Ever After? Maybe I missed something. Maybe he finally had enough of me. And maybe that really was Raj that my mother saw in London with that redhead. I ran at least three stop signs on my way to Sheila's place after work. Oddly, the door swung open before I could even get my finger to the doorbell.

"I'm pregnant!" she squealed, grabbing me by the shoulders and snatching me inside.

"Are you serious?" I stumbled into the foyer and blurted, "That's great! Oh my gosh, congratulations!"

"I'm pregnant, I'm pregnant, I'm pregnant!" she sang, forcing me into a dance. "Aaaaaaaahhhhhhh!!!!!!!"

She was about fourteen weeks along, and absolutely beside herself. And she hadn't told Joshua yet.

"Actually, I just found out myself." She hopped onto the overstuffed sofa, sat cross-legged and rested both hands across her belly. "You know how I'm on that three-periods-a-year birth-control pill? Well, I guess it's not a hundred percent effective, because my gynecologist called to tell me that he ran a pregnancy test along with everything else since I mentioned that my boobs were sore last week!"

"So, I take it this is good news?" I asked cautiously.

"Yeah," she replied, with an affectionate glance at her belly. "Yeah, it is."

"You're gonna be a great mom," I said, reaching out to hug her again. And I meant it.

"I can't wait to tell him." Her eyes were welling up.

I imagined her meeting him at the door, overflowing with excitement, throwing her arms around his neck. He would put down his briefcase, rattled by her emotion, confused and concerned by this swell of feeling from his capricious young wife. She would savor delivering those precious words to her husband for the very first time. *We're pregnant.* And it would be perfect.

Or it would have been, were it not for the fact that while my forehead was sweaty, my throat had completely dried up, tucked inside my happiness for Sheila, was jealousy. And I hated myself for it. I couldn't even look her in the eye because seeing that kind of joy up close only made it that much harder to ignore the possibility that it might never happen for me. So it turns out that while I may have cleaned up nice enough, deep down I was still an ape in a tailored suit, exactly like everybody else.

I pulled my suit sleeve lower, attempting to cover the fur sprouting from around my wrist.

"Monica, what is it?" Sheila asked after a moment.

"It's nothing." I swiped at my eyes. "I'm…I'm so happy for you. I can't wait to start buying baby clothes!"

"Oh my God!" she shrieked. "I didn't even *think* about that! How fun!"

"Yeah," I said with some relief, knowing that I was actually sincere. "But we'll have to wait until we know the sex of the baby, right? So that means we'll have to limit ourselves to toys and cribs for now."

"Okay, but we have to keep it quiet. I don't want to

"Yeah," she chortled. "Me and the rest of L.A. I'm addicted to that show. Probably because it punks regular people, instead of celebrities. That's very satisfying for me."

"Always glad to help," I sneered.

"Not only that, but you got my respect now, for real. I never had the balls to break up with someone through to a television show. Even when my publicist told me it would sell more albums." She laughed. "But that's not why I'm calling."

Right around the moment when I had inadvertently decided to throw my own relationship out the reality TV window, it turned out, Cameron and Lydia had decided to step back from Steel and think things over before moving any further with their divorce proceedings.

"And I know I don't have to remind you that we chose Steel Associates because we expect discretion," she told me, while I slumped over my desk, dreading the process of getting to know a new client once I told Niles that I had lost Camydia. "So of course we will expect Steel not to comment on our marriage, or on whether or not we've ever consulted you, okay?"

"Of course, Lydia," I said, wondering why she felt the need to reinforce the point. "And good luck."

"Yeah, thanks. And, hey, if it's any consolation…it definitely looked like that guy *wanted* to kiss you back," she said before hanging up.

Trust me, it wasn't.

thirteen

ANYBODY UP FOR A LATE LUNCH AT SPAGO'S? JONATHAN replied within seconds of my e-mail announcing Camydia's attempted reconciliation.

"They'll be back within a month," he predicted, heaping three layers of beef carpaccio onto his fork, and then shoveling them into his mouth.

"So this is what Steel has reduced us to? Hoping that people's marriages fail?"

"I don't hope it," he told me midchew, "I recognize it."

"Such an optimist," I observed.

"I am pessimistic where pessimism is due." He snapped a breadstick, sending little bits of it flying into my martini. "And I am an optimist about things that are worth being optimistic about."

"Like?" I swirled the thin layer of pumpkin soup around its oversize bowl, wondering whether the chef had chosen the bowl to imply that a measly twenty dollars only earned you *half* a bowl of a soup this good, or to give weight-conscious diners the illusion that they were eating less.

"*Like*...I am optimistic about my chances of drinking you under the table today." He leaned in and raised his eyebrows. "And...I am pessimistic about your chances of making it big as an actress...however impressive your reality TV credits may be."

"Oh, crap," I said too loudly. "I didn't think you watched reality TV."

He sniggered. "You know, I've never seen you kiss anybody before. May I say, nice form."

"Thank you. But this is not funny!" I insisted, gulping down half of my martini. "Raj might see this. Then what happens? We haven't been having the best relationship lately. I don't know how I'm gonna explain this. I never thought I was gonna be one of those people who claims that it *'Just happened.'* That sounds so weak, but I have no other way of explaining myself. I don't even think I can forgive myself."

"Maybe he didn't see it. He's overseas, right? What are the chances?"

"Wait a minute." I tilted my head, while a waiter replaced my empty martini glass with a newer, fuller one. "How did you know about this? Don't you normally have a date on a Sunday night? On *every* night?"

"Well, that's kind of why I'd planned on taking you to lunch today. I thought you might prefer to hear it from me."

"Hear what from you? Oh God, what happened?"

"I don't really know how to tell you this, Mon." He looked like he had smelled something rotten. "Someone sent the online clip around the office this morning to all the attorneys, anonymously."

"Even the senior partners?"

"Afraid so," he replied. The waiter appeared at our table.

Struggling to balance two water glasses, my steaming salmon and Jonathan's heavy Osso Buco all at once, he never had a chance. In one swift move, he laid my entrée before me, Jonathan's plate before him, and knocked my glass of Perrier right off the table.

"It was Stefanie," I said, paying no attention to the commotion, as if I'd just awakened to what had been right in front of me all along.

I was in grade school the very first time that I can remember another woman trying to ruin my life. At thirteen years old, Vicky had the nicotine habit of a supermodel, a body that I'm still hoping to develop myself and the distinction of being the most popular girl at Hermosa Junior High School. I had the misfortune of being new to the school, having the least generic last name, and therefore I instantly became the target of her aggression.

By the end of September, I was used to the snickers

whenever Mr. Weiss mispronounced my name during attendance for fourth period art class. To this day I wonder why he failed to hear the laughter, and insisted on inserting random *S*'s and *J*'s into my last name where my parents had not. A bad eyeglass prescription? Perhaps. But I'm quite sure that his ears worked just fine. Then again, childhood always screams much louder at the person living through it than at anyone seated nearby. After a number of years in the system, children who are in any way "different" learn the drill.

Like any relatively scrawny newbie being transferred from one prison to another, I expected a certain amount of disdain from the other inmates. At least until I had the chance to show my colors (student government or mathlete?), establish my alliances (who would share their seat on the bus?) and be publicly accepted into any particular gang, that is. So far, the worst of it had been sitting alone or with the pocket-protector and retainer-set at lunch, while waiting to be invited to a more normal table. But it was precisely the moment when I spilled bright green paint onto the floor during fourth period, that I knew I'd made my fatal mistake. Honestly, I would have preferred for the paint to have splattered across my face than to have had one drop soil Vicky's spotless, pearl-pink Candie's.

Clupta-Gupta, she sneered, and everyone in the class burst into a chorus of laughter. *Why are you so clumsy, Clupta-Gupta?*

And that was pretty much it. The name calling over the

next few months was almost as brutal as the fact that even the non-English-speaking exchange students refused to sit with me. Aside from the occasional distorted face or the fact that she stopped speaking in order to sneer at me whenever I walked by, Vicky never directly engaged me again. The problem was that neither did anyone else. Ever. And social isolation for a sixth-grader is about as bad as if a lover starts withholding sex when you're about thirty; you just don't know what to do or who to tell, but you are sure that something is very wrong. I kept it from my parents at home, and mastered the art of moving among my peers almost undetected at school. It wasn't until the school guidance counselor Mrs. Loeb got fed up with my weekly sobbing in her office that she finally hauled Vicky in one day, despite my protests.

I didn't mean it, Vicky told me in the waiting area through tear-soaked eyes an hour later. She'd emerged from what must have been a very intense little chat with Mrs. Loeb. *I'm sorry. Let me make it up to you.*

You know what you can do for me? I was as defiant as was possible for my age. *You can just shut up and stop making fun of me and let me make some friends. I don't need your help. I need you to leave me alone!*

And she did. Somehow, even in the pre-e-mail era, she managed to get the word out overnight. Because the teasing ceased immediately. Despite her remorse, however, forgiveness wasn't an option. I just wanted her out of my life. I declined her invitations to go to the mall, join her table at lunch, or work with her on any class projects. Slowly but surely I gathered the nerve to put myself out there. To make friendships that were strong enough to last through the rest of high school. Vicky's parents divorced soon after the third of her increasingly infamous parties that she threw whenever they were out of town.

By the time she dropped out of high school and went into rehab during our senior year, I remembered feeling something resembling sympathy. At the very least it was clear that there really was nothing personal about why she had singled me out. We were simply children then, and children are as cursed with awareness as they are infuriated by the recognition of what little power they actually have at their disposal. Vicky exercised her popularity as the tool to extract some marginal sense of control over a life that she must have known was spiraling beyond it. I was mere collateral damage in the story of that life, and in the end, I think we both knew it. Although, I am sure that I slept with a smile on my face. I'd already lived long enough to see with my own eyes that sometimes karma works. True, for me it was only one half of a hellish year, but what I had always hoped it had taught me was that living well really was the best revenge.

And I've not dignified any woman's pettiness or attempts to undermine me with anything other than complete composure ever since. I've either ignored these women, or tried to reason with them instead. Failing that, I felt well-assured with the idea that karmic retribution was always on my side. The more Stefanie pushed me, I thought, the more likely it had to be that the universe would give it back to her ten-fold. But then again, how long could I wait until I'd have to take matters into my own hands?

On the way back to the office Jonathan agreed with me that the best response to the scandal was no response. In front of the senior partners or anyone else.

"The less you talk about it, the quicker it will go away," he said, leaning into my door frame.

"This came in for you while you were at lunch." Cassie slid past him to drop off a fax.

"Hey," she said over her shoulder.

"Hey, uh." He rubbed at the back of his neck, taking surprisingly little notice of her cleavage, and searching suddenly for something on the ground. "Hi. Anyway, I've got some paperwork to catch up on, too. So I'll see you later."

"Look," she said, closing the door gently after he'd left, "you're not gonna let Stefanie get away with this, are you?"

I exhaled. "This is not *Melrose Place,* Cassie. What do you expect me to do? Sleep with her boyfriend on the conference table?"

"No, not that. Besides, I don't think she has one." She examined her fingernails, and then smirked. "But you could spread a rumor that she's a lesbian."

"Yeah, sure. Surrounded by an office full of attorneys who attend lifestyle-sensitivity-training seminars every year. Brilliant plan."

"It's not the lesbian part that would cause the scandal."
She came closer, not even trying to stifle her excitement.
"It's the fact that she would be having an affair with one of
the partner's wives!"

"You've lost it." I laughed.

"Actually, I'm thinking a lot more clearly than someone
who just had a three-martini lunch. Nobody would even
have to know that you started the rumor. It's the perfect
crime!"

"It's character assassination."

"You know she deserves it."

"I'm not saying that she doesn't, Cassie. And I appreciate
the loyalty, I really do. But—"

"Monica, stop making excuses for her. She's not just
bitchy…she's bitchy with an agenda. And what she did by
sending that video around demands retaliation."

"Cassie," I tried again before she cut me off.

"No, you don't even see all of it. I mean, I've never really
liked Stefanie—you know that. It's not just that she's the
only junior associate who talks down to me because I'm an
assistant. I can handle that because I don't care what she
thinks. But she always finds a way to make some small
comment to make me look like an airhead in front of the
male staff. She never does it in front of the women. I think
she wants the men to think I'm incompetent. Like it's a
threat to remind me that I'm not a lawyer and I don't really
have as much right to be here. To keep me in my place."

She was getting more agitated by the second, and I

wanted to let her know that I could relate. No woman could claim to be unaware of what it felt like to be made to feel as if she should be grateful for what she knew she deserved deep down.

"I understand, Cassie. I do. I've never exactly fit in anywhere, either."

And it wasn't just the corporate environment I was talking about, either. I was an Indian woman, assertive and outgoing, proud of my heritage but using my freedom, and refusing to be constrained socially or romantically to any one ethnicity. I didn't need to justify myself to anyone, or wave a banner to prove who I was because it was as much a part of me as was my every breath.

I continued, "No matter what, I'm different, and everyone sees that when I walk into a room. And just because I don't go out of my way to act apologetic or particularly aware of the differences, not everybody likes me. I get that, but I have better things to do with my time than to dwell on it. And I believe that's why Stefanie takes so much pleasure in making me look stupid by sending that video around. She needs to force the focus onto me in a way that she thinks will make me respond. But I just have to believe that my work speaks for itself, and that people will eventually get over it. It's not like it was a sex video."

"I agree. I think she wants a rise out of you. But no offense. It's not just about you. She's one of those women who doesn't like other women. Look, I know I'm a little louder than the rest of the women here. Fine, I like to have a good time. So what? She's never said anything directly, but she just makes it seem like I'm…I don't know… Like she thinks that I never could have been a lawyer, even if I tried. She makes me feel like I'm less than everyone else in this place. But there's nothing I can say, because the bottom line is that she's an attorney and I'm…not. And when people like you don't even stand up to her, either—"

"Okay, first of all, what you do for a living is not the bottom line by any means." I walked over and put a hand on her shoulder as she focused on something in the distance outside my window. "But I get it. I hear you."

I understood better than anyone. And it was obvious that Stefanie had gotten what she wanted, whether or not she put much thought into it. So all that was left was for me to decide when and where I would strike. Because I was Mrs. Loeb this time around. And what I really needed was a can of bright green paint.

Stefanie could beat her chest and try to undermine me all she wanted. But going after my troops was one step too far. This was war.

A few hours later in my apartment, Cassie passed me the last of the quesadillas before heading off to the bathroom. We had spent the better part of the evening nibbling on Mexican takeout and sucking down the contents of a dusty old bottle of Coconut Tequila that Raj and I had left over from our trip to Puerto Vallarta. Cassie had made a game out of our mission. Each time we came up with a new

variation of Stefanie's name or critical details to plug into
Google, one of us had to do a shot.

"Private detectiving is fun," Cassie hiccupped, before
laying her face flat on the table in front of her.

We had typed in every combination or iteration of terms
that we could connect with that woman. We tried her full
name, the state where she was born, her birthday, her law
school and her year of graduation, along with all the potentially scandalous words we could imagine, from *criminal
record* to *cockfight* to *foot fetish.* And we found nothing.

"This can't be possible," I protested before squirting more
hot sauce directly into my mouthful of chicken and rice.
"How could she never have done anything stupid or
embarrassing in her entire *life?* You would think that at least
we could find some embarrassing photo of her dressed up
like a hooker for a college Halloween Party. *Seriously, anything…*"

Suddenly, Cassie sprang into action. She yanked my
laptop over to her side of the table, licked the corner of her
lip, hunkered down and started typing away.

"Jackpot!" she said, and then tilted the screen toward me.
And it was.

Cross-referencing her first name and her year of college
graduation with the word *scandal* was all it took. Because
she didn't go to UC Santa Barbara. As it turns out, our little
miss sunshine went to a small New England college where
she was at the heart of a million-dollar embezzlement
scandal while chairing an alumni fundraising committee.

The reason why we didn't find it at first, besides the wrong school, was because we had been including her last name, Saratakos. Back then, however, Stefanie went by a different last name—her maiden name—Landry.

"So she was married?" I thought out loud.

Cassie just winked and poured us each a congratulatory shot.

We dug around in the college newspaper and eventually found out that Stefanie was accused of embezzling by the school, but she was never formally charged due to a lack of evidence. The funds were never recovered, and Stefanie spent her senior year in a state of disgrace. Immediately after graduation, according to a local newspaper that chose to follow up on the story, Stefanie married the faculty advisor to the committee which had organized the fund-raising initiative. The couple left New England for parts unknown, and—we had to assume—decided to move out West.

"And then she went to law school in Los Angeles," I completed the story out loud. "Which is how she got the summer internship at Steel."

"So I guess that means she must be divorced," Cassie added. "Because I've never seen a ring on her finger. But then wouldn't she have gone back to *Landry?*"

"Not necessarily. When you get married you don't automatically change your name. You have to go through a process to obtain the legal change. And if you divorce, you also have to formally change it back. I guess she just never did."

"And why would she?" Cassie shook her head. "As long

as she started practicing law under her married name, she would never have to answer questions about the scandal."

It was better than the jackpot. In fact, it was the silver bullet which we needed to finally take her down. Even though she had never been prosecuted. Even though it was so many years ago. A documented history of questionable morality, combined with a tendency to engage in inappropriate relationships with men in positions of power, was likely to get Stefanie fired at the *very least* on the grounds of omission. Even if Steel were uncharacteristically forgiving, and the news didn't get her fired, these skeletons in Stefanie's closet would definitely kill her chance of being promoted to senior associate.

Cassie was ready to wallpaper the office with this information; to tape glossy, full-color flyers bearing the story to every attorney's computer screen. But I knew that I had to be the one to pull the trigger: in one anonymous gesture I could defend myself, boost my career and annihilate my personal nemesis. I could do more than my part in the fight against all of the Stefanies and Vickys of the world. I could, in some sense, finally right those wrongs.

fourteen

THE ONLY REDEEMING QUALITY OF THE ENORMOUS ILL-FITTING
Gucci sunglasses Raj once bought me was that they practically
covered my entire face. Even looking like a bug on the drive
to work was better than risking the sunlight's contact with my
precaffeine eyes after last night's fun. One much-needed
grande double-shot latte later, Niles stomped into my office.

"Ready for your new client?" he yelled into my ear.

Or at least it felt as if he was shouting in my ear, although
he was technically still standing ten feet away. I must have
accidentally swallowed the worm in that tequila.

"Come in," I said, rounding my jaw as a way of combat-
ing the echoes inside of my skull.

"So, Gupta. Now that Camydia's gone, we're assigning
you to the firm's newest case. As is customary, I'm rotating

the junior partner teams, so you won't be working with Jonathan this time. You'll be teaming up with Stefanie. Sound good?"

On the inside, I swear I was laughing.

Like most men, he took my lack of response as an indication of excitement. "Great! It's not our typical case though. This is not a celebrity couple interested in mediation or an amicable parceling out of the assets. This is a celebrity screenwriter. And he's retained our services on his own. He wants to ask his wife for a divorce, but beforehand, he wants us to help him understand where the divorce would leave him financially. I've spoken to this guy over the phone…and I gotta tell you…he's just not cut out for this cutthroat Hollywood stuff. I feel kind of bad for the guy. Fine, the marriage is over, but he doesn't have a bone in his body that would go for the jugular. Maybe I'm getting soft with age, but anyway, I thought an all-female team was the kindler, gentler way to go. Plus, the kicker is that he recently came into some new projects that will be very lucrative, so timing's everything with this case. Can I turn you loose on it?"

"Of course, Niles." I rose to my feet, praying he would take the hint and leave me to scour my desk for an Advil. "And by the way, does he have a prenup I should be looking at before we meet?"

He raised an eyebrow. "Didn't I just tell you the guy's not Hollywood?"

Poor sap, I shook my head, as I watched Niles walk out of the room.

If this guy worked in entertainment and hadn't known better than to marry without a prenup, then either he was an idealist or a moron. Either way, he was as unlucky to have married the wrong woman as he was lucky to be coming to me to handle his divorce.

As I was pulling one of my casebooks off the shelf a little while later, I caught a glimpse of Stefanie through my open doorway, walking swiftly across the office with a pile of law books cradled in her arms. Stefanie may have been jealous, manipulative and unfair, but she was also really working her butt off for this promotion. Which meant that neither one of us would risk looking petty by asking for a different partner.

She was as serious about her career as I was, and the fact that she seemed to be willing to work with me on this case made that clear. As if there was ever any actual doubt—I now knew for sure that I could never really out her for her past. Besides the fact that I believed I could beat her out for the promotion fair and square, I knew I just wasn't that sort of person. The moment I decided to tell Cassie, I noticed my headache instantly began to dissipate. I caught up to her at her desk and tried to prepare myself for how disappointed I knew she would be.

"We have to talk about last night, Cassie." I leaned into her cubicle and tried to explain. "I can't do it. I can't ruin someone's career like this. Maybe it would be easier if I could, or maybe not. I don't know."

She folded her arms, unconvinced.

"Look, I was raised Hindu. And as nonreligious as I am, I still kind of believe in karma. That means if I do this to Stefanie, I'll have to pay for it later. And even if I don't pay for it later, it's just not how I want to win. I've got to at least believe in myself enough to think that I can get this promotion by doing better work, anyway."

"Or maybe," Cassie suggested in a whisper, "you're so fundamentally Hindu deep down inside that you can convince yourself that her hatefulness will eventually come back to bite her in the ass *with* or *without* your having to get your hands dirty."

"Or maybe you and I should switch desks, since that spin-doctoring was so swift I think you've given me whiplash." I smiled. "Well played."

"I thought so," she said to pat herself on the back.

"I know you're disappointed, babe. And I'm sorry."

"I am. A little. But you're right. I was actually thinking the same thing in that goddamned back of my mind. Or at least the angel and devil sitting on my shoulders were having a pretty heated debate. I guess in the end it's also nice to know that we wouldn't stoop to her level."

"I hate that about us."

"Me, too, Mon," she decided, and then held up a finger while she answered her ringing phone. "Yes, send him up. That was security. It looks like your new client is here."

Already?

I sped over to Niles's assistant, grabbed his preliminary file and barely had time to flip it open before crashing into a potted plant on my way into the conference room. The client was kind enough to rush to my aid in gathering the folder and paperwork off of the floor. He was patient enough not to laugh at me while I stood the pot upright and brushed the bristly leftover leaves off of my skirt. And he was the last person I ever expected to see standing in Steel's offices.

"Monica," Alex said, smiling. But he appeared equally surprised to see me. "How long has it been? Two years? Well, how the hell have you been?"

Two years and seven months. And would you please excuse me while I find a nice quiet place to throw up?

I decided to apply to law school three months after my father died, and one month after I had said goodbye to Alex.

Just think about it, Renu Auntie had explained, sliding the USC application across our dinner table one night after we had put my mother to sleep. *Deciding to apply is not the same thing as deciding to attend. But before you know it you will have passed your first year after college, only to remember that your life must continue. Your father would not want to see you falling behind in life.*

Studying for the LSAT turned out to be my one respite from my mother's crippling depression in those first few months, which might explain why I scored so highly on the exam. Thanks to that score I managed to pay for law school through a combination of scholarships and loans, without burdening my mother or tapping into whatever little nest egg my father had left behind.

And Renu Auntie was right. By the time my acceptance letter arrived the following spring, it was exactly the lifeline I was looking for. My mother took the news of my acceptance by announcing that she was moving back to London, since we had so much family there. I told myself it didn't bother me at all. Maybe this was the way it was supposed to be. Because without a father, law school came to represent the kind of stability that would guarantee I'd never again need to depend on anyone aside from myself.

The work kept me busy enough, but law school was far from the romantic playground that a movie like *Love Story* would have you believe. I dated here and there, from an aspiring senator who seemed like he even slept in cufflinks, to a fellow student from Amarillo, Texas, who came from "oil money," edited our Law Review and then hightailed it off to Washington. I didn't see Alex for the next three years, but I did get the occasional update about him through Joshua, since the two of them had become friends while we were still dating.

He had bartended at various clubs around Hollywood and written three more scripts while honing his craft and repolishing *Like You Mean It*. By the spring of my last year in law school, I had almost managed to convince myself that I was completely over Alex. Until Josh made the mistake of mentioning that Alex had gotten so desperate to be discovered that he'd taken a job as a valet at The Peninsula Hotel. It wasn't because he needed the money; he was hoping to pawn a script off on one of the many film executives who stayed there. I was as proud of him for committing so completely to his calling as I was sad that our lives had grown so very far apart. For months after I drove by the hotel whenever I was in the area, hoping to catch a glimpse of him, just to reassure myself that he was all right.

Three months before law school graduation I signed the commitment letter to work with Steel. It was my dream job, and it came with more money than I would ever need to take care of myself, and more prestige than I knew how to handle. Although that young Texan was still technically in the picture I suddenly found that I couldn't stop thinking about Alex. With every momentous event that passed, I realized what was missing; the right person to share it with.

I started wondering if the right person had been Alex. So what if he was still bartending and pushing his scripts? So what if I was going to make more than three times as much as him? Weren't we mature enough not to make it an issue? Wasn't what we had in college worth trying to see if we could make it last?

Of course, Sheila reminded me when I confided the night before my graduation that I was considering giving him a call, *a lot of time had passed. Surely, he'd been through a lot in his life as a struggling screenwriter. Possibly, he would resent me for having abandoned him at the beginning.*

Right when I decided not to pursue it, Sheila and Joshua announced their engagement. This meant there would be a wedding. And this meant I would have to face Alex again. I decided it was a sign and that I had to take a leap of faith in his direction at their wedding. I bought a new red dress which I thought he would like, assuming his taste hadn't changed. I spent an entire morning at the salon having my hair blown out the way he used to like it. And I scoured the back of my closet until I found the gold bracelet he had given me for our first anniversary.

Imagine my surprise when I flipped on my television the week before their wedding to see Alex's face smiling back at me. According to his interviewer, he had finally sold the screenplay for *Like You Mean It* to a major studio.

For $500,000.

And the glimpse I caught of him that morning while brushing my teeth was a far cry from the one I had expected to find outside The Peninsula Hotel a few short months before. He looked so happy, so relieved, so effusive and so justifiably flush with success, that I felt like a parent crashing the graduation ceremony of the child they gave up for adoption. How could I reach out to him now, after all this time? Why wouldn't he assume that I only wanted him now that he was successful? Sure, I wanted to believe that he would've known me better than that, but given what we'd been through and the last thing I'd said to him, I couldn't take that chance.

I just can't risk having him laugh in my face, I explained to Sheila at her bachelorette party. *And I don't want to do anything that might rain on his very well-deserved parade.*

Instead, I greeted him as warmly as I would any old friend when our paths crossed beside the guest book at the wedding....

"Congratulations, Alex." I cupped my hands together

before me, since I wasn't sure what else to do with them. "I heard the wonderful news."

"Monica." He enveloped me in a hug that seemed to startle him in its familiarity, causing him to detach swiftly and awkwardly. "Thanks, thanks."

"You deserve it, Alex." I stifled the pained expression I could feel creeping onto my face.

And I am prouder of you than you will ever know.

"Yeah, well," he murmured, then shoved one hand into a pocket and rubbed at the back of his neck with the other.

Silence while I shifted my weight from one foot to the other, and we both stared at the floor between us.

"Anyway, I should be congratulating you, too, Monica. Josh tells me you just finished up law school. Your mother must be very proud. How is she?"

Before I could answer him, his date strode over and he introduced us. I don't remember what her name was. It's not important. But in that moment, as he waved goodbye, I could have sworn that he lingered in a stare. Or perhaps I was assuming too much. Either way, I knew whatever chance we might have had was gone.

And about a month after Josh and Sheila's wedding, Raj moved back to Los Angeles.

"Alex?" I clutched my papers to my chest, unabashedly horrified. "*You're* the client?"

"Are you disappointed?" he asked, with a smile that was a little too cozy.

I huffed and moved over to the conference table, plunking the papers down and tucking my hair behind my ear.

"Surprised is more like it." I smoothed over the silk of my shirt at the stomach, as if to hold my own guts in. "Or at least, caught off guard."

"It's nice to know that Steel really does its homework, then." He took a seat opposite me, weaving his fingers together and planting them on the table.

"Seriously," I tried, though I was still dumbfounded, "this is so…I'm sorry."

He looked like a lightbulb had gone off in his head. "Monica, I am just as surprised as you are. It's not like I was trying to hide behind that mini-palm tree or anything."

We both laughed. Alex and Monica. Laughing together. As naturally as if the world wasn't standing on its head.

"Besides, if I was trying to surprise you, don't you think I would have come up with a better disguise than that? A mask, at the very least?"

Wait a minute…was that a reference to the Fete?

Was he the werewolf?

Was I on *Smacked!* again?

My eyes darted around the room, searching for any hint of a candid camera.

"Um…*hello?*" he asked. "I'm trying to break the ice here. I hope this doesn't have to be awkward."

"No reason for it to be awkward." I pulled myself together and started flipping through his file. "I'm sorry to hear about your divorce. Actually, I didn't even realize you were married. To, uh…"

"To Carolyn," he said, shaking his head. "You met her at Josh's wedding."

Of course.

"Well, I'm not sure it's the best idea for me to handle this. In case there is a mediation it's very important—"

"This is not a mediation." His voice was resolute. "This is the end of a marriage that never should have happened in the first place. I wasn't ready for marriage. I was simply crazed over all the success and I guess I needed someone to hold on to. And she had demons of her own. We were impulsive, but at least we never had any kids."

Fascinating, I thought. *And you know what else would be great? If you could tell me all about just how often she cooked for you in the nude.*

"Be that as it may—" I adopted a more formal tone to distance myself "—I think that given our history…"

"Given our history, I think I would feel more comfortable having you help me with this, rather than some stranger. I want it over quick and easy. Like ripping off a Band-Aid. So, will you do it?"

fifteen

"SHH!" SHEILA PRACTICALLY YELLED THAT EVENING, AFTER ripping the front door open and doubling back toward the television. "Don't talk to me until *Extra's* over!"

In fact, she was so vehement in her shushing that she spat on me a little bit just then. But whatever. In the wake of her debacle with the in-laws, I felt a tad selfish running over to her place right after work to spew about Alex at Steel. Naturally I picked up a couple of tiramisus on the way.

So I was bribing a pregnant lady with food. Don't act like you're above it. At least the fact that she was so transfixed on the television meant she was no longer apoplectic over her in-laws. Hence we would be able to focus the conversation on me. I slipped the desserts out of the Whole Foods bag and set the plastic forks alongside them, while she turned up the volume.

"I can't believe this!" She gestured at the screen with the help of a pickle wrapped in cheese and exclaimed, "Can you believe this?"

I grimaced at the sight of pound cake and a small tub of olives on the corner of the coffee table.

"I'm sorry. I can't stop farting. It's disgusting, I know."

"Actually, I hadn't noticed. But thanks for pointing it out. I was making a face at the little picnic you've got going here."

"Oh. Okay. Well, did you want one?" She indicated her pickle.

"I'll pass." I dug into my tiramisu and asked, "What's so unbelievable?"

"Ooooh, that's right. You wouldn't care. I always forget that you're *above* celebrity gossip." She tightened her jaw, I suppose to indicate that I was British?

"I never said that."

"You act like it. Just because you work with these people."

"Okay, I'm gonna chalk that up to pregnancy crankiness. But anyway, speaking of work…"

And then I noticed the headline as it flashed across the screen. "Camydia's Latest Outbreak!"

Yes, you read right, folks.

The host explained with a bawdy grin, a bustier, and a nose that I am sure cost her at least ten thousand dollars, *"That hot on the heels of rumors Hollywood's Prince and Princess of Drama have been working on a reconciliation, basketball super-star Cameron Johnson has been spotted around town by the papa-*

razzi again with the same unidentified blonde we've been hearing about for months."

"Monica?" Sheila snapped her fingers before my face. "Earth to Monica?"

"What?" I waved her away, sinking back into the couch.

"What *about* work?" she asked, sniffing at her tiramisu.

"Oh, um…"

"Oh. My. God!" She dropped the container and grabbed me by the shoulders, yelling, "Tell me that Camydia is not your client!"

"Camydia is not my client," I simpered.

"Bullshit!" She slapped her own knee, hollering some more. "I'm calling bullshit! I cannot believe that all this time you didn't tell me!"

"I still haven't told you," I warned her.

"Not directly." She scarfed down the remaining nub of her pickle, and then licked her fingers. "But I'll take that as a *yes.*"

"Look, Sheila. I came here because I have some big news. And normally you know I wouldn't talk about a client. But in this case, I just can't not talk about it."

"I'm listening." She wiped her fingers on her pants.

"It's Alex. He's my firm's newest client. He's getting a divorce."

"Mon-i-ca." She raised her eyebrows.

"What?" I was defensive.

"Monica, you cannot represent him," she insisted. "I'm too pregnant to remember my husband's cell phone number or to think that there's anything wrong with mixing tiramisu and pickles…but even I know *that*."

"Does pregnancy kill brain cells?"

"Possibly. It's like having a parasite inside of you that you love with all your heart, although you know it is slowly draining all of your energy and resources for its own use. Literally. Some women never recover, even if they make it through it alive."

"Okaaaaaaay…"

"I'm serious. Like, did you know that if a fetus demands too much nourishment, then the pregnancy is full of complications, like maternal diabetes and high blood pressure? It's no wonder I'm so tired. I'm in a battle for survival!"

"You've been watching PBS again." I scraped at the remaining bottom layer of the tiramisu I had just torn through.

"What else am I supposed to do? I can't sleep because my mind is racing and I can't have sex because I disgust my husband and I can't go outdoors because my gassiness will disgust everyone else and I can't leave the house anyway because I might forget where I live and never be able to find my way back!"

"You could always write your address on your hand," I yelled from the kitchen before pouring us each a glass of water. "Or hang it on a dog tag around your neck."

"That's a lovely idea."

"I'm kidding." I set the glasses on the table and sat back down beside her.

"Okay, okay. Stop trying to distract me." She gulped half her glass of water at once. "Don't take advantage of a pregnant woman's scattered brain. That's bad karma. Listen very carefully—you cannot represent Alex."

"Why not?"

"Because one of you is still in love with the other one."

"Sure," I said. "And also, I'm due for a breast reduction."

But she wouldn't be dismissed. "It's true. I'm just not sure which one. Not the breasts. Your breasts are fine. Which one of you, I mean. You and Alex. You know what I mean."

Damn her and her telepathy-inducing pregnancy.

All right, so perhaps there were still feelings.

Maybe even issues.

Possibly even of the unresolved variety.

But was that really such a surprise? Or even a crime? Are these feelings so dangerous that all former lovers should be condemned to a lifetime of averting their gazes and keeping at least a five-hundred-foot distance at all times?

I voted No.

And I cast my vote by choosing to tackle Alex's case head-on when I got back to the office the following morning. Not to prove that I felt nothing for him, but to prove that I could work the case *despite* those feelings. I had to believe that we are not slaves to our instincts any more than we are ruled by our neuroses. That while our desires may be governed by the animal in all of us, our actions most certainly were not. That we all had a series of choices to make every day, and that it was those choices, rather than the instincts, which distinguished the Stefanies from the rest of us.

The more I thought about it, the more I was resolved. Not because I *wanted* to dive into the details of his marriage to that horrible slut, you understand. But because I *could* spend time with him, without it meaning or turning into anything. Why couldn't a friend help a friend in his time of need?

Like, for example, his time of divorce.

Because in my opinion, the lingering emotions for former lovers are no more indicative of a propensity for sexual indiscretion than the cultural vulgarity of Los Angeles is indicative of a propensity for its residents to eat their own young.

The argument made total sense. Trust me. I'm a lawyer.

I will scrutinize and sift through every detail of their finances in search of inconsistencies, I told myself, while zipping down Wilshire Boulevard the following morning.

I will inspect and interrogate every mole, paparazzo and passerby in their world until I find irrefutable proof of her sordid past, I mused while awaiting my Grande White Mocha at the Starbucks.

I will pull out all the stops and make use of every underhanded technique that Steel has ever unofficially employed, to make sure that Carolyn doesn't get the best of Alex, and to make good on the terrible thing that I said to get rid of him all those years ago, I decided while logging on to my computer.

This mission kept me energized for most of the day, while Stefanie presumably buried herself in the relevant case law. Sometime around 3:00 p.m., my eyes started glazing over. I decided to take a break, and tilted my head backward just for a minute. And about a millionth of a second had presumably passed when…

"Nice to see you contributing, counselor."

I didn't need to open my eyes to know that it was her. I smelled the malice the instant she entered the room. I also noticed her new haircut, which was actually quite flattering. But I didn't tell her that.

Instead, I weaved my fingers behind my head, clear my throat and asked, "Anything interesting so far in the precedents?"

"Monica," she said, hovering in my doorway as if crossing the threshold would trigger the door to slam shut and lock us both inside, "let's not act like we enjoy each other's company. Why don't we just e-mail each other our findings by the end of the day, and then we can conference call it tomorrow morning?"

"Fine by me." I stared at a spot to the left of her chin, to test the theory that refusing to look someone in the eye would necessarily make them nervous.

"Fine. Okay then," she concluded with an almost imperceptible shake of the head.

Maybe I was the one with the powerful eyes. Maybe she wasn't as tough as she looked. But the pep in my seat lasted for just another fifteen seconds because that's how long it took for the subject matter of the next folder I lifted from my discovery pile to register in my mind: It was Alex and Carolyn's list of assets.

Their two bedroom condo in the Hollywood Hills.

Their hunter-green Range Rover SUV and white Jaguar convertible.

Their stock portfolio.

The heirloom furniture from his family's side.

The century-old bone china from hers.

Their stereo system.

Their wall tapestries.

Their entire kitchen full of pots and pans and ladles and melon ballers and chicken skewers and lemon zesters and baking pans...

...all of which were intended for a life they just weren't meant to live together. Because someone messed up. And according to my paycheck and to what I had been told, that person was her. But was divorce ever really one person's fault? And did it matter even if it was? I thought about it the rest of the workday and through my entire drive home. Something about the process of poring over the details of Alex's married life to another woman must have made me feel even more nostalgic for Raj. By the time I made it to San Vicente Boulevard, I was in tears.

What would Raj be doing at exactly that moment? I wondered. *And with whom?*

I couldn't call him this time because I couldn't handle the possibility of having him send me to voice mail *again*. And

Sheila would probably force me to make some sort of sense, or find some way to twist it around and make it about Alex. So I headed home with the radio blaring, grateful to be living in a city where nobody ever looked closely enough into anyone else's car to notice such a tiny detail as a steady stream of mascara leaking down someone's cheek.

Some women reject flowers on the principle that they are wasteful because they will die within days. I suspect these are the same women who deny that faking an orgasm is a masochistic gesture on the principle that it is better to spare a man's ego.

I am not one of these women.

My attention can almost always be had for the price of a fistful of blossoms. And it's not just because someone might have wanted to beautify my world. Truth be told, it's the gesture of offering up a pretty, living thing, solely for my fleeting entertainment.

How poetic.

How decadent.

And how very non-Hindu of me.

But anyway.

I bounced down my hallway with all the grace of a soccer mom in a mall on Black Friday. I'd spotted the bouquet of flowers waiting in front of my apartment when I got home that night. It was a bundle of white roses wrapped in a generous silk bow. And everybody knows that white roses symbolize new beginnings.

At least Raj does. He's thoughtful that way.

I swooped my pretties up into my arms and whisked them inside, as if I were about to make love to them. I dropped my bag on the floor, closed my eyes and shoved my nose deep into one of the buds to take an enormous whiff of its fragrance.

It's dizzying. And almost as satisfying as knowing that this means Raj must be coming back to me.

As an afterthought, I dug out the minicard and read. But it wasn't from Raj at all.

Monica,
I really am sorry.
It was all just for the show.
Any chance that we can start over?
Luke

Luke? But how did he even know where I lived? And what about Raj? I fell into a chair and promptly slammed the traitorous roses down on the table. I was racking my brain with millions of questions and rubbing my face over and over with both hands when my cell phone started to ring.

And it wasn't a number that I recognized.

"So…" Luke began before I could even say hello. "Get any interesting deliveries today?"

Pushy, presumptuous bastard.

"Luke, what the hell is going on?"

"I wanted a chance to explain, Monica."

"Tell it to the tabloids," I snapped, realizing instantly that it was a bit melodramatic and that none of the tabloids were actually even the least bit interested in me.

"Wait. Please. I'm not that obnoxious guy from the house. It was all an act. I was under contract and I was doing what I had to do."

"And that makes it okay?" I yanked out a petal and began tearing it in half.

"I just thought of you as the mark in the beginning. But I started to really get a kick out of you. And then when you kissed me back…I was surprised…*pleasantly* surprised."

The nerve.

"Big surprise. I'm a good kisser. Everybody knows that." I knew I sounded more ridiculous by the minute, but I needed fuel for my indignation, so I used what I could find.

"Maybe we can meet in person and talk about this. I don't want you to run around Los Angeles hating me forever."

"Don't flatter yourself, Luke, and…wait a minute. How did you even get my address? I know Steel would never give it out."

"Monica, let's meet and talk about it. Can we do that?"

Was he asking me out on a date?

"Are you actually asking me out on a date?" I was incredulous.

"I'm trying."

"And I'm hanging up."

Rock bottom was a lot warmer and blurrier around the edges than I thought it would be. I was soaking in the tub, picking at the grout between the wall tiles with one hand and wielding a half-empty bottle of Shiraz menacingly at my reflection in the faucet with the other when, for some reason, I finally broke down and decided to call my mother.

Loneliness does not get much worse than when an Indian-American woman decides to lament her romantic woes to one of the people who made her. Not because they don't care, mind you, but because she has already recognized by the age of fifteen that traditional, and even not-so-traditional, Indian parents relate to the complexities of single adult life about as well as albino chimps. But the other thing about them is that they are almost always grateful to have been invited to try.

I eyed the grisly and dismembered remains of those pretty white roses, now strewn across my bathroom counter, and readied myself to be massively irritated by how my mother would likely interpret the delay in selling her house as an indication of my disloyalty to her.

"I was wondering when you would call," she answered haltingly on the first ring.

This was strange because my mother always told me as a child that to answer on the first ring was to give the impression that you had been waiting, fingers crossed, for someone, *anyone* to call.

"Mom." I was also somewhat surprised by the concern in her voice. "Hi. Listen, I have bad news about the house. It turns out that your contractor was…"

I paused, trying to find the most appropriate way to

describe to this very proper lady her only daughter's very improper and very televised behavior.

"I know, sweetheart." She interrupted my fuzzy and circular attempt at coherent thought.

"You mean," I said, whispering, hunching my shoulders just a little bit, getting ready to cringe, "you saw it on TV?"

Silence. Meanwhile someone was tightening miniature screws into the left side of my neck.

"Mom?"

"No." She hesitated. "I did not actually watch it yet."

I must have missed something.

"You mean you are planning on setting aside time to watch your daughter's public humiliation?"

"This was not what we had expected. Didn't that Luke fellow explain everything to you yet?"

I bolted upright in the tub, dropping the bottle into the bath and splashing soapy water all over the place. The deep red of the Shiraz mushroomed out like a little explosion. But I couldn't stop it. The record playing in my brain kept skipping over the same damn word.

Did she just say "we"?

sixteen

IN SOME ANIMALS THE TENDENCY TO CARE FOR THEIR YOUNG is instinctive. In others, not so much. I won't say which side of that fence humanity falls on because I'm sure that it depends on the person. I will tell you that it has long been suggested that the extraordinary plumpness of newborn humans (typically much fatter than other infant primates) is an attempt to convince their parents that they are worth the effort of rearing. Even an infant's smile, according to some sociologists, is little more than a part of its strategy to seduce its mother. Because woe be to the child who fails to curry the favor of those who have the option of sacrificing it to the lions, just to save themselves.

All right. Maybe she didn't exactly throw me to the lions. But she did sacrifice me to reality television. And honestly, wasn't that worse? All I knew was that if she thought she had grandchildren coming anytime soon after the stunt she'd pulled, well then *think again, old lady.*

Not that I had much control over my chances of child-bearing at that point. The flowers weren't from Raj, since he'd apparently decided to break off our engagement without even so much as a goodbye. Not that I necessarily deserved one. But this wasn't about Raj. It was about my mother, who in my book was permanently grounded. Because she may not have thrown me to a predator to save herself, but she had definitely used me to get herself a little head start.

Or more accurately, a little property appreciation.

I should probably explain. It went something like this…

My mother was involved in the prank from the beginning. She saw an episode of *Smacked!* on television and recognized it as her chance to turn a quick profit on a real estate flip. Namely, a house flip in Brentwood. Specifically, by making it the scene of a television moment starring her unwitting but slap-happy daughter, and then flipping it for a handsome profit.

"Honestly, darling," she said, acting as if it all made perfect sense, while I watched the last of my wine blend in with the water, "I expected you to slap him right across the face. I was banking on it, in fact. I never would have dreamed that you would kiss that man back. You're always so…well, you know…*levelheaded.*"

"Maybe that's my problem. And maybe you should sell

the stupid house yourself, Mom," I added before slamming down the phone.

Okay, it was my cell phone, which you can't exactly slam down. But I did press that red button hard enough to make it clear to anyone watching that I really meant it. Almost as hard as my slamming the snooze button when some obnoxious tune yanked me back into consciousness the following morning. The only thing worse than waking up hungover, nauseous and terrifyingly unsure of exactly what it is you're ashamed about, is waking up hungover, nauseous and painfully aware of exactly what it is you should be ashamed about.

If I was so levelheaded, then why would I have allowed myself to kiss Luke? How could I have believed that working on Alex's case would possibly mean nothing to me? When did I grow so cold that I failed to recognize that all Raj truly wanted was some hint of a real commitment with him? And when will I accept that I cannot drink red wine? Not only does it drain the moisture from my head, but it creates a faint ringing that usually persists throughout the following day.

Except this time it was actually the vibration of my cell phone against the bedside table. Always the consummate professional, I burrowed farther under the covers and let it go to voice mail. I thought I was in the clear until a few seconds later, when my wily adversary tried again. I lay perfectly still, holding my breath, hoping the phone wouldn't notice that I was still there. Hatefully, it *brrrrrrrred* again. Finally, begrudgingly, I snaked a hand out from underneath the duvet and pulled the accursed electronic gadget to me.

"What!" I barked, after noting the *unavailable* number and assuming that it was my mother.

But it wasn't. It was Raj. And I had the sensation that I had just stepped off of a Tilt-A-Whirl. Dizzy, giddy, and quite sure that I was about to hurl. Worried that I might frighten him away, I chose to play dead rather than respond to his *Hello.*

…*The savvy male alligator is careful not to surprise his intended mate with any bold gestures or swift movements.*

"Monica," he began, and I was sure I would pass out from holding my breath for so long. "I'm coming back. Back to L.A."

…*The female, having deemed her suitor to be innocuous, rather than potentially infanticidal toward her existing offspring, indicates with a shake of her tail that it is safe to approach.*

"Great!" I blurted but then bit my lip to calm myself down. "I mean, I'm glad. I…I missed you."

…*The mighty male makes his way into her immediate perimeter, breathing heavily enough to indicate that his purpose is mating, but taking care to keep his normally aggressive posturing in check. He does not want to disrupt the rhythm of their dance.*

"Okay." He cleared his throat. "I apologize for the silent treatment, but I was hurt, Monica. And I had to question whether you want to be in this thing with me at all. But then I just retrieved your last voice message, and I was touched…by the emotion that you showed. It was rather unlike you, and I understand that it isn't always easy for you. To share your emotions. For God's sake I'm practically

British, so obviously I can understand it. But perhaps that was all I really needed to know…that you could make that effort for me. For us."

…Once within arm's length, the female is careful not to display her backside to the male at first. She greets her suitor face-to-face, looks him in the eye, and emits an almost imperceptible, guttural growl. It is an invitation as much as a warning, and the male must proceed with caution toward her, while voicing his own might.

"Then why did you wait until now to call?" I pressed him, wincing preemptively in case I was about to get the verbal thrashing I knew I deserved.

…The female, having had a better look at him by this point, makes her final decision. Will she beat a swift retreat in the hopes of finding a more powerful partner? Will she growl louder and begin circling him to indicate that some sparring (or foreplay) is in order before they can begin their mating dance? Or will she simply lick his face and then twist to one side, displaying her readiness to be mounted immediately? The tension is thick…and uncharacteristically, the female is unwilling to commit with any standard gesture. The staring contest could last for hours, unless one of the animals chooses to break the tension. In this case, it seems it will be the male…

"I was stubborn, Monica. Just like you. I really wanted to call. But I would prefer to talk about this in person. We have a lot to discuss. And I would like it if you could pick me up at LAX this Friday."

Being as much the optimist as I am the consummate professional, which is to say, occasionally, I took this conversation as a sign that:

1. He hadn't seen *Smacked!,* since he would have mentioned it if he had.
2. He missed me and loved me and wanted me back, (Yeah!) and
3. It was time for a bikini wax.

For most of that week I was grateful the division of labor on Alex's case kept Stefanie out of my hair. The last thing I needed to bring along when I met Raj at the airport on Friday was an enormous stress zit. You know the kind. It forms right in the middle of your cheek, is magically resistant to all forms of cover-up and concealer and routinely threatens to swallow the rest of your face.

Anyway, Stefanie volunteered to keep the partners appraised of our progress (no doubt to take the bulk of the credit), and was in and out of Niles's office frequently. I was so preoccupied with Raj's impending arrival that I had mostly been on autopilot. When Alex came in to sit down with me on Thursday, I was energized and ready to push this divorce seamlessly through. All that was left was to prioritize the marital assets in their order of importance to him, take his deposition and set up a timeline within which we would promise to deliver a final settlement proposal.

Easy as pie, right?

"So should we order in?" he suggested, two hours into our meeting, before I even had a chance to look up. "For lunch, I mean. I'm starved."

"Sure!" I was so bright that I hurt my own eyes. "Why not?"

"Great, how about Thai?"

"Sure. But no peanuts on the pad thai," I said offhand, feeling a pang of guilt wrapped in a rush of affection for Raj.

"Huh?"

"Nothing, nothing." I shook my head, retrieving the book of menus, yanking out the one for *Sweet Basil* and handing it over to Alex. "How about this place?"

"Looks good to me." Tilting his head, he squinted at me and asked, "Chicken with basil...and...something with green coconut curry sauce, right?"

My eyebrows made a break for my hairline.

"You didn't think I'd remember? C'mon, we must have ordered in Thai food for every final exam you helped me cram for."

"Yeah," I replied, musing how long ago that life seemed. "I guess we did."

"You helped me with a lot of stuff back then, Monica. You were always great that way."

I waved his compliment aside, slipping my glasses back on and leaning into the documents before me.

"Seriously," he paused, looking away, "I don't know if you ever saw *Like You Mean It,* but...well...I never could have done it without you."

"Alex." I studied him over the rims of my glasses. "I was long gone by the time you made it."

"Yes, but you were there when I was getting started. And besides, I think I was writing for you."

Poor thing. You know how patients routinely believe they

are in love with their psychiatrists? Well, when it happens in the world of divorce litigation we don't call it "transference" we just call it sad. Some people will grasp at anything, rather than be alone.

He continued. "Maybe I still…"

I opened my mouth, but then noticed that he wasn't making eye contact with me anymore. He looked stunned. And he was staring…at my cleavage?

"Umm…Monica…is that…"

That massive zit wasn't the only thing that was in danger of popping out that day…my engagement ring had jumped from the inside of my blouse, and was staring us both in the face.

"Are you *married?*" he asked finally, finishing his thought.

What could I say? That I had bought it for myself, hoping it would attract an eligible man the way that red attracts a bull? Instinctively, I planted my hand on top to cover it up.

"No!" I blurted, and felt instantly as if I had cheated on Raj.

Out, damn spot! Or better yet, I thought… *On, damn ring!*

I slipped it onto my finger so hastily that I forgot it was still connected to my neck. So I had to reach around and unclasp my chain in front of Alex, which naturally caused me to choke myself.

Yes, I am the queen of the elegant gesture.

"I mean, I'm engaged," I explained, gagging a little bit, wishing I could crawl inside the dirt of the potted plant that had so abruptly heralded Alex's disruptive return to my life.

"Well." He nodded aggressively, looking anywhere but directly at me, as if the sparkle of that ring might turn *him* into stone. "That's great. Really. Congratulations, Monica. He's a lucky guy, whoever he is."

It was ironic. In preparation for Raj's arrival I had acquired his favorite wine, had my apartment professionally cleaned, set out fresh flowers and scented candles, spun myself into oblivion at the gym every morning that week and booked myself in for the total treatment at the salon. But it still hadn't occurred to me to slip that ring onto my finger. And it was probably the gesture that would have meant the most to him.

Maybe Raj was right not to want to marry me.

And maybe I needed to figure out whether I was more ashamed about neglecting to put the ring on after all this time, or about wanting to hide it from Alex.

Nobody likes waiting in line. I have at least three pairs of pleather pants tucked into the back of a closet somewhere that can attest to that fact. *Oh, come on!* They were *the thing* back in 1995. And don't act as if you've never wiggled into anything way-too-tight and leopard-print just to make it impossible for the bouncer to consider making you wait in line with the huddled and less fashionable masses.

Anyway, patience is not a virtue with which my people are more than passingly familiar. And by *my people,* I mean Indians. Tolerance, deference, and in some cases even abstinence, sure, but not so much with the patience. So is it any wonder that I'm usually unable to wait more than two minutes for my morning latte without imagining several ways to disembowel either the cashier, the barista or the person standing before me in line? Of course it doesn't *start out* that way in my mind. But if you know that there are five people in line behind you, and you know that finding your wallet inside your massive purse will require a search-and-rescue team, and you plan on paying with exact change, which will be scooped from the bottom of your handbag, then *why oh why* would you wait until you'd ordered to think about unzipping your purse?

My anger management skills aren't my favorite thing about myself, but I swear it's a genetic predisposition. According to Hindu mythology, one of our gods had asked her son to guard her privacy while she bathed one morning. When her husband returned from a long battle that same day, her son neither recognized him nor was prepared for his arrival. True to his mother, her son refused to let him pass and see her until she was fully decent. True to our impatient nature, (and furious to have been told to wait) her husband was so infuriated that he pulled out his sword and lopped off the head of his only son. *And bouncers who have to deal with sloppy investment bankers think they have it rough.*

All right, so I have yet to decapitate anyone at a Starbucks. But I had huffed more than my fair share of discontented breaths, and was distracting myself with a glance at my *Pucker* horoscope—tucked inside a folder of legal briefs, of course—while waiting for the unbelievably slow line to lurch forward when Jonathan suddenly materialized.

He caught me completely off guard by waving a twenty dollar bill in front of my face. It wasn't a sword, exactly, but still. My people don't appreciate surprises before we've had our morning coffee, either. And by *my people,* I mean women.

"Umm…is this the part where I'm supposed to shake it like a salt shaker," I asked, as sarcastic and defensive as was possible without the benefit of any fuel in my stomach, "Or is that your way of implying that maybe this skirt isn't age-appropriate?"

"Can't a guy buy a girl a coffee?" He joined me in line.

"What's your angle, man?" I squinted sideways at him. "Do I have some hot friend you want to be introduced to? If so, it's gonna cost you a lot more than a latte."

"I had no idea you were so cynical," he mocked, as we inched forward and then stopped again.

"Just a small-town girl," I pleaded, and put my hands up, "trying to protect myself in the big, bad city."

"Does that make me a city boy, born and raised on the wrong side of the tracks?"

"I don't think the wrong side of the tracks would know what to do with you, Jonathan." I shook my head, seriously hoping that he wasn't about to break into the chorus of "Don't Stop Believing."

I love him like the cousin I tried to smother in his sleep. For the record, he started it when he hid a bullfrog in my underwear drawer. But I am quite sure I would have had to chop off Jonathan's head if he ever did that. No singing before morning coffee, either.

"Granted. But L.A. has its hands full with women like you running around."

This was information that I did not need. In my mind, up until that moment, I was able to believe that I don't run. I *glide*.

"Meaning?" I snatched the cash from his hands, deciding that he was gonna have to buy me a blueberry scone, as well, for punishment.

"Meaning…nothing." He fiddled with the bags of coffee beans lined up beside the counter. "Meaning that you're cute and you're spunky. So you usually get your way…two grande lattes, please."

"Toying with my emotions before I've had my morning coffee may not be the safest life choice, Jonathan," I warned while handing over his cash. "If there's something you want to talk about, spit it out."

"It's Cassie," he stated, while we moved down the counter toward the barista.

"Ooooh." I remembered the two of them laughing together at the Fete, and how quickly he had left my office the last time she walked in. "Wait. What's going on with you guys? Are you guys…"

"No. We're not. We're not…anything. Anymore, I mean."

"You were a thing?" I gasped.

"Not really." He seemed to be trying to figure it out.

"You slept together?" I lowered my voice, feeling terrible that I could have been unaware of an office romance blooming right under my nose. So now I'm ungraceful *and* self-involved.

"No…we didn't." He glanced to both sides, and insisted, "We, uh…never got that far."

"So what does that mean? Does that mean that you're actually…*dating?* I thought you didn't do that. What happened to love 'em and leave 'em Jonathan? If you go all decent on me then I'll have to start believing in love, which will mean I'll have nobody to blame for my fiancé's disappearance but myself. Don't do that to me."

"Two grande lattes?" the barista announced, and handed them over.

"Monica, keep it down!" Jonathan clenched his teeth as we made our way toward the condiments. "We went out a coupla times. Nothing big. But I guess I thought it was going somewhere, and now I know it's not."

"What happened?" I popped off the lid and began dousing the foam with sugar.

"All of a sudden she doesn't want to go out anymore. All of a sudden she's just busy."

"Did she say she'd never go out with you again? What did you do?" I spoke to him as if to a child who had been sent home early from school without any explanation.

"Nothing." He stopped midstir. "Why did you assume that I did something wrong? Besides, she didn't say never again. She just…cooled off."

"Jonathan," I said, and faked a huff, "how many times have we been over this? Women are not race cars…"

But I could see that he wasn't in a playful mood that morning. He was actually hurt about this one. So I changed my tune.

"Look, I don't necessarily think that means…" I began, and then paused to check the message buzzing on my Black-Berry. "Hang on a second."

It was a message from Alex, including an attachment of the first draft of his latest screenplay. And the e-mail asked me to read it and to give him my honest opinion. *For old time's sake.*

It was an olive branch, obviously. And I was touched that he still valued my opinion after all this time. I was getting ready to respond and let him know I would be happy to give it a read-through, when I felt Jonathan's hand on my arm.

"Monica," he whispered. Clearly it was taking a lot out of him to ask me this. "Would you just…try to find out what went wrong?"

seventeen

MY JAW WAS CLENCHED SO TIGHT I WAS WORRIED I MIGHT actually crack a tooth. By 6:00 p.m. I'd finally taken the Los Angeles International Airport exit off the 405 expressway. And within ten minutes of idling outside the Lufthansa arrivals terminal, I had chewed my lower lip practically raw.

How was I going to explain myself to Raj? *Never mind the little matter of my newest client being the only other man I have ever loved. It's nothing for you to worry about. I'm just reading his screenplay because I can't find anything worthwhile at the local Barnes & Noble. And you mustn't take my brazen public intimacy with a complete stranger as any indication that I gave up on this relationship mere moments after you left for London. I was just bored. Did I mention the intimacy had been televised?*

The main question was: Would it be more humane to get

him drunk before telling him everything, or would that be just plain selfish? I didn't know the answer, but I did know that I had to admit to that on-air kiss before Raj found out about it for himself. Still, there was no real need to tell him within the first five minutes of seeing him. After all, I had him all to myself until the following morning. One thing at a time, I decided. Like maybe I could make sure we were back on solid ground about the whole *pad-thai incident* before bringing up anything else. I checked my watch. His plane had landed twenty minutes ago, which meant that he could be coming out of those sliding doors at any second.

I considered opening with a joke. But all those years in England had rendered him practically immune to knock-knocks, and sadly they were all I had. I thought about greeting him with tears as a distraction, since he could never focus on anything outside of fixing it when I cried. But that was a little too low, even for me. So I decided to distract him with sex. Luckily, I was wearing a red and black lace push-up number I had gotten just for the occasion. I was unfastening the second button on my blouse when a knock on my car window startled me and made me look up.

There he was, and for a moment I felt as if nothing had changed. I unlocked the door, let him into the passenger side, and leapt instinctively across the divider to smother him with kisses.

"Thank God you're home," I managed, in between ravenous mouthfuls of his face.

"Charming ring." He lifted my hand out and stared,

creasing the skin around his eyes in exactly the way that I remembered falling in love with. Then he dropped his gaze to the south. "And is that a new bra? Because I quite like it."

Everybody knows that make-up sex is fantastic, but I didn't realize it could actually render me blind, deaf *and* dumb. Blind, because I was down on all fours, squinting across Raj's beige carpet, scanning for any signs of the pearl stud that had popped from my earlobe one of the many times we showed that headboard who was boss the night before. Deaf, because I didn't hear him calling my name from the kitchen the first two times. And dumb, because I genuinely believed there was still some chance he hadn't seen my humiliation on *Smacked!*

Goddamn the Internet. And goddamn whoever designed the backs of earrings to be so tiny and easy to lose.

"Monica." He poked his head into the bedroom and stated, "I was calling you."

"Sorry." I pouted like a naughty girl who was kind of hoping that her fiancé might teach her a lesson. "I was looking for the pearl earring that you knocked right off of my ear last night, you stallion."

His grin and the arm he extended to help me back up to my feet was all the reassurance I needed. I was in the clear.

"Darling, I'll buy you a new pair. Are you hungry? I've made pancakes."

I brushed my teeth, slipped on one of his T-shirts and

snuck up behind him in the kitchen. Wrapping my arms around his waist without a word, I pressed my cheek up against his shoulder blade. My eyes were shut, and I was savoring the moment. God, he was so cute when he wore nothing but the bottom half of his pajamas. God, I was lucky to have a man who actually took the time to slice up strawberries and fanned them across our pancakes. And God, I was planning on making it worth his while when we hopped back into bed after breakfast.

"In case you were wondering," he mentioned over his shoulder, as casually as if he were asking me to get the powdered sugar, "I saw you kiss that construction bloke."

Living with my mother had taught me that standing perfectly still wouldn't make the comment go away. Instead, I took a big step back.

"Relax," he said, spinning around with two plates of pancakes and walking them over to the table. "Eat your breakfast."

He sat down and motioned me over. I walked slowly, keeping my eyes on him the entire time. He just hacked into his breakfast like a serial killer opening his mail calmly amidst the bodies.

"What?" he asked, noticing that my mouth was still open, and that I had yet to touch my food. "Cat got your tongue?"

"Bloke?" I blurted out. It was all I could manage at the time.

"You know that whenever I'm in London I fall back into the Queen's English." He squirted maple syrup rather inelegantly across his breakfast.

"You weren't gone for that long." I crossed my legs and tucked my hair behind an ear, trying my best to remain stoic.

"I've always been an overachiever," he said, and spooned another sloppy mess toward his mouth. "Besides, what else would you call him? Not exactly a *barrister*."

I couldn't take this anymore. And I wasn't sure which part to react to first.

"Raj!" I slammed my hands onto the table, setting the silverware aquiver. "What's going on?"

"What do you mean?"

"Raj!"

"Look." He put down his fork and furrowed his brow as if suddenly deep in thought. "You don't need to worry about anything, Monica. I've decided that I'm not going to be angry with you."

Rather than relieved, I was surprised. Surprised and disappointed.

"I'm not happy about it," he continued. "You made a poor choice. But technically I suppose we weren't together at the time. Neither of us really knew where we stood. So in a sense, we were on a hiatus."

We were?

"Raj, I'm…"

"There's no need for that, Monica." He waved away the beginnings of my apology before reluctantly forcing a reassuring smile in my direction. "Perhaps this separation was what we both needed. To be sure about us. And now we are. So why don't we move on?"

★ ★ ★

If I hadn't still felt guilty about Luke, I never would have agreed to dinner with Raj's colleagues the following night. As I donned the new pearl earrings that he bought me a few hours before, while we strolled hand-in-hand through Nordstrom's at The Grove, I reminded myself that nobody sleeping in the doghouse had the right to make any decisions on her own. He had assured me that his coworkers were *not the sort of people who would spend their time watching reality TV—even if they had been stateside at the time.* And I had no choice but to trust him. It was either that, or send him off alone to a dinner full of couples and effectively confirm what many of them probably already suspected: that we were over.

It's just one evening, I repeated in my mind, while he helped me on with my coat, and I gave myself the final once-over in my hall mirror.

And then he chortled.

I questioned him with a glance.

"Imagine," he mused out loud while unlocking the bolt on the door, "*you,* leaving *me,* for a *construction worker.*"

"What does that mean?" I asked, standing firm against the hand on my waist that was trying to guide me through the open door.

"I suppose it means that…you're not like that." He thought about it a second before looking me in the eye. "You're reasonable."

This was certainly a less-than-appealing color on him, but

worse than that was what sort of a shade it implied about me. The man who supposedly knew me better than anyone had been willing to dismiss my indiscretion not because he believed I was sorry, but because he couldn't imagine me taking a "construction bloke" seriously. I wasn't totally sure which part of my brain to file that in, but I was sure that somehow I was now embarrassed for the both of us. And since we were running late and the whole situation had become too convoluted to dissect at that particular moment, I made my way outside. As I allowed him to open the car door for me, to spirit me away to dinner, I wondered: was this what marriage would be like?

Never before had I been so pleased to have a gorgeous, buxom redhead towering over me.

"And this is Rogier's girlfriend, Inga," Raj explained while we were meeting and greeting at the bar of the Napa Valley Grille. "Why don't I get you ladies a couple of glasses of that white from Alsace that we had enjoyed so much? I believe they carry it here. And Rogier? Your usual Glenlivet?"

"Perfect," Inga said, before returning her focus to me. "This way we can get to know your beautiful fiancée. We've heard so much about you, Monica. You know, you've really got a good one there."

"I know," I replied, and smiled for the handsome couple, mostly because it seemed like the logical response.

I hadn't realized until that moment how much my

mother's "spotting Raj's lookalike with a redhead" comment, combined with Raj's silent treatment, had made me doubt our relationship. Maybe I was taking everything a little too seriously. Marriage was a big-picture endeavor, anyway. Now that I had evidence of the irrelevance of my mother's sighting standing before me, I couldn't help but laugh at myself.

I locked eyes with him while he ordered our drinks, and felt more in sync than I had since he'd returned. It was the small, truly intimate glance which is almost imperceptible to anyone other than the two people involved, but which means so much more than all the others. It was a connection across the crowd. A reminder that we were still us. A reassurance that the connection had not been severed. And the screws in my neck began to loosen for the first time since the previous call with my mother.

Maybe Raj and I *were* getting off on a stronger foot now that we had been through something rough. They say that the only way a desert fighter pilot knows he's crossed over something important in the dark is because all hell breaks loose. Maybe Raj needed to see that I had other options in order to convince himself I would never really leave him for anyone. Maybe my suspicion about Mom's comment would have eaten away at me from the inside unless I had met Inga and seen for myself that the mysterious redhead was actually very happily involved with somebody else.

Soon enough, we were ushered to our table. We ate. We

laughed. General merriment all around. Somewhere between the pumpkin tortellini appetizer and the second bottle of wine, Raj placed a hand over mine and tilted his chin in the direction of an impeccably dressed, unmistakably miserable couple seated a few tables away. It was a ritual of ours; whenever we were at a restaurant where a couple looked particularly unhappy, we pointed them out to one another as a reminder of how glad we were to be on our date rather than on theirs. We would keep an eye on them for the rest of the evening, go out of our way to eat off each other's plates, and then gossip about the miserable couple all the way home. It provided hours of entertainment in a city full of relationships that were little more than a way to kill time on the way to a bigger, better deal.

"Shane and Eliza," Raj whispered into my ear, indicating the names of tonight's anonymous couple.

"Professional baseball player and aspiring actress from Wisconsin," I explained to him in return, with a mischievous grin. They were a life-size version of Malibu Ken and Barbie, down to the anatomically impossible measurements and almost entirely plastic faces. They had yet to look each other in the eye, or say more than a few words by the time our entrées arrived.

A few more glasses of *that wine from Alsace* and our table was erupting in laughter at Rogier's jokes concerning the foibles of the British. But things were a lot less fun over in Shane and Eliza's corner. Raj had nudged my attention toward them when a waiter walked over to the table, handed

Eliza a note, and pointed to a plump, balding gentleman smoking a cigar at a large table at the far end of the restaurant. Despite Shane's mounting irritation, Eliza had perked up, scribbled something on the opposite side of said note, and sent it back to the gentleman by way of the waiter. Promptly, Melvin (which was what we decided to call baldy, having determined that he was a dirty old movie producer who wanted to get the young Eliza onto his casting couch) belly-laughed at her note and made some hilarious comment to his friends, all of whom suddenly raised their champagne flutes in Eliza's direction.

Raj and I exchanged confused glances. *Was this the end of the road for Shane and Eliza's relationship? Did this mean that she was accepting a part in an X-rated movie despite his protests? What about the pomeranians?*

Shane was pissed. Eliza was defiant. He threw his napkin down on the table, dropped some cash on top and made his way out the door.

Being on my third glass of wine, I decided it was time for me to make *my way* toward the powder room. I did my business well enough, but was really in no condition to deal with a test. While I appreciated the beauty of the shiny copper bird fountain/sculpture/sink, I was about ready to give up on my search for the faucet when someone else flushed and came out to help me.

"It's down here," Eliza told me, swiping a delicate and bejeweled wrist across an invisible sensor at the base, causing water to spring forth. "These things are so annoying."

"I know." I started washing up alongside her, wondering how I had morphed into such a hick. "Thanks."

"You got a light?" she asked, handing me a towel and grabbing one for herself.

"Sorry, I don't smoke."

"Figures." She exhaled and leaned against the sink, clearly anxious about something.

"Are you okay?" I asked her reflection, while I checked my teeth in the mirror.

"No," she said, rummaging around inside a purse smaller than my fist for the matches she was already sure she did not have. "But I will be. As soon as I cut that guy I came with loose and get back to my career. Three years without a ring. Can you believe it? What an asshole!"

"I dunno what to tell you." I gave her my best shrug of anonymous female solidarity.

"Well," she said more to herself than to me, while leaning over and giving her boobs a final adjustment in the mirror. "It doesn't really matter. There's a movie producer who just recognized me from a B movie I did before I met this idiot. I think it's a sign. Maybe that tacky producer might be able to give me something I need."

"You're really leaving with him?" I asked, dumbfounded.

She winked, tossed her towel into the basket, and sauntered out of the room. I was still absorbing what I had just heard when after another flush, Inga appeared alongside me at the sink, grinning and shaking her head.

"Wow," I tried, while she dried her hands and then

puckered up to her own reflection. "I guess there are those women who have no problem walking away from a relationship at the drop of a hat, huh?"

"This is true," she answered, while smearing candy-apple red across the rim of her mouth. "But there are also many others who stay in the relationship though choose to stray instead. They are merely lucky enough never to be caught in the act. Or on tape."

I looked up and we locked eyes.

"Or on *television*." She leered.

Now it could be argued that Inga had no real designs on my man. Of course, it could also be argued that I was the reincarnation of Mary Magdalene. But the truth was that the way Inga said it made it very clear that she was just waiting out my relationship with Raj. In fact, she was so confident of our split that she was telling me as much to my face. And at the risk of embarrassing Raj in front of his colleagues, who probably hadn't seen *Smacked!* and had no idea what was going on, I had little choice but to just stand there and take it.

It just goes to show you, you should never trust any woman who doesn't know you from a hole in the wall, but still seems a little too enthusiastically happy about your relationship. Lydia wasn't the only one who had to learn to sleep with one eye open.

eighteen

"YOU KNOW WHAT WOULD MAKE YOUR LIFE A LOT EASIER?"
Cassie planted herself before my desk on Monday morning and crossed her arms at me. "If you finally accepted relationships for what they really are—a brief period of pheromone overload followed by a sustained mad grab for emotional superiority."

I shook my head like a dizzied cartoon character. "What the hell are you talking about?"

"What did he do?" She was unmoved.

"Who?"

"Raj!"

"Nothing." I looked back at my computer screen.

"Bull." She squinted, and said, "You never close your office door without even saying good morning to me unless you're trying not to deal with something. And since Raj came into town on Friday…"

"Nothing happened." I tried my best to focus on some spam about male enhancement that had gotten through our IT filters. "Don't we give you enough work to do?"

"Why are you so crabby?"

"I am not crabby, I am busy. Now shoo." I lowered my chin and raised my eyebrows.

"Then he's pissed off at you." Her eyes went wide with a gasp. "Oh my gosh, he saw you on *Smacked!* before you had a chance to warn him!"

"No!" I said. "I mean…yes, he saw it, but no, he wasn't pissed off."

"Really?" She was confused.

"Really." I was as enthusiastic as a tax collector at a speed dating event. "About that, or about anything else."

"Then what's wrong?"

"What's wrong is Alex."

"The client?"

I exhaled, dropped my shoulders, and decided to let her in on my personal hell: "The *ex-boyfriend* who is now the client. I used to read his screenplays for him in college. He asked me to read his latest for old time's sake. The working relationship is totally professional, of course."

"Of course," she added.

"But Raj caught me reading it yesterday," I persisted despite the smirk in her voice. "And when I told him whose it was, and that I was working with my ex, he didn't even bat an eye."

"I don't get it. What did he say when you told him you used to date?"

"That's the problem." I shook my head. "He knows our entire history. All I had to tell him was that it was Alex."

"And what did he say?"

I almost laughed. "Not much."

"Oh." Cassie took a seat opposite me and leaned forward, forming a steeple with her fingers. *"That's* what he's doing."

"What?"

"He's smarter than I gave him credit for." She nodded, ignoring me like some self-satisfied movie villain. "Way to go, Raj, growing a backbone on the other side of the pond."

"Okay, I'll say it again—Cassie, what the hell are you talking about?"

"He's turned the tables. He still loves you, but he needs you to be aware of how much you care about him. He's making you aware of it now. This is all about control, babe. And as much as you will refuse to admit it, it turns you on."

"Much in the same way as telling me that I'm fat turns me on." I rolled my eyes.

"He's a desperate man." She shrugged.

"You're a fruit loop," I said, trying to dismiss her.

"And you're deluding yourself, Monica." Her voice was adorably tough love. "Why would he stay with you if he wasn't even interested enough to give a damn about the fact that you're consorting with the enemy?"

"I am not consorting!" I was indignant, and then unclear. "What does that even mean?"

"I don't know. But it has something to do with war."

"This is not war, it's my love life."

"Love is a battlefield, Monica. And Raj is fighting for you."

"Love is not a battlefield!" I insisted a little too loudly. "And have you been watching *MTV 80s Pop-up Video* again?"

"Okay, first of all, yes it is, and yes I have. Also, did you know that Pat Benatar wrote "Love Is A Battlefield," and that *Tell my wife I love her* are the most common last words of American soldiers in combat, but that Pat Benatar's own first marriage to a guy in the military actually ended in divorce?"

"Well there's fifteen seconds of my life that I'll never get back," I told her. "Can I please get on with work now?"

"Not until you open your eyes, Monica. When have you known Raj not to be passionate about you?"

She had a point. And it made me feel better in a twisted sort of way, so I asked her, "When did you decide that relationships are all about control?"

"I didn't decide anything. I just admitted it, because it's exactly what I'm doing with Jonathan. Look, nobody wants anything that comes easily, at least not for the long term. So I'm reminding him now that he needs to win me. That I have other options."

"Well, then all I can say is that my cousin Sheila could learn a lot from you. She can't even control herself, much less any of the people around her."

"Fine, I give up on you." She stepped back, seemingly exhausted by my persistently skewed worldview. "Speaking of people who have a lot to learn, what do we think has been keeping Medusa so quiet lately?"

"I'm not sure exactly, and I don't care, as long as it keeps her out of my face. I have enough to worry about without trying to protect myself from the evil eye of some maniac who is jealous of me for no reason. You're the one dating Jonathan, for God's sakes."

"But that's how you think, Monica, not how she thinks. I've been pondering this and I figured it out. You don't have to feel better than her to be happy. You're fine feeling equal. She's not. And knowing that you won't compete with her is what's really making her angry. So she can only tolerate you by telling herself that you're smug."

"I'm smug because I don't base my life around her?"

"No. But being around someone who doesn't consider her a threat eats into her comfort zone. You are very similar to her, but you're also different, and that's all right with you."

"So?"

"So if she was you, it wouldn't be all right with her. And she knows that. So what she's jealous of is your confidence."

In high school everything is personal. Even the way that someone eyes you across a crowded gymnasium, no matter if the reality is that they were checking the clock above your head.

Everything is magnified when your world consists of the five-mile radius of your parents' home. And so, fortunately, are the lessons that people try to teach us in the precious last moments before we leave high school and emerge into the world. I remember my senior year like it was yesterday....

"But how can you let her get away with it?" I pounded an idealistic fist down onto Mr. Tonin's desk one afternoon late in April. As faculty advisor to the school yearbook, he was the only person with the power to censure Carolina for what she had done.

"Monica, you have got to calm down," Mr. Tonin insisted, as if he had seen this all before. "It is not the last time something like this will happen to you."

Not exactly the response I had been expecting. Carolina and I had been co-editors of the yearbook. We had been co-cheerleaders on the squad. And we had both competed for the same college scholarships. But it had never turned personal between us until then.

"Sit down," he said, and indicated a chair across from his desk. "Monica, you must be aware of the fact that you...you don't blend into the crowd around here. And I don't mean that simply for the obvious reasons."

I glowered, waiting for him to continue.

"Look, I can understand why you are upset. Carolina had no right to publish senior superlatives without polling the class."

"So?"

He smoothed over his moustache and sighed. "You are always going to be a visible person, Monica. And along with visibility comes scorn. You're going to have to get used to it."

I looked out the window. Clearly, Mr. Tonin was on her side.

"And that is not your fault. You're just being yourself. But it is, unfortunately, a fact of your life. Unless you decide to become a shy, quiet, in the background sort of a young woman. And I don't think that's you, which is why you're going to go far in life, Monica. I can promise you that. But there are more Carolinas in your future, kiddo."

"Great." I was supremely sarcastic, even with a pink scrunchie in my hair.

"I'm not telling you that you're wrong. But to save yourself a lot of grief and frustration, I urge you to choose now, Monica. Choose today how you will handle people like this. For the rest of your life. Are you going to let them distract you from being who you are and from doing what you're doing? Or are you going to do the smart thing and ignore it?"

"But she called me *Most Likely To Die Alone!* It's not *fair!*"

"No, it's not fair. But Monica, what she wants from you is a reaction. And if you've learned nothing else from my class this year, please take that little piece of insight with you."

"So you want me to do nothing?"

"I want you to rise above it."

"So you won't help me?"

"I hope I just did."

"It's not confidence, it's self-assurance," I told Cassie. "They're two very different things."

I wasn't always the only Indian girl in the class, but I was a lot of the time. And it wasn't that I never saw anyone who resembled me on television in the seventies and eighties, but if the truth be told, it was rare. And it wasn't that I didn't have an Indian community to identify with for the better part of my life, because I did. But when the majority of the people you interact with on a daily basis, and can safely expect to interact with for the first thirty years of your life cannot properly pronounce your surname, it makes an impression. If you're wise, you decide early on that comparing yourself to "the norm" is about as clever as doing your own dental work. So you start comparing today's version of yourself to the version you were yesterday, and you learn very quickly to be grateful merely for progress.

"Whatever you want to call it," Cassie went on, "you can't buy it."

"What do you want from me?" I asked, hoping that my return to the computer would signal her to be on her way.

"You know what I want to do," Cassie said, forcibly deeming my rhetoric literal.

"No, Cassie." I bit my lip. "I can't. I won't. I don't want to ruin her career."

"Then what do you want?"

"I want her to see that she's a bad reflection on all of us."

"I've got it!" Cassie almost jumped.

"What?" I was ready to dismiss whatever it was.

"You can go over to her apartment, show up on like a

Sunday morning, ring the doorbell, and when she answers…
punch her in the nose! And then turn around and walk
away!"

"Hmm, now I think you're actually getting a little scary."

"Consider it." She was totally serious. "She would come
in to work the next day with a broken nose, and she would
be running around telling everyone that Monica showed up
on her doorstep and punched her in the face without a
word, and then calmly took off…nobody would ever be
able to believe that you were capable of it. Everybody would
think she was insane. And you would get to punch her in
the nose. *It's the perfect crime!*"

At the very least, it was a beautiful daydream…

Ski mask (to ensure that Stefanie's nosey neighbors could
not identify me in a lineup): $10.

Outlast boxing gloves (to protect my knuckles and
prevent her having any proof): $50. (Or free, if I could
borrow them from Lydia.)

Blank videotape (with which Cassie could immortalize
the event, so that we can enjoy it for years to come): $3.

Knowing somewhere deep inside that not only had I
scored one against the Stefanie in every woman's life, but
that Mr. Tonin would be oh-so-disappointed in me: *Priceless*.

nineteen

I KNOW HOW TO CHECK MY LIPSTICK IN THE REFLECTION OF MY cell phone's time and date screen when my compact is nowhere to be found (say, because I was so drunk that I accidentally dropped it into a toilet at a club in Vegas). I know how to stare directly into a stranger's eyes for long enough to figure out whether he's got something to hide (I am The Queen of visual "chicken"). I even know how to tie my hair up with my thong before stepping into an unfamiliar shower the morning after (in the absence of a rubber-band, who's gonna risk an awkward conversation just because one's waiting for her hair to dry?). These are only a few of the handy little tricks that any capable woman masters after a sufficient number of years of living and loving in the ethical funhouse that is Los Angeles.

What she apparently does not learn, however, is how to

maintain her composure when confronted with an ex-boyfriend and a couple of pitchers of sake. As it turns out, fifteen years of living and loving in Los Angeles is no real protection against feeling like a fumbling, geeky amateur every once in a while.

Case in point: there really is no way to describe the dis-tasteful sound my lips made while I sucked the last sesame seed out from between my teeth as Alex approached the table at The Ivy the following afternoon. It was sort of like the sound of a bathroom drain expelling a clumpy, hairy clog, backward. Even a few of the bitchy waiters turned around to look me up and down.

"Wow, so it was that bad, huh?" Alex took a seat and grinned at me.

"No!" I smoothed over my printed copy of his screen-play while cursing my flapping lip as much as the sesame seed that did me in. "Actually, I really enjoyed it."

It would have been nice if I had been able to resist the warm bread they set out while I was waiting. It would have been nice if I hadn't torn into it like a prisoner into the first woman he's seen after being paroled. It also would have been nice to have been reincarnated as Aishwarya Rye. But there was no time to dwell on the past. And the present was much more pressing. I cleared my throat and ran my fingers through my hair. He tilted his head, obviously awaiting further praise. Why are men always such whores for positive reinforcement? Never mind, I told myself. Just throw the guy a bone…

"You're really very funny, Alex," I told him while a waiter with a tattoo of what looked just like Gianni Versace's face on his forearm tipped water over the edge of the pitcher. "Really."

"Really?" he mocked me in a high-pitched voice.

Clearly flirtatious. Clearly testing the waters. Clearly, this was the moment for me to draw my line in the sand. I was spoken for, after all.

"Really." I was monotone and intent on delivering some useful feedback. To stall for time so that I could come up with some, I guzzled the entire glass of water before me.

Why had I agreed to read his screenplay? Why did I care whether he saw a sesame seed in my teeth? How could I feel this way when I was so sure about Raj? Had I become one of those people who claims to be able to love more than one person at the same time? But that was impossible! I had always eyed those sorts of women with the same suspicion that I usually reserved for vegans and men who wore pink shirts in public while insisting that they were heterosexual.

Regardless, Alex was waiting for my feedback. And if I could visit a strip club for Bruno and crawl into a changing room for Lydia, then this was the least I could do for Alex. But the truth was that I was nervous about giving him my thoughts on his new screenplay, *Tell Me More About My Eyes,* because it was unlike anything I had ever expected him to write. It wasn't just funny, frothy and a little tongue-in-cheek. It was the love-child of satire and sarcasm. It was...

"It was well-organized," I said. "The plot, I mean. It

flowed and maintained dramatic pace throughout. The humor was appropriate for the subject, but it was definitely a lot darker than I remember you being."

"Well, it's been a long time, Monica." He reached for his menu. "Some of us have become dispassionate and others have just gotten darker."

Huh?

"I guess that's what age does to people, right?" I tried to keep things light. "So where did you come up with these characters, anyway? They were pretty…umm…extreme."

And that was like saying that your first trip to a gynecologist was sort of *surprising.* On the surface the story was simple. The screenplay follows two strangers through a one-night-stand on New Year's Eve where they meet, dance and decide not to ruin the magic of what seems like the perfect, no-strings-attached liaison with silly details like where they're from or what they do for a living. But the question that lingers throughout the script is why Lenny (the tall, dark man in the three-piece suit) and Veronica (the petite, perky brunette wearing a little black dress and "a smile saying she's looking for trouble") are both so desperate to connect that they're willing to set their usual getting-to-know-you questions aside.

What begins with an air-toast and a wink across the ballroom of a black-tie New Year's Eve ball in Chicago proceeds to Veronica telling Lenny that rather than hearing any of the details of his life she would prefer that he "tell her more about her eyes." And as the screenplay progresses there are flashbacks to episodes of each of their pasts, laced with witty but evasive banter that manages to heighten the suspense as much as the sexual tension. In the end we learn that nearly five years into widowhood, Veronica has yet to forgive herself for cheating on her late husband. Lenny was recently paroled from prison after it was proven that the hit-and-run in which a girl was run over was not his fault. For both of them, it's the first time to have been intimate in years.

Somehow, Alex had managed to make all of this seem funny. Lenny's hair gets tangled in Veronica's earring as he tries to nuzzle her neck. Veronica treats herself to an eyeful of soap in the bathroom while freshening up when the dispenser accidentally misfires. And there is the part when Veronica, making her best effort to unzip her dress and have it fall seductively to the ground, instead gets her zipper stuck in her nylons and winds up gasping for air while Lenny yanks it tighter around her waist in a botched attempt to come to her rescue.

"Life is extreme, right?" He aligned the silverware on both sides of his plate in a transparent attempt to avoid eye contact. "Love has as much power to hurt as it does to heal."

"You always go back to the same theme, don't you?" I stated, as the waiter laid our chopped salads before us.

"You always did think I was a dreamer, didn't you?" He smiled, somewhat sadly.

No, I didn't always think that. But I do now.

"Alex," I said, and dug into my salad, "I think this movie is gonna do well whatever the message is."

"The message is what I've always believed, Monica." He reached across the table for my hand to force me to look up from my plate. "Idealism is what I've got. Wasn't that always what you used to say that you loved about me?"

I tried to pull away and then found that I was fixated on the image of our hands clasped together again. It all seemed so artificial. Who was this man? It had been years since we were in a relationship, and although I still knew he was decent and would always share memories of the childhood we had ventured through together, something was off. And it wasn't just that he was no longer the same Alex. It was that I was no longer the same Monica. Nor did I want to be.

"Why are you being so academic and nonemotional with your feedback on my screenplay? I didn't show it to you for your opinion on plot structure. Come on," he whispered and lowered his head. "It's *you and me*."

And I could see how much he wanted it to be. But it was like watching someone who just got voted first-runner-up; the tightness of her face as she smiles for the camera only reinforces how sincerely she feels that it's not turning out the way that it should. I softened, and clasped my hand on top of his instead. *He didn't even know me anymore, I was getting ready to tell him. And this wasn't about me. It was normal during the course of a divorce to wind up clutching at anything that seemed familiar.*

But I didn't have the chance.

"I have a confession." He furrowed his brow before

looking up at me, saying, "I saw you on *Smacked!* And…I hired Steel specifically to get back in touch with you."

Suddenly, I felt like all eyes in the restaurant were on us. Was he about to say what I thought he was about to say? And if he did, was it partially my fault? Had I been leading him on? Oh my God, was I *that girl?*

"Hey, where is that waiter of ours?" I scanned the patio, trying to make a joke to stop him from finishing his thought. "Is he actually picking the parsley for the garnish himself or something?"

Alex leaned across the table. "Monica, I was more than disappointed when I saw that ring appear on your finger the other day. I assumed you were single when I saw you kiss that guy on television. And at first, I was even more disappointed to find out that you're engaged. But then it occurred to me that your kissing that other guy must mean this engagement isn't right for you."

"Well, I don't think that's necessarily fair." I pulled back.

"I want to give us another chance."

It's not as if I was completely unaware of the flirtation going into this lunch. And as uncomfortable as the situation was, I was prepared to do whatever was necessary to diffuse it without insulting him or losing my firm a client. But to think that he would actually move beyond flirtation to make a move on me while he was still married and I was still technically engaged? I was disgusted. Disgusted, disappointed and at the same time, thrilled. Because my ire came directly from how protective I felt of what I had with Raj.

And the moment I realized that was where my indignation was coming from, I also realized that I could not keep my mouth shut.

"So," I said, folding my arms across my chest, thinking about the poor woman he was trying to cheat on with me, "how is Carolyn doing anyway?"

"What?"

"Your wife, remember? The woman to whom you are still married."

"She's all right." He blinked and stiffened. "She's fine."

"Alex, I have to say that this is very unlike you…plotting to get ahead of the possible failure of your marriage? You know, most clients who have gotten this far with Steel have already told their spouses and at least been formally separated. But you haven't even brought Carolyn into the office. Should I assume that this means you're trying to salvage things? To be *adult* about the situation?"

His silence made me wonder if I had overstepped my bounds. He was a client. I had to fix this, find some way to play it off. For what felt like ten minutes we just sat there glued to our chairs.

"Are you in couple's therapy?" I finally asked.

"We tried that, actually." He gulped down the remains of his sake without looking at me. "But it didn't work. I just can't seem to get past it."

"Past what?"

After a while, he answered. "She cheated on me."

And he seemed so small, so tired. For the first time since

he had walked into Steel, I was really thinking of Alex not as my ex, but as somebody else's husband. He had taken vows and heard someone else take them in return. He had planned for his life to turn out very differently than it had. He probably didn't feel very good about himself at that moment, and now to top it all off, I had rejected him. Again. I felt more than sorry for him. I felt protective. Sorry, protective, and even guiltier about Luke.

By the end of lunch I found myself counseling Alex more like a family minister than an ex-girlfriend. Not as his lawyer, and not as his former flame, but as a friend. I really wanted him to know that he was not irrational because he was unable to overcome her infidelity.

"I guess it really has been a long time," he said through the last mouthful of salad. "Because this is the last conversation I ever expected to be having with you."

twenty

"I MEAN, OBVIOUSLY I WOULDN'T HAVE SLEPT WITH HIM THAT first night if I had any interest in seeing him again," a bottled and botoxed blonde quipped to her friend in the elevator later that afternoon.

"*Du-uh!*" her friend with the pastel nails and the spray tan immediately concurred.

Alex and I shared a smirk but kept our thoughts to ourselves.

"So what do I do? The idiot has sent me flowers every day this week."

"*Actors,*" Spray-tan spouted. "That's why you should only have one-night stands with agents—they never bother you again. Actors are too emotional."

"So…"

"So, actors are for hot, short, summer relationships. Agents are for one-nighters. Bodybuilders are for quickies."

"Then where do women in L.A. look for real relationships?"

"Hell if I know," she shot back and shrugged, before stepping off at their floor.

"Maybe I'll just tell him I'm pregnant," Bottled-and-Botoxed decided while following closely behind her friend. "That was always the quickest way to get rid of a man in Atlanta."

We waited until the doors had closed to finally burst into cackles.

"So should I take it as a compliment that you didn't sleep with me on the first night we went out back in college?" Alex asked.

"Absolutely," I replied, smiling, as the doors opened on our floor. I motioned toward my office, since we had some more paperwork to finish.

"Is there some correlation between how long you made me wait and how seriously you were planning on taking the relationship? Because those were the longest three months of my life!"

"Yes, there is," I said, as we rounded the hallway leading to my office. "And for the record, I took you more seriously than I had ever taken anyone else in my life."

"Monica," he began, but paused and looked down for a moment, while holding the door open for me, "in case I forget to mention it later, I really want to thank you for your help. Honestly. I know that…you and me… It was a long time ago. But we still do have a history, and…well…you can't blame me for getting nostalgic."

I tried to wave it away, and get past him into my office, but with a hand on my arm and a more earnest look than I'd ever remembered, he held me to the spot.

"I know you, Monica. And I know you're not all tough-as-nails. So thank you, as usual, for being the…voice of reason in our…err…whatever this is."

"Friendship, Alex." I smiled up at him.

He nodded. "Yeah, friendship. Let's go with that."

"Besides, I'm tougher than I look, remember?"

"Yeah, yeah. I remember that tough girl very well." He reached a sentimental hand up to touch my face.

It was the most relaxed and familiar that I had felt since Alex came back into my life. And for a second I thought things could be that simple. Why shouldn't we be friends? Why wouldn't we still care about each other? Why couldn't we be around each other without things becoming romantic?

And why was everything suddenly in slow motion?

Alex was shooting me a smile that meant he was on the same page. As I was getting ready to step back, something I sensed over my shoulder made me turn around and look.

It was Stefanie. With her arms crossed and her smirk cemented, she must have been watching us from the other end of the hallway the entire time. And from the looks of it, she had been far enough to miss the words, but close enough to take presumptuous note of the tenderness in our exchange.

She looked up from my shoulder and into my eyes. The smirk spilled outward into a way-too-satisfied smile. And before I could even turn around completely, she had twisted on her heels and gotten a running start in the other direction.

Oh, no, no, no, no, no! She was heading straight for the partners' offices, and all I could do was practically sprain an ankle trying hard to catch her. No matter what the truth was, Stefanie was about to plant a seed in the partners' minds that I might have to spend years trying to erase. I had to convince her that what she saw was an innocent exchange between old friends.

Time caught up with itself a few seconds later, and sensing this, she increased her speed. I rounded the corner at the far end of the hallway in time to see her snicker and leap-frog those stairs. Damn the open floor plans in this place. Nobody could have ignored the sight of two junior associates in heels leaping three steps at a time toward the partners' suites on the second floor. She got to the top as I made the last step, and at that point, she broke into a sprint. If I had taken a moment to think about it, I might have slowed down. I might have acknowledged the eyes assaulting us from open-air cubicles scattered below. I might have recognized that the glass walls were making for a very public chase. Instead, I had to struggle to catch my breath because a woman on a mission like hers was superhumanly fast.

There was no way I would reach her in time, so instead I did the only thing I could think of.

"Stefanie!" I yelled, doubled over at the top of the stairs. "You can't do this!"

"You don't tell me what to do," she spat the words at me, in between heaving and gasping for air. She may have been fast, but she definitely wasn't pretty with pit marks full of sweat.

Then again, judging by the expressions of the office full of witnesses, neither was I. I staggered, swallowed and took a step back from the violently charged situation. Plus, I had the sensation that Stefanie might have bitten me if I got too close. We were beyond animosity, and whether or not she had anything real to tell the partners, she was clearly planning to try. Knowing that, I had to stop her.

"This isn't right." I reached out physically, adopting a more civilized tone than the roar I was holding inside, and took a small step in her direction. "This…this has all gone too far!"

And then I made the biggest mistake in the world. I touched her arm.

"Get away from me!" she shouted, and jerked at the elbow, knocking over a tray of Starbucks being carried past her by an intern too focused on avoiding spillage to have taken note of the situation.

The coffee flew everywhere, almost as if it had exploded. It was on our clothes, on the floor, on the walls, and all over the poor, shivering intern. With my mouth agape, I looked from Stefanie's clothes, to the intern, to the floor and finally to my own shirt, which was bisected by a splash of what must have been an iced mocha only a few short seconds before. Rather than stopping at all, Stefanie smiled maniacally and turned to run away. *Damn it!*

"Will you just listen to me?" I yelled, just to make sure that *the entire office* was listening. Brilliant move, Monica.

But she wouldn't.

So I lunged for her.

And I caught her…

…by the hair.

This meant, in effect, that I yanked her to the floor. Cavewoman-style.

Not my proudest moment.

Immediately, I snapped back and instinctively tried to reach out and help her to her feet. But she recoiled, and seemed hyperaware of our growing audience. Then she smiled, telling me this was not going to be pretty.

"Ask and you shall receive, Monica," she buzzed, with one eye narrower than the other. Was she having an epiphany or an aneurism?

"What?"

"You wanted me to say what I'm thinking to your face, right? Well, here it is. I am going to confront you, exactly as you wish, to your face, in front of everyone, you self-important bitch!"

"Stefanie, I…"

"So counselor, what exactly was the meaning of the

client gently stroking your face back there?" She planted her hands on her hips, clearly savoring the view from what looked like a position of moral superiority.

"You don't understand." I swiped whipped cream from my blouse and splattered it onto the carpet.

"So you're denying it?"

"No! This has gone too far!"

"What?" she mocked me, licking some of the coffee from her own face. "Your professional relationship with our client? Well, that's pretty obvious."

"No! What has gone too far is this unnatural hate that you have for me." I pulled myself together and decided she wasn't the only one who was going to work the audience. "And I'm sick of sweeping it under the rug! And I'm sick of worrying that if I acknowledge it then everyone will think I'm a hyperemotional child! And I'm sick and god-damned tired of putting up with it! That's what has gone too far. As for Alex, it was nothing. There is nothing be-tween us. And you cannot walk over to the partners' offices and imply that I would do something so unethical. I shouldn't have to watch my own back so fiercely because of your obvious insecurities!"

"So then there is absolutely nothing between the two of you?" Niles, who had by that point emerged from his office, interjected.

"Well, no. I mean, not really," I fumbled, squeezing coffee from my skirt and noting the incredulity in the dozens of eyes piercing me from every direction. "We dated. Years ago. Back in college. I haven't seen him in years. And I know that I should have mentioned it when he became my client, but I knew that it wouldn't interfere with my work because it's ancient history. There's nothing there between us."

Silence reigned while Niles studied me. Someone coughed, Stefanie huffed and the intern started collecting the cups.

"For God's sakes, I'm engaged!" I continued, laughing nervously. "So let's all calm down. I mean, it's not like I was *sleeping with a partner* or something."

That's when the silence turned a corner of its own. In fact, I think it went and hid behind the intern. The blood had drained completely from Stefanie's face, and rather than looking at me, Niles was staring at the floor. When I saw that, it hit me.

"Oh my God," I said. *"You?"*

twenty-one

You know how the rule is *never answer a cell phone call from a private number?* Well, my new rule is *never answer the door if I haven't invited anyone over that day.* I felt badly enough about myself a week later, without the added pressure of having to deal with the opinions of unwelcome visitors. I was decked out in bunny slippers, a housecoat and a week's worth of leg stubble, eating stale cereal out of the box in front of *The Montel Williams Show* on a Friday afternoon, when there was a knock at the door.

Hey, you do what you want with your personal days, and I'll do what I want with mine.

I hunched my shoulders, snapped one eye shut and tried my best to act as if I hadn't heard it. I even froze in place, as if remaining *vewy vewy still* might make whoever it was go away.

"Hey!" Sheila shouted and kept banging on the door. "Monica? It's your favorite cousin. Lemme in!"

Resentfully, I headed in the direction of her voice. She should have known that I was I no mood for company. I had my hands full just dealing with all of the self-recriminations. Stefanie had left Steel voluntarily the morning after our very public cat-and-mouse game, via an e-mail claiming she was taking a position at a rival firm. I had removed myself from Alex's case, without so much as an explanation. In fact, I had been so horrified at having accidentally outed Stefanie's relationship with a married partner that I would rather have eaten my own foot than set it in the office for the next few days. Thankfully, Jonathan had been willing to deliver the news to Alex personally, in return for my help in getting Cassie to give him another chance. And I had been planning on existing solely within the confines of my apartment for the next few "personal days." I would live off delivery and frozen dinners, gorge my mind on dating TV shows and refuse to tolerate direct sunlight until either I managed to get over this or the Steel Image Consultant Team threw me into a van and dragged me forcibly to the nearest full-service-spa for an intervention.

Don't laugh. It really happens.

Oh well, I told myself as I reached for the lock, *at least Sheila usually brought bagels when she knew I was upset.*

The problem was that she also brought along something else…

"*Da*rling," my mother began, with a smile and a hug, but

then pulled a face meant to convey that my disarray was somehow a personal attack on her. "How are you?"

It was a good five minutes before I could get Sheila alone in the kitchen, while my mother took her suitcase to my spare room.

I punched my own palm for extra effect. "You have ten seconds to explain yourself."

"She swore me to secrecy!" Sheila explained, raising her hands and backing up against the counter.

For an instant I was offended that she actually thought me capable of physical violence. Then again, if I was capable of ruining someone's career, then maybe I was also capable of throwing a *beat-down* fit for reality TV. I wasn't really sure what I was capable of, and I didn't want any help figuring it out. I just wanted to put one foot in front of the other one until this whole Stefanie thing seemed like a distant memory. I hadn't even told Raj any of the details besides that she had left the firm, that our client had been reassigned and that I was taking a few days to relax. For some strange reason, Raj had been particularly happy-go-lucky the past while, and I didn't want to bring him down. Regardless, none of this was my mother's business; she was still on my hit list.

I was loading our teacups into the dishwasher after an hour of conversation about Sheila's in-laws when my mother snuck up behind me. I must have been in my own world because I squeezed the dishwashing detergent so hard that it slipped right out of my hand.

"Oh!" She stepped back as we both gasped, acknowledging how unfortunately awkward we were around each other. "I'm sorry."

"It's fine." I bent down to grab the bottle. "I didn't see you coming."

"Can I help?" she asked hopefully.

"No, Mom. I've got it."

"All right." She searched for another way in. "And how is work? Is it going well?"

"Of course it is, Mom." Suddenly I was captivated by the need to hand scrub every last bit of tea leaf off of my Williams-Sonoma copper pot. "I've got everything under control."

"Of course you do, Monica. But you do seem to be under some pressure. Is it because of my visit?"

"No, Mom." I propped my hands on the sink and craned my neck toward her. "You should do whatever suits you. It's fine."

"This is about that television show. I am ready to sell the house myself... But I...I feel that we should talk about it."

"Mom, that's the last thing I want to talk about right now." I wiped the hair from my eyes with the back of my hand.

"But Monica, *beti,* I'm..."

"I've got to go out for a run." I snapped off my gloves and made my way out of the kitchen. "I haven't had any exercise all week. I'm sure you can entertain yourself."

At that point, even the prospect of exercise was better

than the possibility of having a heart-to-heart over her apologizing for getting me mixed up in that TV show in the first place. What she did was insensitive, but what I did was my own fault. Too much was going on, and the situation with my mother was only one small part of it. Besides, whatever she had to say, I really didn't want to hear.

If Beverly Hills is plagued with ridiculous housing prices, cultural vulgarity and too much focus on the bigger-better-deal, then Marina Del Rey also has its fair share of problems. Like the confusing layout, the plethora of family-style chain restaurants, and way too many liver-spotted retirees looking for the best early-bird dinner and a place to dock their boats, for example. But it also boasts one of the loveliest brunches in Los Angeles, namely, at the Ritz-Carlton overlooking the water. You toss your keys at the giddy valets, stroll past the grand lobby and through the sumptuous, wood-paneled lounge, and into the breakfast piazza, where a maitre'd is always really convincingly happy to see you. There are white tablecloths, French-pressed coffees, and various types of caviar and champagne just to amuse you while you work up the energy required to tour the buffets. My usual tactic is not to eat for a good twenty-four hours beforehand, in order to prepare for the smoothie, sushi and omelette bars, the tables full of meats and cheeses, and the massive central display of at least fifteen different types of dessert arranged like a protective moat around their three-tiered chocolate fountain. Leave it to my mother to ruin even my most reliable pick-me-up.

Normally, I cannot help but leave that place feeling better about my life. But normally, I'm not flanked by my spaced-out fiancé and my interfering mother, seated across from my bubbly cousin, her spineless husband and both sets of their supremely annoying parents. *M-more m-mimosas, anyone?*

"I have told my Monica that when she and Raj have their first child, that is when I will move back here to Los Angeles to be closer to them." My mother prattled on, gesturing with her fork while the rest of the table nodded, and I shoved my mouth full of eggs Florentine. "Although I will so miss London in the springtime. But then how will the kids manage a child without some help? *Hai key nah,* Renu?"

My mother was convinced that everyone was dying to hear all about the fascinating new friends she'd made in London, you see. But I knew that Josh's parents, while they had their faults, were far too polite, and impressed by what they perceived as her globetrotting lifestyle to interrupt.

"Absolutely," Sheila's mother assented, while the waiters refilled our coffee cups, lest we sprain something trying to lift the French presses all of three inches. "The kids will always need our input. Even if they don't see it now."

And with that, she winked at Sheila in a way that was clearly intended for everyone to witness. I assumed that Sheila suggested the Ritz-Carlton for brunch because it's neutral territory, rather than someone's house. Plus, she knew it was the only suggestion that might actually get me out in public. By the time I had inhaled the last bits of my first plateful of food, I was almost convinced that this could go smoothly. *Stupid, stupid girl.*

"What was that?" Karen asked Renu, helpfully.

"Karen." Her husband tried in vain to warn her off.

"What?" She was indignant. "It's my grandchild, too. And if you're not going to speak up for Josh's side of the family, then I have to make sure that *someone* does."

Call me old-fashioned, but I have always believed that certain ground rules for life are both universal and sacred. Among the most obvious are:

(1) That future contact or even recognition on the street are neither required nor expected after a one-night stand

(2) That what we do in Vegas does not stay in Vegas; in fact, it usually winds up on the Internet, and

(3) That Saturday morning brunch is not the time for discussions of anything more serious than the latest news of an engagement of a friend of a friend of a friend.

Apparently, no one in my family had gotten the memo.

"There is no *grandchild!*" Sheila slammed her palm down onto the table.

Raj dropped his cheese-schmeared cracker, Josh's mouth fell open, and I had stopped midchew.

"Look—" Sheila held the floor "—the grandchild isn't even born yet. There are a lot of things that Joshua and I did not discuss before we got married. And we should have. I know that now. But we are still the only two people in this marriage. We're gonna make these decisions now, and figure out what's right for us, as a couple. We're not interested in the input of anyone else…even our parents…from *either* side."

I swallowed and glanced to Raj, who indicated with a shrug that he didn't know what we should do. Renu seemed to be seeing her daughter for the very first time. Karen folded her napkin across her plate, folded her hands across her lap, and made it clear with her posture how displeased she was with the entire exchange. Sheila looked to her husband, who simply sank deeper into his chair.

After about ten more seconds of the most painful silence, Sheila stood up and stormed off. I would have run after her, but I had had too many mimosas at that point to get enough speed to catch up. Instead, I smiled sloppily at Raj, who cleared his throat and thrust his neck forward like he expected me to intervene.

And he was right. If I wasn't going to stand up for Sheila when she couldn't stand up for herself, who would? But then I realized something….

"What is wrong with you?" I accused Josh, a little too loudly. "Why can't you ever support your wife?"

"Monica, this is between us." He blinked, but insisted.

"Umm…no…since it has ruined more than one of my meals at this point I think it's between all of us. And besides, welcome to an Indian family. It has always been between all of us."

"Okay," he countered, seeming almost as surprised as he was embittered, "if my business is your business, then I guess it works both ways, *cousin-in-law*. So tell me—why hasn't your fiancé even set a date yet for your wedding?"

"That has nothing to do with anything," I replied, while my mother shook her head helplessly at Renu Auntie, who was hunched over, rubbing her temples.

"Oh, I think it has plenty to do with why you are so focused on *our* marriage."

What the hell was he talking about? How did this become about me and Raj? And how could Josh be this quick with a comeback at me while he routinely let his wife flail around alone?

"Okay," I asked, "so suddenly being married for five minutes gives you a Ph.D. in relationships?"

"Actually," Raj spoke up, taking my hand in his, "I was planning on waiting until the dessert course, but…"

But I couldn't let it go. "Raj! Not now, please! Don't you see what you're doing, Josh? You're acting like a boyfriend, instead of a husband. Right or wrong, justified or not, she's not supposed to ever be the only one in her corner anymore now that she's married. That's the whole point, isn't it? The rest is window dressing. And I don't know much about marriage, but I do know that these resentments don't disappear, Josh. They fester and explode."

More resonant than the dead air between us on the way home from brunch was the fact that Raj didn't even try to fiddle with the radio setting. And what my mother lacked in sympathy toward her daughter, she apparently made up for in sensitivity to the mood of her son-in-law-not-necessarily-to-be. On the pretext of taking a nap, she headed straight for her room the moment we got home. Unfortunately, I was totally sober by that point, which meant I couldn't deny that something was wrong with Raj. So I waited until I heard my mother's bedroom door shut, and then went over to Raj, who was thumbing through a copy of *Pucker,* which he knew I hid under the ottoman in my den.

"Since when are you interested in that celebrity stuff?" I asked, kicking off my shoes and hopping up beside him on the sofa.

He tossed the magazine onto the ottoman before looking back and examining me, exhausted.

"What is it?" I asked. "What's wrong?"

"Shouldn't I be asking you that?" He ran a handful of fingers through his hair, and then back down over his face.

"Honey, so I got a little sloppy at brunch and snapped—"

"I don't care about that. I know you by now." He shook his head at nothing in particular. "I was trying to set a date for our wedding…and you ignored it completely, Monica. Tell me, how am I supposed to feel about that?"

"I…" I floundered. "I didn't mean anything by it. I just didn't think it was tactful to do it in the middle of Sheila's marital problems."

"Don't do that. Don't try to distract me like that. I deserve better."

I didn't know what to say.

"There's something else going on here." Raj started wringing his hands. "I thought we were on good terms, you and I. I thought we were back on track, but you're not behaving normally these past few days. Please tell me that something else is wrong, because otherwise I'll have to assume you weren't excited to set a date because you aren't really interested in *us* anymore—"

"I'm sorry. You're right," I cut him off, but to reach out, to try to bring him back to me. "It's something else. It's not about us."

"Is it your mother?"

I couldn't lie. Not entirely, at least.

"It's not just her. Mainly, I think it's Stefanie."

Judging from the look on his face, he had no idea what I was talking about.

"My coworker," I elaborated, leaning back and pulling my feet onto the couch so that I was facing him.

"The one that quit?"

"The one that I got fired."

Another blank stare.

"Raj, I need to help get her job back."

"But she quit, you said." He visibly relaxed, pulling my feet onto his lap and leaning against the opposite arm of the couch.

"She quit because she had to." I got more animated,

"Because I messed up and accidentally revealed that she was having an affair with our boss."

"But why do you care?" He smiled, as if I'd told a joke.

"What do you mean, *why do I care?*" I took my feet back.

"If she's gone, then doesn't this mean that you have a better shot at senior associate?" He stuck his neck out, as if I was missing the obvious.

"So you think I should gain from the fact that I got her fired? Do you really think I'm that much of a jerk?"

"No, baby." He gave me a wide smile and began massaging my knee. "You're a shark. And that's part of what I love about you."

For a shark, I should have had a better response than to just sit there dumbfounded.

"I just mean that you get what you want by any means necessary," he added, as if this clarification might have helped the way I felt about his opinion of me.

"What does that mean?" I took my knee back.

"Nothing, Monica," he said, rolling his eyes. "It doesn't mean anything."

"You think I'm cold."

"Not cold, no. I think you do what needs to be done."

"Like get someone fired even though they're good at their job?" I stopped and then made a realization that forced me to stand up. "Oh my god, do you think I got her fired *on purpose?*"

"That is not what I said." He stood up to face me. "It's that I don't see why you should care what happens to this woman. You said she was terrible to you for a long time. Maybe she got what she deserved."

"But this isn't about her. It's about us." Suddenly I felt as if I was all alone in my corner again, boxing gloves and all. "After knowing me for so long, how could you possibly imagine that I would do something like this on purpose? Or that I would be able to live with it even if it was an accident?"

"Monica." He reached out.

But this time I wasn't drunk enough to think that I could cut him off—I was sober and angry enough to know that I *had to.*

"Raj, I don't think I can be around you right now."

"What?" He pulled back. "Monica…"

I stood up and crossed my arms.

"You're *serious?* This is unbelievable. You actually think we're gonna *break up* over this?"

Actually, that wasn't what I was going to say. What I wanted was to be alone. To work things out on my own. But now that I could sense he was leaning more toward walking away than toward making it work, something changed. I wasn't proud of it, but I knew that I couldn't give an inch. So rather than replying, I stood firm.

"Monica if you want to end this engagement," he paused, "then at the very least you should be woman enough not to hide behind some stupid excuse."

And then he walked unceremoniously out my door.

twenty-two

INDIAN MYTHOLOGY IS CHOCK-FULL OF STORIES ABOUT women who didn't need boxing gloves—bejeweled or otherwise—to do their damage. In fact, in the case of the Vishkanyas (loosely translated as poisonous women) the only weapon they needed was themselves. The story goes that hundreds of years ago, the kings of various Indian princely states recognized the power of seduction as the ultimate weapon, especially when it came to outwitting their warrior adversaries. In order to make use of this knowledge, kings made a habit of kidnapping the daughters of beautiful peasants and rearing them in their harems. From the earliest age, these girls were fed nonlethal but increasing doses of poison on a daily basis. And by the time they had grown into beguiling young women, they were virtually immune to the powers of the arsenic that was coursing through their veins. When an enemy captain was known to have set up camp nearby in preparation for an impending attack, the king simply dispatched a Vishkanya disguised as a local prostitute to infiltrate the camp, seduce the captain and lure him toward her kiss of death.

Poetic, no?

Growing up, I always took this as a straightforward, chauvinistic, cautionary tale, warning men to be weary of the hypnotic powers of a beautiful woman. But was that really the moral of the story? Is it that women cannot be trusted? Is it that men cannot be without weakness? Or is something more complicated than that? Because if you take it just one step beyond the poor warrior who dies for a kiss, you are left with the image of a beautiful young woman who will surely be killed for her treason by his guards mere moments later.

So maybe the point isn't that men should be wary of women with inviting lips. Maybe Raj should have known better than to let me blind him with a brand-new bra and reign him in for the emotional kill. Maybe the flare of his nostrils wasn't directed entirely at me because he was really just angry that he let himself be lured back into my web. Or maybe, the point is that any man who thinks himself beyond reproach should fear what temptation might reveal to him about himself. And that an otherwise good woman, who decides she is looking for trouble, is ultimately likely to wreak far more havoc on herself than on anyone else.

★ ★ ★

They say that the older you get the better you know yourself. But if that were true, then unlike a jilted teenager, I would have been smart enough to have myself chained to the radiator, instead of letting loose and playing with fire that night. Experience had taught me by now that I always end up getting burned.

Always.

When I realized that Raj was gone, it was a little bit too much for me to take. Should I wait for him to come back, or should I go after him? If and when I caught up to him, should I explain myself or wait for an apology? Did I really even want him to come back, or did I just *want to want him* to come back?

I figured that Sheila might have the answer to that question. But I knew she had problems of her own. And even if she wanted to give me a glimpse into the reality of my own psyche, I really didn't want to hear it. Not that night.

So I called Cassie instead.

Or more accurately…after twenty minutes of pacing my apartment and talking to myself while biting my fingernails…followed by a long shower during which I nearly scrubbed all of the hair off of my own head…followed by the realization that staying in the apartment that evening would necessitate engaging my mother in conversation at some point…I called Cassie.

"What are you doing?" I asked, chewing on the edge of my lip.

"Hello to you, too," she answered lazily.

"Dude, I'm…I need to do something tonight." I knew I sounded like I was about to have a panic attack. "I need to get out of my apartment. What are you doing?"

"I was having a cup of tea, actually," she said. "It's white pomegranate. I just love it."

"What? Yeah, that's great, Cassie…"

"It's really very calming," she continued. "And you sound like you could use some."

"Fascinating. Listen, I meant what are you doing *tonight?*"

"What's wrong?"

"Nothing. I don't want to talk about it. I just need to go out. Now."

I blame George Michael. I don't know if it's the silky voice, the permanent tan, or the lingering hint of a carefree-1980s feather in his hair, but George Michael songs always make me feel invincible. And everybody knows that the notion of one's own invincibility is best left in high school. Along with dry-humping and wine-in-a-box. But they were playing "Fastlove" on the speakers in the bathroom of The Skybar that night, so on some level, they were setting me up.

Who are *they?* I don't know. Try to keep up.

So what if I was wearing a backless, sequined top that also introduced anyone who was interested to my navel? My fiancé had stormed out of my apartment mere hours earlier without mustering up so much as an elevated tone. What was I supposed to do: take up needlepoint?

Yes, I said sequined. Deal with it. Unlike today's college girls, at least I had the decency not to try to resurrect leg-warmers.

"You look hot tonight!" Cassie told me before swiveling around to check out the reflection of her nonexistent butt in the mirror. "Whatever it is that's pissed you off, I'm glad."

"It's Raj," I said, unscrewing my lipgloss and yanking out the wand. "I think it's over."

"What?" She stopped.

"I don't want to talk about it now." I puckered.

"But Monica…"

"If you make me talk about him, then I'll make you talk about Jonathan," I threatened, waving my wand at her. "So do you want to fight me, or do you want to have fun?"

"Masala magic?" She smirked, referring to her belief that two Indian women on the prowl possess special powers which no mere mortal can resist. As if we were some sort of Sexual Power Rangers.

I laughed. Two tall women emerged from the stalls, checked themselves in the mirror, and then walked out without washing their hands.

"*Ieeeewww.*" I shook my head. "They didn't even run some water over their hands!"

"Maybe they were just snorting, not squatting," she offered, powdering under her eyes.

"Well, in the scheme of things, I guess that's better." I slipped off my ring and dropped it into my purse before clasping it shut.

"The world is a cesspool," she observed as nonchalantly as someone pulling out their dentures.

"So then," I said, pleased at the idea of mocking Raj at a moment like that, "fancy a dip?"

"Sorry I'm late." Some guy that reminded me of the lead singer of Midnight Oil slipped an arm around my shoulder and gazed out over the same view of West Hollywood that I had been admiring.

He wore a suit jacket over a tank top and a pair of jeans, and his sunglasses, which were rimmed entirely in silver, sat atop the shiniest bald head I had ever seen. He was oddly intriguing, much like a naughty version of Mr. Clean. Yet his lack of body fat had rendered him so lean that I probably could have snapped him in half and used him for kindling. Just in case you were wondering. Despite all of this, since it was The Skybar, and since Cassie was already engrossed in conversation with a wall of a man a few feet away, I decided to play along.

"Took you look enough!" I said, exasperatedly. "And where the hell is my vodka and cranberry?"

"I forgot!" He smiled and played up the part of the put-upon boyfriend. "I'm sorry! Damn, woman!"

"Well, go get it then!" I folded my arms across my chest and pulled a pouty expression.

"Fine!" he said, grinning while he pulled away and turned in the direction of the bar. "We've only been together for a year and already with the nag-nag-nagging!"

"You've always said I was worth the trouble," I insisted.

"That's true, gorgeous." He paused and kissed the back of my hand before bouncing dutifully off in search of my libation. "I'll be right back."

Men are so easy.

Cassie wrinkled her brow as if to ask *what's going on with you and the pirate, over there?*

I shrugged, winked and then pivoted to scan the bar. I thought I sensed someone staring at me, but before I could find any reason to be gone when my pirate returned, he found his way back, vodka and cranberry in hand. Or, more accurately, beer in one hand and vodka and cranberry in the other. Weaving through the growing crowd had jostled him enough to spill some of my drink onto his hand. After handing me my drink, he then took the opportunity to lick it off.

…With a tongue roughly the length of my arm. And he looked me in the eye for the duration of the lick.

Sure, it was kind of sleazy. Still, it took me a second to shake the feeling that someone was singing "The Look of Love" directly into my ear.

In the fifteen minutes that followed I found out that not only did he have that tongue, but he also had a place with a hot tub on the beach in Malibu that I *was welcome to use any time.* He also had a thing for Latina women (which he assumed I was, being a typically lazy and culturally oblivious native Los Angeleno), and that he'd recently wrapped up a low-budget film that was being vetted for the Sundance Film Festival.

"It's called *Release,* and it's about inmates finding redemption internally," he said pridefully. "I play the leader of the Aryan Nation gang in prison who has the biggest change of heart."

"Of course you do," I said, stirring my swizel stick around the ice remaining in my glass.

"What do you mean?" he asked.

"Just that a girl never runs the risk of meeting the normal guy who plays a social worker on *Lifetime* at a club in L.A. She only meets the guy who plays the incarcerated Head of the Aryan Nation."

"So you've decided that I'm not normal." He raised an eyebrow without moving any of the rest of his face. Maybe it was the ability to do that which allowed men to age so much better than women.

I made a mental note to learn how to do that, before returning my attention to the pirate.

"Who says that normal is necessarily better?" I answered.

"I knew I married you for a reason," he said, slipping an arm around my waist in that intimate way that men do to force you to believe that your comfort zone includes them.

"So now we're married?" I laughed.

"We are for tonight."

"Then I'll have to admit that I've been cheating on you," I said.

"It's understandable. I was locked up for years. A woman has needs."

After a pause, we both cracked up. We were midgiggle

when his phone beeped. He paused to check the text. I considered mixing drinks to speed along my ascent. George Michael gave way to Gwen Stefani, who was singing about bananas, I think.

"Damn it. I gotta take care of this. My buddy's in line outside and I need to get him in. I'll be back, okay? Don't run off on me or anything."

"Geez! I run off with one mailman for one weekend in Cabo and I'm paying for it for the rest of my *life!*"

"Oh, I'm gonna have fun with you," he said, before walking off in the direction of the entrance, and taking his eyebrow with him.

And I thought I was going to let him have fun with me. At least a little bit. But then I saw who was lying on one of the platform beds spaced throughout the club just beyond where my pirate had been standing.

"So are you gonna kick me in the balls if I ask you to join me in bed?" Luke asked sheepishly.

"Not tonight, Luke." I plopped down beside him and leaned onto a mountain of pillows. "Tonight I'm not kicking anyone. I'm a bit *knackered,* as the British say."

"And was that scary-looking guy British?"

"Who, him? No. He's a pirate."

"A what?"

"At least in my mind he is. Don't ruin my fantasy," I slurred.

"Are you drunk?" he accused.

"Are you pushing forty in a leather jacket and a ponytail?" I shot back.

"Hey, I'm only 33," he defended then let out a sigh. "But I know I have to start thinking about letting go of the eighties. I'm just not ready yet."

"That's okay. I'm not drunk yet, either. But maybe we can help each other with the transition." I slurped at my drink before dropping it onto the tray of a perky waitress who had climbed into bed with us to take our order. "Can I get…umm…a glass of champagne?"

"Are we celebrating you learning to accept me and my ponytail?"

"Nope."

"Are we celebrating you finally forgiving me?"

"Nope." I was as resolute as a woman can be while she's lying on a bed in a bar and yanking at her skirt in hopes of getting it back to the vicinity of a PG-rating.

"Seriously though." He laughed. "Who was that guy?"

"He was my boyfriend. But we just broke up. You saw those silver sunglasses. It never would have worked."

"I'm sorry to hear that. And what does your…fiancé… think about it?"

"Oh, him?" In my haze I had forgotten that Luke knew I was engaged. "I don't know. It's sort of…off."

I hiccupped and was in danger of actually thinking about that fact when the waitress came back with our drinks.

"You know you really do have a beautiful smile. Beautiful teeth."

"That's a new one," I said.

"I'm a sucker for the details, I guess."

"Well then don't look at my nails, because I've bitten them down to the stubs."

"Better small and real than big and fake."

"Are we still talking about nails?" I whispered, gesturing with my chin at the well-endowed redhead who had draped herself across the next bed.

We were sharing a snicker at her expense when we were interrupted.

"So I leave you alone for a minute and now I find you in bed with another guy?" The pirate was back. And was trying to make light of the situation, since he probably couldn't figure out what was going on between myself and Luke.

Fueled by the vodka, the champagne and the altitude of the hills, I swung a leg over Luke's ankle and shrugged. "What can I say? A woman has needs. Right now I need to be with a man who has hair on his head. And then I see this guy, and his hair is almost as long as mine. There's something very hot about that."

"That's cold," the pirate said good-naturedly. "And after I stayed faithful to you even while I was locked up."

"I'll always love you for that, pirate guy."

"Pirate guy?" he asked.

"Never mind."

"You snooze, you loose, man," Luke chimed in playfully.

"Not necessarily," I said, propping myself up on my elbows when I spotted Cassie on her way over. "Have you met my friend Nina? She's a stewardess for Air-Mexico, and she's in town for two nights on a layover."

"Where have you been all my life?" he asked her, before taking her by the hand and leading her off to admire the pool.

"Is that true?" Luke asked. "Is that friend of yours a stewardess?"

"Shh," I told him. "Too much talking."

"I'm confused." He wrenched his gaze from my thigh back up to my eyes. "Are you single, or what?"

I took a deep breath, pulled my legs together, and mustered up what energy I had within me to address the reality. And it wasn't even a very deep breath, considering how tightly the straps of that shirt bisected my back, making it so that I had to choose between wearing it and actually taking a complete breath all evening. Being the class act that I was, I chose the shirt over the oxygen. Which may have had something to do with my behavior in the moments that followed. But you'll hear all about that soon enough.

This time, I blame Messieurs Moët & Chandon.

"Luke, I'm not in the mood to really get to know someone deeply tonight, all right?"

He laughed.

"What?"

"Nothing." He shook his head like I was adorable. "You just seem like such a nice girl…or…err…you know…a good girl. And then you say things like that and it seems like you have no idea how funny they seem coming out of your mouth."

Oh, puke. I always resented the way that men presumed my innocence.

"Have we not already established that appearances can be deceiving?" I charged.

"Good point. So what are we gonna do about it?"

Dear God, why was it that when you wanted someone to take you seriously, there were only pirates as far as the eye could see, but when you wanted a little anonymity men always insisted on getting to know you? It was the curse of the nice girl, I thought. God's way of reminding us that we are meant to be mothers one day and should think twice about doing whatever it is we were about to do.

And you know what the antidote to that sort of divine intervention is? Vodka with a champagne chaser.

"Why don't we try something new?" I had a flashback to Alex's screenplay and suddenly the words were ready to come spilling right out of my mouth.

"What did you have in mind?" Luke propped his head on his hand and gave me his full attention.

"Instead of telling me all about yourself, and where you grew up, and if you have a dog, and blah blah blah…." I flashed my most girlish smile. "Why don't you just *tell me more about my eyes?*"

"Okay, you're the best person ever," he said, beaming.

"I know."

A half hour and another champagne flute later, I wasn't feeling so badly about Raj. In fact, I wasn't feeling much of anything. Truth be told, I had kicked off my shoes, and was lying on my back next to Luke, looking up at the stars.

"And anyway, in my opinion reality TV isn't the plague

on society that it's made out to be. In fact, it's more like the mirror society is uncomfortable yet fascinated with having held up to its own bloated, puss-filled underbelly."

"You sure know how to romance a girl."

He rose up to hover above me. "I wasn't sure that I was allowed to romance you. What with you hating me and all…"

I was drunk enough where I would have been equally satisfied getting lucky as I would have been going right to sleep. Well, almost as satisfied. I was numb enough where I wasn't worried about bumping up against my feelings about Raj at any point that night. I was attracted enough to Luke to have noticed that he smelled like baby powder, that his camel-leather jacket brought out the flecks of gold in his eyes and that he wasn't looking away. But I still wasn't sure.

Then I noticed the redhead from before, glowering at us from her perch on a barstool nearby. So I reached around Luke's neck, weaved my fingers in to grab a tight hold, and literally yanked him down onto my face by his ponytail.

And there was nothing remotely *good girl* about it.

twenty-three

THE LOBBY OF THE MONDRIAN HOTEL, WHICH FEATURED THE entrance to The Skybar, was packed with the usual Saturday night mix of security-flanked celebs, Hollywood industry-types and college kids looking for trouble. Unless Luke and I had set ourselves on fire, nobody would have paid us any attention as we made arrangements and headed for a room. Still, we both felt the need to maintain our composure. At least until we stepped into the elevator.

I slammed him against the opaque glass wall with the weight of my body once the doors slid shut behind us, while Gnarls Barkley wailed overhead about losing his mind.

"Ouch!" Luke complained about the barely perceptible little nibble I took out of his lip.

"Take it like a man!" I ordered, giggling and going in for another bite.

I can only imagine that from the perspective of the security guards, watching the elevator security camera, I must have looked like a deranged midget-dominatrix attempting to climb on top of this strapping, panting man. And he acquiesced, wrapping his arms around me and kissing me with lips pulled taut in a smile.

God, I had forgotten how much fun it was to be carefree. I couldn't remember the last time that Raj and I had a night like this. The best part, I reminded myself as Luke and I stumbled down the hallway without breaking the kiss, was this brief period between giving yourself permission to do something like this, and having to deal with it later on.

He swept me up into his arms newlywed-style, and whisked me into the room. He grabbed a bottle of champagne from the minibar and treated the both of us to a mouthful. And then he dove into my cleavage like an Olympic swimmer, sending shivers up my spine and lots of heat everywhere else. Moments later he was rustling my hair into a veritable bee's nest of knots, but I couldn't have cared less. He lapped sloppily at my neck, swallowing some of my hair and getting a good taste of my chandelier earrings.

"Man," he said, "you're driving me crazy!"

And to be honest with you it felt a little bit like an accomplishment.

So, apparently women are easy, too.

And men are able to sprout multiple arms on call. I could've sworn there was a hand on my butt, another in my hair, a third on my breast and yet another one sliding up my thigh, which is probably why I didn't notice in time to stop him from getting to that spot. The one below my right ear that immediately sends my eyes to the back of my head and my self-control on a one-way trip to Mars.

"Wow!" I hunched over and tried to refrain from having an orgasm right then and there. "What's the rush? Let's… uh…umm…slow it down a little."

I took a deep breath and what I could only hope was a graceful step back. He was panting and looking at me like a confused and lipstick-covered bull who had been re-strained, midcharge. Seeing him like that I decided I wanted to have some fun with this. Simplicity was so hard to come by that I wanted to make this last. To seduce him. To make this movie scene a little more cinematic.

And what could be sexier than a striptease?

For once in my life I was going to be *that* girl. That effortlessly sexy, genuinely spontaneous girl. The one who took off after graduation with a backpack for parts unknown and returned a year later with a palpable calm, a permanent grin and a much wiser veneer. The one that jumps on the mechanical bull at a Western-theme bar without a moment's hesitation and leaves the crowds hooting and hollering for more. The one who knows what she wants and takes what she needs without a second thought. Just once I wanted to feel like the kind of woman who can actually pull off an impromptu striptease without blinding anyone with a pro-jectile button, failing to move to the beat of the music in the background, or snagging any zippers or straps on her stockings and tripping all over herself.

Wait a minute. I wasn't wearing any stockings. Beautiful! I turned up the volume on the wall stereo.

Luke dropped onto his elbows on the bed behind him, and started loosening his tie. I twisted and I turned, putting on a pretty good show of arousing myself. And the grin on his face only encouraged me.

Casting him a "who's a naughty boy" look over my shoulder, I reached back to unlace my shirt. I paused for a second before yanking it off, and waving it above my head like a sign of surrender. I even sent it flying over a lampshade, all the while keeping my girls covered with my other arm. And then I managed to unzip my skirt and suck in my belly long enough to have it drop to the ground in one elegant flourish.

Mentally, I high-fived myself. Physically, I acted as if this was just how suave I always was.

"Well," he said. "Happy Birthday to *me!*"

"Is it your birthday?"

"No, but I didn't know what else to say." He reached out and pulled me toward him by my hips. "It's not Christmas, either."

As he turned me around and kissed up the length of my back I closed my eyes long enough to keep myself in the moment. To savor the feeling of his hot breath, his deliberate hands, and his pillowy, gentle lips and teeth on my neck while he forced me to lean back into him, and Gnarls suggested that perhaps we were all crazy.

I noticed the view beyond the balcony that looked down

over the lounge of The Skybar…*as well as into the windows of other guestrooms!*

You know how they say that most managers rise to their level of incompetence within a company? Well, I think most good girls similarly rise to their line of personal craziness on a night of low self-esteem, and then try to claw their way across it. My line, as it turns out, was the one marked exhibitionism.

I stiffened. "Is that… Do we have *shades* for those windows?"

He laughed. "We made out at the bar and you violated me in the elevator, but now you're shy?"

I nodded, covering myself with his arms.

"Man, you're cute," he said, hopping off and grabbing a fluffy white robe. "But I guess you'll have to wear this and then make a mad dash for that hot tub on the balcony."

"But this is The Mondrian!" I said, while he wrapped me in the robe and pulled me close. "The place is crawling with paparazzi!"

"Paparazzi who are looking for celebrities," he clarified, brushing some hair from my neck, pulling off his shirt and then taking me by the hand. "Not for us."

"Hey," I said and dug in my heels before we made it to those sliding doors. "I'm not taking the chance that they see black hair and brown skin and mistake me for somebody else, and then my butt winds up on the cover of *Pucker*."

He tilted his head, grabbed the champagne off the dresser and then swept me off my feet again.

"It could happen," I said, apparently to myself.

★ ★ ★

It's a lot like telling someone that you've never been un-faithful. Even if it's the truth, nobody ever believes you when you say it. Especially because you said it. But still.

"I don't normally do this, you know. Go back to a hotel room with some strange man, I mean."

"Of course not." He yanked my foot out from under the water, propped it up against his chest and began massaging it. "Me, either."

"No, I'm serious," I said, grabbing the nearly empty and condensation-covered champagne magnum and tipping it back.

"Well, tonight you've been an absolute tigress," he com-plimented me with a sinister glint in his eye and all of the cockiness of a lion who had already cornered his prey. "And what makes me so special?"

This has always been a big part of my problem: I listen to people when they talk. So when someone tells me that they don't deserve me, I believe them. And when someone reminds me that I'm acting out of character, I reconsider. While the bubbly suds simultaneously made their way around my body and swished inside of my mouth I paused to think about it. I looked beyond his smiling face and steaming shoulders to the skyline of the City of Angels. I listened to the giggles of the women at the lounge below our sheltered perch. And I felt something I hadn't felt in quite a while. Sober.

Those twinkling lights seemed as close as they were far

away…and so did this man, who was right there for me, just like all the rest of the readily available excess in this town. I could have told myself that I was merely dabbling in the insanity, merely dipping my toe in a world full of divers. But the truth, I realized with a shudder, was that I was on the verge of submerging myself whole. How had I gotten myself into this hot tub just a few short hours after Raj left my apartment? Had Alex come back into my life to become a part of it, or just to shine a mirror on my own dissatisfaction? Who was this strange man rolling my big toe around on the tip of his tongue, and why had I felt the need to convince him that I was taking him seriously just to get through this night?

The truth was that I didn't want him. I didn't want any of this.

"Luke, wait," I began, taking my foot back, much to his disappointment. He looked like a child whose newest toy had been snatched away.

"What is it?" he asked.

I stared at him while the jets whirred in the background. This wasn't about Luke. And it wasn't even about my mother, or Raj, or Alex, or anyone else. It was about me. Me and how I felt about that redhead at the bar. Of course I was attracted to Luke, and of course I was hurting from what had happened that afternoon with Raj. But tonight was about reinforcing my status as a sexual alpha female. The worst part was that I wasn't even reacting against the redhead in particular. I was battling directly against my own weakened self-perception. I was battling myself.

Knowing that, I couldn't go forward with this. I may have been an ape deep down inside, just like Stefanie and every other woman in the world, but unlike them I was going to choose to walk away from it. To walk away from him. Right now.

"I'm sorry, Luke. I…I have to go." I hoisted myself out of the hot tub, and started toweling off. "I can't do this."

"Why not?" he asked, alone in the hot tub.

I avoided eye contact while I zipped up my skirt. "This is not me. I'm just not myself tonight…around you."

"Or *maybe,*" he coaxed, "this is exactly who you are. Did you ever consider that?"

"I just can't go through with this, okay?" I attempted to refasten my blouse while searching for my heels.

He climbed out of the hot tub, swaddled himself in a towel and came toward me. "Monica, you take yourself too seriously. And then when there's finally a glimmer of your real, playful self, you pull her away!"

"I'm sorry, Luke. I really am." I yanked my arm out of his grasp and turned for the door.

"No, you're *not!*" he yelled, and reached out to grab me again.

And what I saw in his eyes wasn't anger; it was hurt. But I just didn't have it in me to deal with it. I had enough of my own problems already.

So I unbolted and ripped the door open, launching myself into the hallway.

"Why are you so freakin' closed off?" he yelled at my back.

He might not have been poisoned, but I knew I had left a bad taste in his mouth. I tried my best to walk calmly down the hallway with its blue lights, nightclub color scheme and thumping music. I knew that I had been about to do something we both would have lived to regret. There was a chill in the air of that hotel hallway, but I didn't shiver. I just stood there calmly at the elevator, staring ahead even as the heat was still rising from my body.

twenty-four

ACCORDING TO THE ANCIENTS, SONS BELONG TO THEIR PARENTS, while daughters are only on loan. At the end of any traditional Hindu wedding the bride's family will collapse into mourning over what is seen as the literal loss of their girl. *May your new family treat you so well that you never think of us again,* they sing, in the hopes that they have entrusted her to the right hands. Off to a new home, with a new family, in a new village perhaps hundreds of miles away, a village girl of my grandmother's generation could expect to be renamed and to remain with her husband's family for the rest of her life. Depending on the day, the lighting and the position of the moon, the relationship between a mother and her daughter can resemble anything from prisoner and captor to sister and sister to master and marionette. But common among all these variations is the fact that no matter how far apart they may seem to have grown, mothers elementally understand their daughters.

When I was about four years old, my mother discovered me alone in our kitchen one afternoon. Surrounded by a mountain of shredded tissue, I stood tall, pulled in my chin and pierced her with a defiant stare.

Monica, she asked in a warning tone, *who made this mess?*

I don't know. I dared her to contradict me. Being knee-deep in the evidence proved nothing.

Monica. She stooped down to meet me at eye level. *You are going to have to clean up this mess.*

Your kitchen, I answered after the world's most intense staring contest, *YOU clean it.*

What was a mother to do? Raise her voice? Slap her child? Send her to her room?

She got down on her knees, dragged the wastebasket between us and placed one scrap of tissue into the bin. And then she waited. Soon enough, I was cleaning the rest on my own.

Thwappp! Thwappp! I awoke to the swift clapping of my mother's hands beside my head.

"Hello?" she said, as if I were on the other side of a door. "Hello, hello?"

"Mmmmmmhhhhhhhh," I moaned in protest, hoping it might scare the crazy lady away.

"Monica?" she asked as if she wasn't sure it was me. "Monica, what are you doing?"

Why do mothers do that? I forced my eyes open and twisted to face her for long enough to let out an extended yawn and another growl.

"I'm sleeping."

I must have looked like a zombie given the way that she recoiled. And I have to admit I found it more than a little bit satisfying. Snapping my tongue against the paper-dry roof of my mouth, I sat up and got a better look at myself in the massive mirror opposite my bed.

Which, as I had explained to my mother, *was only there so that I could get dressed while…standing on top of my bed.*

I really was a sight. My mascara had mushroomed into a cloud of gray around my eyes, made murkier by the globbed-together patches of once-creamy gold-and-glitter eye shadow. My hair, while pouffy on the top, curly in the back, and dried to straw at the tips, still managed a particularly aggressive showing of bed head. And my lipstick, I imagined, was still making its way through Luke's small intestine. Basically, it looked like a cosmetics bomb had gone off, and the focal point had been my face.

Somehow I had managed to swap the backless blouse from hell for a thin T-shirt, but had fallen asleep with my skirt still on. By now, of course, it was more like a belt around the middle of my belly and was threatening to cut off my air entirely.

Good times.

"You are obviously not sleeping. You are awake and you are talking to me. And darling, you shouldn't sleep in such thin shirts," she said. "Anybody can see your…your *parts*."

"Who's anyone, Mom? You're the only one here."

"But it is not decent at all to sleep like that." She tightened the belt on her housecoat.

"Mom, did you really wake me up to talk to me about the indecency of my breasts?"

"Don't say it like that," she winced. "It's vulgar."

I lay down and pulled the covers back over my face.

"I thought you were awake," she defended herself.

Sure, Mom. *And the only things inside my bedside table are a copy of the Mahabarat and a jar of multivitamins.*

"I don't want to talk right now, Mom. Can I please go back to sleep? Please?"

"Monica." Her voice was stern enough to make me think that perhaps after all these years she was finally getting ready to give me the sex talk. "Monica, I was not trying to listen yesterday, but I overheard your argument with Raj."

I pushed the covers down around my shoulders and let out a very long breath to indicate how little interest I had in where this thing was headed. She took one close look at the damage to my face and winced again: "Oh my God, Monica. Get that gunk off of your face. Here, I'll get you a tissue."

And in that instant when she reached out for the top drawer of my bedside table, I considered letting her go through with it. Feast your eyes on the contents, Mom! Body chocolate, flavored condoms, sexual dice and various lacy thongs sporting slogans like It's Not Gonna Lick *Itself!* She would have gone immediately blind and hopped the next mule, puddle-jumper or rowboat back to London.

But as much as I wanted her to leave, I didn't want to give her a massive coronary.

"Mom," I said, and held the drawer shut. "I don't need anything."

"Yes, *beti*. I am sure that you know what is right for you." She sat on the bed and looked down at her hands. "You don't need my advice. You never did."

"Mom, do we really have to…"

"Listen, Monica. I just want to give you my opinion. I know that you are an adult. Can I just give you my opinion? And you can do whatever you want with it?"

No matter what she had done, she always managed to make me feel like the guilty one. *Brava, Mother,* I thought, while I hung my head and awaited her advice.

"I know that when Daddy died, I could have…or I *should* have been stronger for you. And maybe you would have felt more secure at that time in your life. But you see, I have never felt that being emotional is a weakness. I always thought, even when you were a little girl, that if I showed my emotions, then my daughter would see how liberating it is. To let these things out so that they cannot control you."

I fingered the gunk out of the corners of my eyes. "Mom, I have no problem with the way that you live your life."

"Yes, you do, *beti*. But that's okay. All daughters judge their mothers. But the more you react against me, the better

I understand you," she explained, smiling warmly. "You are a very strong person, and you are your own person. You always have been. Yet Monica, you are not your own mother. I am. Please believe me when I tell you that sometimes it is good to soldier through. However, in the long term, if you keep your feelings inside, they do not disappear…they will emerge at some later time, in a way that you cannot control. Whatever it is with you and Raj, you should discuss it. You should *talk*."

"I understand that, Mom."

"Good, *beti*. Good." She rose to drop the shades before she headed for the door. "Now I will let you sleep all day, like a schoolchild, *na?*"

"So you want me to make it work with Raj." I turned on my side, wrapping myself in the comforter like a nasty, hungover, champagne-and-hint-of-regret-soaked pig-in-a-blanket.

"I don't remember saying that," she said, before closing the door behind her.

Any other day, the Santa Monica beachfront overlook on Ocean Avenue would have been invigorating. But that morning the combination of crisp air and orange light was only oppressive. I raised a hand to block the sun from my heavy, tired eyes. There was something about being surrounded by chipper joggers and power-dogwalkers that made me feel like a degenerate. It was possible, I thought, that I had suggested the location deliberately to chastise myself. It was also possible, I reasoned, that I had wanted a location conducive to my breaking into a dead sprint in the other direction in case Raj wasn't willing to accept my apology. No, neither I nor my vulgar breasts could have bared that.

I knew that I wasn't at my best that day, but I felt as if it just couldn't wait. I hadn't even been brave enough to call him; I just sent a text message laced with hidden meanings that only he would understand.

Me: Can we talk?

(Meaning: I'm an idiot with a hangover who is too ashamed of herself to call you right now. I fear that you will read my stupid behavior in my voice, and choose never to speak to me again. Also, I don't want to confuse the issue of my general stupidity with my particularly classy behavior last night. Nobody needs to know except me and God and the elevator-security-camera screeners at The Mondrian. Is there a convenient time for you to sit back and watch me grovel?)

Him: I don't know. Can we?

(Meaning: I am not correcting your grammar merely to imply that the few years I spent in England have made me more articulate. I am correcting your grammar to be snide. I'm aware that you are an idiot and I am glad that you realize it. In fact, you are such an idiot that I am not entirely convinced you are capable of a rational conversation with me. And even if you are, I'm not sure that I'm interested. But maybe if you grovel a little more through text messages, I'll consider it. Like, for example, if you admit in writing that you were wrong.)

Me: I'm sorry. I was wrong. But I think we need to talk. Maybe today?

(Meaning: I'm sorry. I was wrong. But I think we need to talk. Maybe today?)

Him: Where?

(Meaning: Your groveling pleases me, but your behavior was so atrocious that it has rendered you unworthy of the effort it would take for me to text you in full sentences. I am meeting you only on the condition that you understand you are terrible. Where?)

Me: Ocean Avenue overlook. In an hour.

(Meaning: Agreed.)

I leaned against the guardrail. Two power walkers with their SUV strollers and healthy complexions passed me by, while a homeless man came out of the public restroom, shook his fist at the sun and walked off, pushing his shopping cart. I still had no idea what I was going to say.

"Hey," Raj called to me as he came down the winding

dirt path. Even in his favorite jeans and that sweatshirt I had worn so many times, he could not have looked less recognizable. That was when I knew it might actually be over.

"Hi." I bit my lip, unsure of what else to say or do.

He leaned over the railing facing opposite me, both of us unsure how to greet each other. Moving backward on the spectrum of affection always feels so unnatural.

"So should I take the way that you look as an indication that you've been up all night crying your eyes out over me?" he asked wistfully.

Meaning: Please tell me that you've been crying your eyes out over me all night, because even though I know this isn't the ideal for either one of us, I'm not sure I'm ready to walk away.

"Raj." I swallowed, feeling my face get hot. "I…I'm not sure that we're in this for the right reasons anymore."

As I said it, it occurred to me how true it was. The thing that felt like it had changed the night before had actually been a long time coming. Despite how wonderful he was, and how good we had been for each other for all that time, this was the end of the road. I could see that he knew what I was thinking.

He looked back out over the water, and nodded. "Is there…someone else? Is it… Is it Alex?"

"No, Raj. No." I shook my head, gnawing at the inside of my lower lip. "It's that…I'm not the end of your story."

Meaning: You're not the end of my story.

"You know I always wondered if on some level we began just as a salve for your relationship with him," he stated, rather deliberately, not in the form of a question. "There was just a part of you that I never reached."

"But that part of me was not with Alex," I said. "Honestly, I don't think it has ever really been opened with anyone."

"I hope you can find someone to open it up to, Monica," he told me, while an in-line skater zoomed past.

It was strange to hear him say my name that way. Almost as if I had been demoted to a more formal circle of acquaintances. *Already?* But I knew he was doing it as much for my sake as for his own.

"Can I ask you something?" I said, after a while. "Inga. The umm…the redhead. Did anything ever happen with her?"

"No," he said quickly, and then thought about it. "She put it out there, while we were in London. But I never touched her. I just…I needed to know where we stood first."

He twirled the class ring on his finger, the way that men do when they're working on a serious thought. This might be the last time that I knew him that well. The intimacy was dissipating before my eyes, and the next time I saw him someone else would know him better than I did. Perhaps he was thinking about it, as well, because we seemed to be sitting in long, comforting silences between our thoughts.

My eyes were moist by the time I reached for the ring waiting inside my pocket. I didn't want to let it go. More because of the gravity of that gesture than because of anything else. We could fight and we could talk and we could make all sorts of proclamations. But until I gave him back that piece of himself—of us—it wasn't real.

"Then you're a better man than I am," I said, thinking about everything I had put him through.

Would I have stayed with someone who refused to wear my ring? Someone who laughed in my face at the idea of moving for my career? Someone who kissed another woman on national television and had an ex-girlfriend as a client? Probably not. Would Raj have been prepared to do his absolute best to make me feel safe and adored for the rest of my life? Probably so. Was there any chance that I was going to leave that overlook with that ring still on my person?

Absolutely not.

Because there are moments in a woman's life when she knows it can go either way. There is no right and there is no wrong; there is only the knowledge that she is what she is about to choose. She can feel her entire future shrink into the space of the decision that she is about to make. These are the tipping points on the karmic map of her life, and they are there to force her to admit what sort of person she is. A woman who can sleep at night, knowing that she has singlehandedly ruined someone's career? A woman who can see her adversaries in herself, but who refuses to be ruled by her baser instincts, even as she learns to accept that they will always be there? A woman who would rather be on her own than be with anyone for whom she wasn't willing to risk it all?

It was time. Forcing myself to look him in the eye, I held the ring out on an outstretched palm. He shifted his weight away from my hand, as if I were holding a tarantula.

"It's all right, Raj. This…this was never really mine."

He took it without looking at me.

"I'm sorry," I said. And I was.

"I'm not," he replied. Then he smiled at me as if we were still sweethearts, for what would, I knew, be the very last time.

twenty-five

"MORE WINE," I ORDERED CASSIE THROUGH THE CELL PHONE
as I burst through her door an hour later.

"I didn't give you any wine," she replied, before snapping
her cell phone shut and following me down her hallway.

"Fine, then." I dropped my jacket and ran both hands
over my face, having no patience for the time it would take
her to catch up. *"Wine!"*

"Coming up. Just let me get Phil out of my bed. He's
been pissing in it every night for a week for some reason."

Since it was a studio, her bed was front and center, and
the stench of cat pee was even worse than it should have
been. She ripped the purple duvet off her bed, sent the virtually hairless mongrel scurrying to the floor, and shoved
the sheets into her hamper. Why she had decided to rescue

that poor specimen from the shelter in the first place, I would never understand. *He may not be pretty, but he's got spunk,* she told me the first time I'd seen him. *And I appreciate his potential.*

Potential, my ass. Her apartment smelled like that homeless guy who had been shaking his fist at the sun.

"I'm cracking a window," I said, heading toward the sill.

"Bad cat!" she scolded over a shoulder, while the rail-thin Phil struggled to hack up a hairball.

She swiped two wineglasses from her cabinet and a half-empty bottle of red from her countertop.

"What's wrong with him, anyway?" I asked, looking for a somewhat sanitary place to sit.

Which was kind of like looking for a somewhat sophisticated way to pull out a wedgie.

"I don't know. I think he's just being a bitch to make my life hell. I woke up with his butt in my face this morning." She handed me a glass, took a sip of her own, and smacked her lips like it was a cold, satisfying beer. "So you really gave back the ring?"

"You say that like you're surprised. Do you really think I have that little class?"

"Monica, come on, everything is not a moral issue. It's not about class. It's…well…nobody ever gives back the ring. It's like, a rule or something. Compensation for the cost of your time."

"But I'm the reason we're over," I said, while Phil eyed me like I was what was making him sick.

"It's never that simple," she said, as if she had been engaged so many times.

"Look, I don't exactly know the rules of etiquette in a case like this. Or in a lot of other cases, either." I thought back to Luke's face as I darted from the hotel room the night before.

She lifted the magazine Phil was curled up on, forcing him off her desk. "Clearly, because there is no rule in favor of doing a striptease to a techno song for a stranger with a ponytail."

"Shut up." I dropped into an armchair, taking a heavy gulp and trying to think of ways to deflect her attention. "What happened with Long John Silver, anyway?"

"Nothing, really." She shrugged. "I didn't want to give him my number, so I took his."

"You gonna call him?"

"Probably not." She twirled the stem of her glass and then noticed Phil trying to nose his way into her closet. "Phil, No! Did I mention he pooped in a pair of my Ferragamos last week, too? Mommy's little angel is going to have to sleep in a shoebox if he doesn't learn where it is not *all right* to relieve himself! He must be depressed. I should Google Kitty Prozac."

I raised my eyebrows, gesturing with the wineglass that that wasn't a good enough explanation and that I needed a lot more wine.

"Don't look at me like that," she said, filling my glass to the rim. "It's not about Jonathan. *Hey! Damn it, Phil!*"

★ ★ ★

Impressively, my mother barely blinked at the news of her only daughter's newfound spinsterhood. I found her in her room when I got home.

I waved a hand before her eyes to make sure she hadn't had a spontaneous aneurism and gone catatonic in her chair.

"You have done what you think is right," she decided, resuming consciousness, folding a shawl over her arm and then plunging it into a travel bag.

"What's going on?" I sat on the bed.

"It is time for me to go back to London," she said, examining the contents of her open suitcase. "And you can take me to the airport tomorrow morning on your way to the office."

"Already?" I asked, surprised at my own reaction to the idea.

She paused, and softened. "Yes, *beti*. You don't need me. But please, check on Sheila. Marriage is not always as easy as it may seem from the outside."

And I did. From my cell phone in the car right after I delivered my mother to the airport the following morning.

"I'm sorry," I blurted out when Sheila answered the phone on the first ring. "I just want you to be happy."

"I know, babe. You were trying to protect your little cousin." She exhaled. "I understand."

"Yeah, but I shouldn't have attacked Josh like that. He is your husband, after all."

"Yes, that's true. But for what it's worth, maybe you're better off. Marriage isn't always all it's cracked up to be."

"Huh?"

"You don't think your mom called my mom right after you told her you broke up with Raj last night? Come on!"

"I was gonna tell you myself, you know."

"Monica, we should talk about this. Are you okay?"

"I will be." I glanced at the rearview mirror before merging onto the 405. "But I can't talk now. I have to get to work. In fact, I wanted to invite you and Josh over for dinner at my place. Josh is family and I don't want things to be awkward. How's Friday night?"

"I'll check with him and let you know later today."

"Be careful with that thing!" Jonathan shoved a briefcase between the closing elevator doors and then wedged himself in beside me. With a nod toward my latte, he said, "You could really hurt someone this time, slugger. And this suit is brand-new."

"Not funny," I complained, taking a large gulp and then shoving half of my cinnamon scone right into my mouth just to do my part in the fight against non-trans fats.

The beep of my cell phone indicated a message from Josh:

We would love to come to dinner on Friday. It will give me a chance to apologize. In fact, I'm going to bring along something that I think will be good for you. Olive branch extended...

I replied:

Olive branch accepted, cousin-in-law. Just bring dessert and we'll be a-o-k!

"Come on," Jonathan insisted. "There was coffee everywhere! It was like a WWE Women's Wrestling Championship, except with a lot less oil and kissing than when you and Stefanie used to wrestle in my imagination."

"Not on my first day back, Jonathan." I closed my eyes.

"C'mon! You know what they say, partner," he quipped. "If you can't laugh at yourself…"

"And how often do you laugh at yourself?" I snapped at him.

He shrugged. "For what it's worth, I know you didn't out Stefanie on purpose. Nobody who knows you would ever think that. You just need to really believe that for yourself."

"Since when are you so Zen?"

"I dated a yoga instructor once," he said. I could tell by his tone that this was meant to be sufficient evidence.

"Since we're not on the topic, what's up with you and Cassie?"

"Nothing. Why?" He got agitated. "Did she say something to you?"

"Oh, this is ridiculous," I said, stepping out of the elevator before him on our floor. "You need some sort of resolution."

"You're one to talk."

"Actually, I am," I whispered, looking from side to side. "I broke up with Raj yesterday. Officially."

"Wow."

"At least it's not being dragged out anymore. Clarity is valuable."

"Good perspective, slugger," he said, turning toward his office.

"Hey, listen." I had an idea. "What are you doing Friday night?"

I had decided that Sheila wasn't the only person who deserved an apology from me.

"What?" Luke answered on the fifth ring later that afternoon.

"Luke, hi." I chewed on my upper lip. "I just called to say that I'm sorry."

"All right," he was short. "Is that it?"

"Luke, please," I tried.

"Please what? You said you were sorry. I heard you."

"You're obviously still angry."

"Monica, I'm not angry. I'm done."

"It doesn't sound like it."

"What do you want from me?"

"I don't want some guy walking around Los Angeles hating me."

"Why shouldn't I stay angry at you?"

"Because I apologized."

"Yes, you apologized, but you're not really sorry. You're schizophrenic."

"I am not!" I was taken aback. "I am not schizophrenic. I was about to make a mistake.... We both were.... And I stopped it. I shouldn't have taken it that far, and I shouldn't have run out like that. It was childish, yes. But I'm not emotionally disturbed."

"Oh, no…not at all." His sarcasm came dripping through the phone. "Not you. You're perfectly stable."

"Luke." I stood up.

"You didn't avoid making a mistake, Monica." He continued, "You ran screaming because you couldn't handle that you were opening up."

"You're wrong."

"You're closed off," he concluded as matter-of-factly as if he had mentioned that he was allergic to mushrooms.

"Luke, I am sorry that you need to accuse me of these things to massage your ego, but I am not closed off."

"Prove it," he challenged.

"What? *How?*"

"I don't know. But if you really mean it, then prove it." He was so smug.

"You want me to prove to you that I feel nothing more than embarrassment when I think of you."

"Yes."

"Fine." I went calm, suddenly seeing the most obvious way to kill at least three birds with one stone. "Why don't you join me and my friends for dinner on Friday night?"

twenty-six

"APPLES AND BLUE CHEESE FOR THE SALAD?" CASSIE HOISTED herself up onto my counter and popped a few pecan-halves into her mouth that Friday night. "This doesn't look very Indian to me."

"You know I can't serve Indian food." I shooed her away from the pecans, handing her a Granny Smith and a peeler instead. "It'll never be as good as my mom's cooking."

"So?" She took a bite out of the apple.

"So...I have no problem serving mediocre French or Italian food, but I will not serve sub-par Indian food."

"Then why don't you learn how to make better Indian food?"

"I will...one day. Why don't you stop eating the things that you're supposed to be chopping up for the salad? What are you, pregnant?"

"No." She pouted, swinging her heels off the edge of my counter. "I'm nervous. I can't believe you invited Jonathan."

I stopped stirring to wave a ladle at her. "You two need to decide whether you're gonna kiss and make up or grow up and move on. No more games. No more wasting time. Stop messing around."

"But…"

"Stop it."

"Well."

"Cut it out."

"Monica, I—"

"Don't make me force everybody to play Seven Minutes In Heaven just to get you two alone together!"

"I miss that game," she said wistfully.

"This is not for fun, Cassie. We all need to get things out in the open and act like adults," I ordered, wondering why I had chosen to step into my party clothes before finishing up with the cooking.

"You're mean." She snatched another pecan.

"And you're tall." I skimmed the recipe for my entrée one more time, to make sure I hadn't left anything out.

"So?" she asked.

"So, that makes you a mutant among Indian women. And it also makes you useful in the kitchen because you can get me another boullion cube from the top cupboard without my having to climb up onto the countertop in my dress."

I was breathing heavily onto one of the soup spoons, so that I could shine it on my apron, when the doorbell rang a little while later. I lined the spoon up with the fork, grabbed a matchbox from my pocket, and lit the five votives positioned down the middle of what I had to admit was an impeccably laid table. After a final once-over, I yanked off my apron and swiveled in the direction of the door, shoving the apron into the closet.

"I don't remember you having such a *domestic* side to you" came a voice from the other end of my hallway that stopped me in my tracks.

"Alex?" I almost whispered.

"And dessert, too!" Josh barreled past him to thrust a cake box at me before heading toward my dining room. "I brought wine. See? Two presents!"

I gritted my teeth and headed for the kitchen.

"Why don't I help you with that?" Alex appeared behind me. "You know you always leave the cork in the bottle."

I didn't like the look in his eyes. Not one bit.

"It's been a long time since you've seen me open a bottle of wine," I said, yanking the cork out in one clean gesture, and then yelling to Cassie, "Cassie, can you please set another place at the table?"

"True, Monica. But people don't change that much," Alex said.

I gently shooed him away from the oven door. "What are you doing here?"

"Is that any way to talk to a dinner guest?" he asked my

behind as I leaned down to check on the chicken in the oven. And to ponder what it might be like to stick my head in.

Inside the oven, not the chicken. Try to keep up.

"Josh told me that you and Raj ended your engagement…and it got me thinking."

Before I could respond, or vomit, or fake unconsciousness, the doorbell rang again. I bolted upright, slamming the oven door shut. *Oh crap. Luke and Alex and me and Cassie and Jonathan and Josh and Sheila musing about the state of the economy over chocolate cake? What could possibly go wrong?*

I was pulling off my oven mitts when I heard Sheila's voice booming through the apartment. Her signaling was about as subtle as a train wreck.

"Oh, hello! You must be Luke!" she bellowed. "It's nice to meet you! And you brought a bottle of wine, too! Well, how thoughtful! What is that, red wine? Is it a cabernet or a merlot? Really?"

"Luke," I called, swooping down the hallway with a glare in Sheila's direction to rescue the confused man who didn't understand why my cousin was trying to deny him entry. "Come in, come in! We've uh…got a full house here, tonight. But I'm glad you could make it."

"Hey, man." Alex offered the first firm, eye-contact-intensive handshake of the evening. "Good to meet you. I'm Alex. Can I take that bottle of wine off your hands?"

His voice must have dropped three octaves. And to drive the point home, he laid a hand on my waist before swinging nonchalantly toward the kitchen. "I got it, babe. I know where you left the corkscrew."

Luke replied with a short, upward nod that men have been using to acknowledge each other for centuries. The kind that says everything and nothing at once.

"Ah-huh-huh-huh" was all the awkward banter I could manage.

"Hey, people," Jonathan cut his wobbly salutation short, having wandered in just behind Luke.

He took one look at Luke, nodded in Cassie's direction, and then threw his coat over a chair with a satisfied and inebriated flourish.

"Awesome," he said. "Soooo, anybody need a stiff drink? No? Just me?"

"Um, Luke," I began. "This is my cousin Sheila and her husband Josh, and Cassie and Jonathan from work, and well…you already met my friend Alex…"

"Friend?" Jonathan guffawed, while blowing into my martini shaker, as if it might be filled with dust.

"Are you drunk?" Cassie came up to my wet bar and accused Jonathan, while Sheila and Josh stared nervously at one another.

"Are you *frigid?*" he shot back, loosening his tie.

"Idiot," she mumbled, before heading back toward the kitchen.

"Tease!" Jonathan called after her.

"Alex!" I said, way too cheerfully. "It's time to bring out the salads. And why doesn't everyone, um…er…have a seat?"

"You invited that guy from the TV show to dinner?" Alex's nostrils were flaring when I got into the kitchen.

"What's with the attitude?" I asked, lifting up the tray of mushroom soup, and whisking them out of the room…

…and almost slamming into Luke, who also suddenly seemed to have developed the need to make himself useful.

"Can I get that?" He took the tray from my hands. "It seemed like your cousin and her husband needed a minute alone, so I thought I'd come hang out in here."

Two men, a hot kitchen, a lot of wine… I think I had a dream like this once. Although I couldn't be sure which one of them would be feeding me strawberries, and which one would be dipping me gingerly into the massive vat of chocolate fondue.

"Thanks, Luke." I slipped on my oven mitts, reminding myself that this was not the time for my imagination to be running wild. "I'll bring out the chicken and we'll get this party started."

"You don't look so good, Sheila," Cassie was saying while I ladled chicken onto everyone's plates.

"Oh, I'm a little distracted. My husband here thinks we should give the baby a Hebrew first name and an Indian middle name, but I think it should be the opposite."

"It's just another one of the many things we should have talked about before we got married." Josh lifted her hand from her belly to kiss it. "But at least we're working through it all now…just the two of us."

I couldn't resist a smile in Alex's direction. Back in college he had always said that he loved my grandmother's name so much that he would gladly have swapped it for the promise of an annual family trip to Italy. He must have been thinking the same thing, because our eyes met when I looked up.

"So, you guys dated in college, huh?" Luke slopped some spinach onto his plate rather abruptly. "Jonathan mentioned it didn't end very well."

"Jonathan, I can't believe you're gossiping like that!" Cassie admonished.

"You don't tell me what to do," he slurred in her direction, while chomping on an olive.

"Honey, don't you think maybe you're overdoing it with those peppers?" Josh asked Sheila.

"Not at all," she replied, before dropping her fork with a clatter and palming her belly. "Seriously, though. Back me up here, ladies. Don't you think I'm justified, Cassie? Monica?"

"So Monica's opinion is relevant, but mine isn't." Jonathan burped.

Cassie shoved a hunk of bread in his direction with a glare that apparently amused him into momentary silence.

"Well, I can see both sides," I began carefully. "I will say that it's gonna be easier for your child to lose out on the Indian part of its heritage in this country than it will be to lose out on the other part…just by virtue of the lack of Indian visibility in the popular media and landscape…as opposed to the Jewish synagogues on practically every street corner in Beverly Hills. So maybe an Indian first name wouldn't seem so unfair. But then again…"

"Seriously, Sheila. Maybe you should take it easy on those peppers," Josh urged.

"I'm *fine*," she insisted. "And don't cut Monica off!"

"You don't have to finish it just for her sake!" Josh pushed. "It's not like she's married and cooks all the time or anything. She's not gonna take it that personally."

"So now single women can't cook?" Cassie sprang to my defense, waving her wineglass at him.

Jonathan grinned, satisfied that her irritation had really been inspired by him.

"Oh…I'm sure that's not what he meant." I tried to keep the peace. "More chicken, anyone?"

"Don't tell me what I meant," Josh said, rendering the table silent.

Until…

"When have you even managed not to burn a *Pop-Tart?*" Jonathan snapped.

"Insults will not win me back." Cassie stood up and headed for the bathroom.

"Then what will?" he mumbled, but she didn't hear him.

"Josh…" Sheila said.

"No, Sheila. If she can speak her mind while we're eating, just because we're *family,* then so can I! It goes both ways!" Josh lifted his napkin from his lap and dropped it onto his plate.

"I already apologized for what happened at brunch!" I said.

"You're doing a lot of apologizing these days." Luke was snide.

"How exactly did you two manage to…er…reconnect?" Alex hacked into his chicken and shoved a heaping spoonful into his mouth. "After he humiliated you on national television, I mean."

"Los Angeles is a small town." Luke took a massive mouthful of his own, before starting to gag on an oversize pepper.

It might not have been Tandoori, but at least it was spicy.

"What's the matter, buddy?" Alex sneered, lifting a similar pepper off his own plate and chomping proudly into the middle. "Can't handle the heat?"

"Excuse me." Sheila stood up and started to wobble toward the bathroom. "I think I'll go powder my nose."

Jonathan dropped an armful of dinner plates into my sink rather theatrically: "Are you going to do something about the situation in the dining room?"

I was hovering over the cake, dropping raspberries onto each plate.

"Monica!" He practically stomped to get my attention. "Are you listening to me? Josh went after Sheila to make sure she didn't fall into the toilet bowl, so now it's just Alex and Luke growling at each other. The tension's so thick it sobered me up."

"Are you gonna do something about the situation with Cassie?" I raised an eyebrow, while drizzling a little too much powdered sugar over the raspberries.

"What can I do? She obviously hates me."

"Yeah," I agreed. "Because women always get that worked up over men they don't give a damn about. Kind of like how stripclub owners with names like Bruno always marry for love."

"I wonder where Bruno is these days." He smiled to himself. "I should look him up."

"Get out of my kitchen," I said, putting on the coffee. "The sooner we all eat this damn cake, the sooner I can kick you all out and move on with my life."

"What's Luke doing here, anyway?" He sprayed whipped cream down the length of his finger, and then licked it off.

"Do you have to be so unsanitary?"

"I think you know that I do." He faked a bashful expression.

"Long story." I counted out the teaspoons. "I kind of almost slept with him this weekend, and then I ran out, and then I called to make amends and he wouldn't accept the apology, so I invited him here as a peace offering. Sort of."

"Almost?"

"What?"

"*Almost* slept with him? What does that mean? I know what it means to me, but I'm pretty sure it doesn't mean the same thing to a nice Indian girl like you."

"It means I mauled him in an elevator, did a striptease in a hotel room, made out with him in a hot tub and then ran away. You know, high school stuff."

"What high school did you go to? All of your old boy-friends must still be blue from the neck down."

"Shut up." I smirked.

"I take it back! You're a bad Indian girl. *A bad, bad Indian girl!*"

"Down boy." I quelched that hungry look in his eyes before sending him on his way with a towel snap to the butt. "Or better yet, *out!*"

"Monica?" he yelled a few seconds later from the vicinity of the front door. "Monica!"

"What now? No, I am not mediating between you and Cassie from opposite sides of my bedroom door. Everybody needs to grow up and stop hiding and take care of themselves!"

"Um…there's someone here you're gonna want to see!" He sounded as if he was trying hard to remain calm.

Which was odd, since I hadn't even heard the ringing of the doorbell.

twenty-seven

"YOU GOTTA HIDE ME!" A FIGURE IN A PURPLE TRACKSUIT bolted toward me, hunched over as if a hail of gunfire was going off overhead.

And they might not have had guns, but the avalanche of flashes that proceeded to flood through my bay windows nearly blinded me.

"Goddamn paparazzi!" she moaned, before yanking off a bobbed, blond wig, dark sunglasses and peeling off a prosthetic nose.

It was Lydia. In my living room. With no explanation and no idea what she had walked into.

"It's like something out of *Alien!*" Jonathan commented, to nobody's amusement.

"Don't just stand there, Jonathan! Make yourself useful

and go and close the damn shades! I'm not paying you for nothing!"

"Actually, Lydia," I said, stepping forward, "you aren't paying us at all…remember? We're off your case. You've reconciled with Cameron."

"Well, it looks like I'm hiring you again." She ran her fingers through her hair, and picked at the last of the faux-skin lingering on her nose. "We need your help tonight."

"Paparazzi scum!" Cassie complained while helping Jonathan shut the shades, and then let out a giggle. "I've always wanted to say that."

"We?" I interrogated Lydia.

She smiled. "Okay, here's the deal. I have a confession to make. But first, are we on the same page that I've hired you again so you have to maintain confidentiality?"

"You've barged in unannounced and ruined my dinner party." I crossed my arms. "I don't think you get to set the conditions."

"Yeah, and it was such a great dinner party in the first place," Jonathan shared.

"Cool, cool. Look." She breathed deep and took a seat at my table. "This whole marital-mediation-thing? It's a bunch of crap. Cam and I are fine. We always were. We're solid. But my career needed a boost, so…and this was all my publicist's idea…so we staged this whole 'rocky marriage' thing."

"And?" Cassie was on pins and needles.

"And," she continued, "my publicist thought my fans

needed a new reason to root for me, and if they thought Cam and I were working through a rough time, and actually came out on top, it would boost record sales. I have a new album coming out in a month, so time's a-wasting."

"Why the wig?" I asked.

"I'm the mystery woman," she said, as if it was obvious. "My husband is cheating on me *with me*. We needed a hussy for him to run around town with, but we couldn't really trust anyone not to leak it to the press."

"And why did you hire Steel?"

"Because it made it look more real. Think about it. If I hired the most private divorce firm in the city, then we must really be on the verge of a breakup, right? I even had to put on that show for you at Barneys because we knew the manager would leak it to *Pucker* immediately. I was expecting them to run photos of me having a meltdown on the floor of that dressing room." She winked and went on. "Pretty good, huh? My agent wants me to do some movies next year, too, once the album's out. I told him I'd think about it."

"That is insane," Josh said from the hall where he had overheard the entire story.

"Hey, what's all the commotion?" Sheila trailed behind him, and then stopped midstride as if one shoe had been glued to the floor. "Oh my God! Lydia Johnson! Oh my God! Monica! Lydia Johnson is in your dining room! Oh my God, what are you doing here?"

"Hiding from people like you," Jonathan answered for her.

"What do you want me to do, Lydia?" I asked. "I still don't understand why you're here."

"I needed to hide, so the paparazzi wouldn't figure out it's me. They never got so close before. We need them to believe it's still some 'unidentified starlet.' So I think I'm staying here for the night because the damn photographers are going crazy trying to find out who Cam's mystery woman is, so they'll probably be camped out on the lawn all night waiting for me to come out."

"I think I'm gonna pass out," Sheila told Josh, who just *shushed* her, before returning his attention to us.

"So you just want to stay here?" I asked Lydia, who had removed her fake eyelashes and deposited them beside the sugar bowl, making it look like a daddy-long-legs was about to crawl its way in.

"Basically." She sniffed, and then leaned toward Alex, eyeing his cake. "Hey, that looks good. Are you gonna eat that?"

"Monica—" Sheila began with a huff, before I cut her off.

"Lydia, you can't honestly expect to barge into my house and take over. This is out of control, even for you."

"Monica," Josh tried again.

"I'm sorry." She raised her eyebrows and her voice, through a mouthful of Alex's cake and with a glance toward Sheila. "But it's not like your friends are disappointed that I'm here. I mean, this chick is about to have a coronary."

"Monica!" Sheila howled.

"What?" I swung in her direction.

"I'm not having a coronary…*phew, phew, phew*…I think I'm having *the baby!*"

"You're what?" Jonathan leapt off his chair as if Sheila were about to blow chunks all over his brand-new tailored suit.

"Don't be a jerk, Jonathan," Cassie said, kneeling by Sheila's side. "Honey, are you sure?"

"Her heartbeat is getting too rapid," Josh said, checking his wristwatch against her pulse. "I need to get her to the hospital, now."

"Monicaaa!" Sheila reached for my arm, and pulled me to her. "You have to come with me!"

"Of course I will. Of course! Let me, umm…let me get my keys."

"No! Don't let go of my hand," Sheila squealed.

"I'll drive so you can stay in the backseat and hold her hand," Alex volunteered.

"I'll come, too," Luke blurted out. "So…so I can help you carry her to the car quicker!"

"You can't leave me here alone," Lydia interjected.

"Well then you'll have to come with us," I snapped.

"But I already took off my disguise!" Lydia freaked out. "The paparazzi will know it's me!"

"I don't give a damn about that right now, Lydia!" I shouted.

"I'm calling 911," Jonathan announced frantically. "I'm calling 911!"

"Get a hold of yourself!" Cassie slapped him across the face. "You're useless in an emergency...*useless!*"

"Actually, he should call 911, since we can't fit that many people in Monica's car," Josh said, grabbing Sheila's purse and coat from the closet.

"Are you hyperventilating?" Cassie asked Jonathan.

"Ooooh!" Sheila moaned.

"I can't get into a car without tinted windows looking like this, Monica. I can't even go from the building to the car without a disguise unless I want the paparazzi getting pictures," Lydia pressed. "They always hide out in the garages... It'll be the end of my career if they find out I was the mystery woman!"

"Wait a minute," Alex said, his eyes alight. "Do you still have all those Indian clothes in your closet? I have an idea."

"I feel so exotic," Lydia remarked about ten minutes later, as we sprinted across the front lawn and into the waiting ambulance.

She didn't exactly look natural swathed in the red chiffon *lehnga* I had picked up in New Delhi on my last visit to the homeland, but at least the traditional head scarf was ample enough to cover her face.

"Just don't get it dirty!" I yelled, gathering up the skirts of my own Sari to avoid tripping over it as the paramedics yanked us into the back of the ambulance, one by one. Of course, Lydia insisted that both Cassie and I also change into traditional garb and cover our faces to further confuse the score of photographers who'd leapt into action the second they saw the ambulance pull up. The only female face they could actually see, in fact, was Sheila's, contorted with a mixture of anguish, fear and pride while being carried out in Luke's arms.

But don't feel so sorry for her. After all, the birth of her first child was about to be commemorated in tacky magazines and tabloid TV shows across Southern California. If it weren't for the pain, that night would have been the high point of her life.

"I'm a doctor," Josh announced to the paramedics, grabbing their CB radio and proceeding to spew a torrent of directions at the hospital staff on the other end of the line.

"Wait for us!" Cassie shoved Jonathan in behind me before hoisting herself in.

Alex jumped in last, pulling the doors shut. "Go!"

"You'll be all right," I cooed, and smoothed the sweat off Sheila's brow. "Everything's gonna be fine."

"It's never a dull moment with you, is it?" Luke asked from his spot to my left, as the siren roared to life and the ambulance leapt into traffic.

"This is Doctor Joshua Weiss, from the UCLA Medical Center E.R. My wife is in labor and we're on our way to Cedars Sinai. I'll need a stretcher waiting outside, and an epidural ready to go!" he barked over the radio. "Over!"

"That's great, man." Alex leaned in from the other side of me, steadying himself as we were jerked left and right. "This is the perfect time to make your move. *Actors…*"

"What is your problem?" Luke grew incensed.

"Shut up! Shut up, everyone!" Sheila clutched my hand so tightly it might actually have burst.

"Do you have an inhaler in this thing?" Cassie grabbed a terrified paramedic by the collar, motioning toward a wheezing Jonathan. "I think he might pass out."

"Just try to breathe, baby." Josh returned the attention to his wife. "Remember the breathing from Lamaze? Hee-hee-hee-hoo."

"You!" She unleashed a voice reminiscent of *Poltergeist*. "Get your hands off of me. So help me *God* I will stab you in your sleep if you ever try to touch me again!"

"Okay, honey." He nodded, stroking her hand. "That's fine. Whatever you say, I know it's the pain talking."

"Shut *up!*"

Clearly rattled, he looked helplessly at me from across her belly.

"Hey, what did you get her as a push present?" Lydia whispered into his ear, thinking that somehow in this five-foot-by-five-foot space, the rest of us wouldn't hear.

"She's dilated too far," the paramedic between Sheila's legs announced before Josh could venture an answer. "We're gonna have to get this baby out now."

"Wait! Let me do it!" Josh tried to climb across Lydia to the other side of his wife.

"No," the paramedic told him and held him back by a shoulder. "With all due respect, Doctor Weiss, you work from the neck up, and let me deal with the rest."

"Wait, what?" I said. "You mean *now?* You mean you're gonna deliver the baby *here?*"

"We won't make it to the hospital in time, ma'am," the paramedic explained. "So I'm gonna need two of you to get down here and grab a hold of her legs so that she can push."

"Lydia—" I swallowed after a pause "—it looks like it's you and me."

"Me?" Lydia was like a deer caught in the headlights. "Why me?"

"Josh has to stay up there, Cassie's trying to revive Jonathan and I'm pretty sure that my cousin doesn't want my ex-boyfriend or my fling from last weekend getting that familiar with her...you know...*parts!*" I explained while climbing across Luke's lap to get to Sheila's left leg.

"My parts?" Sheila questioned Josh rhetorically.

"Your fling?" Alex asked territorially, as if he could possibly have still known me well enough after all these years to judge or be shocked by my behavior. "You had a fling already? In the one week that you've been single?"

"Your *fling?*" Luke repeated, his self-defense instinct kicking in. "Is that what you're telling yourself?"

I had had enough.

"Just get over here!" I ordered, and Lydia reluctantly complied, lifting Sheila's right foot up against her shoulder and hunkering down.

"Now, Sheila." The paramedic eyed us all into silence. "On the count of three, I'm gonna need you to push with everything you've got...."

I leaned my shoulder into Sheila's other foot, shot a steadying glance at Josh, and then nodded at the paramedic, thinking: *May God, Vishnu and Adonai have mercy on us all.*

"Would you like to do the honors?" The paramedic waved a stainless steel clamp in Josh's direction, as we pulled into the driveway of Cedars Sinai about thirty minutes later.

Tearfully, he reached over and snipped off the cord.

"I can't believe I have a daughter." He kissed every one of his wife's white-knuckled fingers. "I'm somebody's *dad*."

"Asha," Sheila whispered. "Asha Weiss."

"Okay," the paramedic said, wrapping the baby up in a blanket before the back doors flew open. "Let's get Mom and her new baby inside that hospital."

"That was amazing," Cassie said, and then hopped out into the throng of waiting paparazzi.

"No," Jonathan said to me before jumping out after her. "*She's* amazing. Did you see the way Cassie took care of me? Where can you find a woman like that?"

Lydia ran right past the paparazzi and into the hospital, bolting alongside the stretcher conveying Sheila, followed closely behind by Cassie and Jonathan. Disappointed to realize that nobody besides Alex, Luke and myself remained inside our clown-car of an ambulance, the paparazzi quickly dispersed.

It looked as if the both of them were getting ready to speak at once, so I held up a hand to silence them. There really was nothing they could tell me that I didn't already know. And there was nothing I needed to hear. They weren't really competing over me that night any more than I had been competing with that redhead at The Skybar for Luke a week before. Alex hadn't known me for years by that point, and Luke had never actually known me at all. This was about territory and instinct, pure and simple. I knew it as well as anyone else because I had been just as guilty of that motivation as them. The truth was not just that all women were animals…the truth was that everyone was.

"No need to say anything, boys," I told them, shaking my head. "Trust me. I get it."

To forgive the animal instinct inside of these men was to admit to the animal inside myself. Survival is more than an instinct; it is an imperative. So maybe it's not about forgiving or denying our inner ape. It's about accepting, appreciating and keeping her on a very short leash, and going along with Alex and Luke and even Stefanie when they occasionally failed to secure said leash.

But I would think more about that later. Right now, I had to drag my knuckles into the hospital and be part of the welcome committee for the newest little gorilla in our pack.

epilogue

ASHA THRUST HER TONGUE OUT AT THE BEADED STRAP ON MY shoulder, while her head bobbled from side to side. Sheila and Josh had decided to raise Asha with exposure to both their religions because as Sheila said, *Life is confusing anyway.* She might as well get used to it. Asha was truly good-natured, even for a one-month-old baby, calm to a fault, probably in direct reaction to her mother's tendency toward the dramatic. I rocked the baby gently, cradling her head, savoring the idea that I could protect for however short a time.

"Here come the *copter-azzi*," Lydia announced, and gestured above her head at what was previously clear blue sky.

All two-hundred seated guests shifted their attention from the altar to the skies above the new Camydia Compound in the Pacific Palisades. Cameron and Lydia's recommitment ceremony came complete with a chartered fleet of limousines shuttling guests to and fro, a split-level platform erected to showcase the smiling couple, and a gospel choir from Lydia's childhood church, singing out over the bluffs at the Pacific Ocean.

And even with all that meticulous planning, someone had forgotten to restrict the airspace around the Palisades for long enough to avoid helicopter-photos that were sure to be splashed across most trash magazines the following morning.

How convenient.

"Do something about them!" Lydia scolded her security manager. After having thrown her hair back, Lydia perked up and gave the vultures her best look of interrupted romantic devotion. "This is a private expression of our love, damn it!"

I smirked at Sheila, who took Asha from my arms and handed her over to Joshua.

"Even *I'm* not falling for that," she whispered, before fishing a bottle of formula out of her bag and handing it to her doting husband.

"You've got to say this much for her, though," I countered. "She plays the paparazzi better than anyone I have ever seen. Her new album is likely to go platinum."

"Of course it is. Everybody roots for love," Cassie interjected, slipping her hand into Jonathan's. "We can't help it."

I also learned recently that everyone can't help but root for the underdog. Because the last thing I expected to feel when I opened a letter from Stefanie the day before was hope that she would succeed at the new law firm where she was starting to practice. It was only an announcement, of course, one of a thousand photocopies she had made and probably distributed without thinking to everyone in her Rolodex. I recognized, too, what this could be intended as. I chose, however, to see it as a peace offering. One which I would return with a congratulatory bottle of merlot.

Maybe after an entire month without any men in my life, I was unfettered enough to see things clearly. *If all of the insanity had been rooted in biological competition, then clearly avoiding men completely would render me genius enough to make partner in no time.* I smiled to myself, tipping back my glass at the champagne toast.

And as always, positive energy draws opportunity to a woman in much the same way as heat draws moths to a flame. The moth eyeing me from across the room was fixated, even winking as the bubbles zoomed to my head. I knew I should have ignored him. Snubbed him. At the very least *definitely not* have winked back.

But what would be the fun in that?

Keep your friends close...
and the blondes closer.

Jodi Gehrman

When her boyfriend, Coop, invites her on a romantic road trip from L.A. to Mendocino where his college chums are getting married, Gwen regards it as good news. After all, she typically enforces a three-month expiration date in her relationships; the open road and some QT just may be the antidote to break her of the cut-and-run cycle this time around.

Enter the bad news: not only will Coop's best friend, stunning yoga celebrity Dannika Winters, be joining them as the blond Satan behind the wheel, but Gwen's about to feel like the third one, so to speak. Hello, jealousy. So in an effort to avoid committing blondeicide, she decides to record her every thought...from the backseat.

Notes from the Backseat

Available wherever trade paperbacks are sold!

A Rachel Benjamin Mystery

Jennifer Sturman

Rachel Benjamin's weekend of meeting her future in-laws turns out to be quite challenging when she discovers her friend Hilary is missing. As someone orchestrates an elaborate scavenger hunt across San Francisco, dangling Hilary as the prize, Rachel must track down her friend while proving to her future in-laws and her fiancé how normal she really is!

The Hunt

"Sex and the City meets Agatha Christie!"
—Meg Cabot, author of *The Princess Diaries*

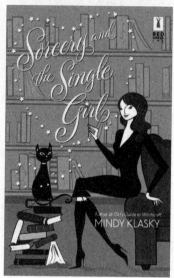